Praise for *Child of My Heart*

"A master . . . As good as any literary novelist writing today, and when I say that I include the big guns: Russell Banks, Philip Roth, Toni Morrison . . . All of [McDermott's] books mirror the central truths of existence so sure-handedly that they are neither comedies nor tragedies but merely true."

>—Anna Quindlen, Book-of-the-Month Club citation for *Child of My Heart*

"We have echoes and stirrings of Hardy, Shakespeare, Dickens, James, Beatrix Potter, Christina Rossetti . . . [Theresa] is a vessel containing a multitude of heroines, a transcendence of ethereal beauties who loved and lived in the minds of their readers and inventors."

>—Laura Kasischke, *Chicago Tribune*

"[A] quietly enchanting novel, graced by McDermott's well-calibrated writing and observant eye . . . Filled with subtle truths and hard-won wisdom."

>—*The Charlotte Observer*

"This is a novel which . . . awakens the senses . . . It lingers over light and shade, the taste of ripe peaches, and the smell of suntan lotion until we lose all sense of boundary between our world and its."

>—*The Times Literary Supplement*

"A terrific writer—precise, immaculate, and with a keen lyrical ear."

>—*The Economist*

"[A] wise, brilliantly observed novel."

>—*Star Tribune* (Minneapolis)

Beowulf Sheehan

Alice McDermott
Child of My Heart

Alice McDermott is the author of nine novels, including *The Ninth Hour* (2017); *Someone* (2013); *After This* (2006); *Charming Billy* (1998), winner of the National Book Award; *At Weddings and Wakes* (1992); *That Night* (1987); and, most recently, *Absolution* (2023)—all published by FSG. *That Night, At Weddings and Wakes*, and *After This* were finalists for the Pulitzer Prize. She is also the author of the essay collection *What About the Baby? Some Thoughts on the Art of Fiction* (2021). Her stories and essays have appeared in *The New York Times, The Washington Post, The New Yorker, Harper's Magazine*, and other publications. McDermott lives with her family outside Washington, D.C.

ALSO BY ALICE McDERMOTT

Absolution
What About the Baby?
The Ninth Hour
Someone
After This
Charming Billy
At Weddings and Wakes
That Night
A Bigamist's Daughter

Child of My Heart

Alice McDermott

Child of My Heart

PICADOR • FARRAR, STRAUS AND GIROUX • NEW YORK

Picador
120 Broadway, New York 10271

Printed in the United States of America
Originally published in 2002 by Farrar, Straus and Giroux
First paperback edition, 2003
Paperback reissue edition, 2023

The Library of Congress has cataloged the Farrar, Straus and Giroux
hardcover edition as follows:
McDermott, Alice.
   Child of my heart / Alice McDermott.
      p.   cm.
   ISBN: 978-0-374-12123-5
   1. Teenage girls—Fiction.   2. Beauty, Personal—Fiction.   3. Long
Island (N.Y.)—Fiction.   4. Babysitters—Fiction.   5. Cousins—Fiction.
I. Title.

PS3563.C355 C49 2002
813'.54—dc21

                                                          2002069764

2023 paperback ISBN: 978-1-250-88837-2

Designed by Abby Kagan

Our books may be purchased in bulk for promotional, educational, or
business use. Please contact your local bookseller or the Macmillan Corporate
and Premium Sales Department at 1-800-221-7945, extension 5442, or by
email at MacmillanSpecialMarkets@macmillan.com.

For book club information, please visit facebook.com/picadorbookclub or
email marketing@picadorusa.com.

picadorusa.com • instagram.com/picador
twitter.com/picadorusa • facebook.com/picadorusa

1   3   5   7   9   10   8   6   4   2

For Harriet Wasserman

Child of My Heart

had in my care that summer four dogs, three cats, the Moran kids, Daisy, my eight-year-old cousin, and Flora, the toddler child of a local artist. There was also, for a while, a litter of wild rabbits, three of them, that had been left under our back steps. They were wet and blind, curled up like grubs and wrapped in a kind of gray caul—so small it was difficult to know if their bodies moved with the beating of their hearts or the rise of their breaths. Not meant to live, as my parents had told me, being wild things, although I tried for nearly a week to feed them a watery mixture of milk and torn clover. But that was late August.

Late in June, Daisy arrived, the middle child of my father's only sister. She came out by herself on the Long Island Railroad, her name and address written on a piece of torn brown paper and attached to her dress with a safety pin. In my bedroom, which she was to share, I opened her suitcase, and a dozen slick packages slid out—tennis sets and pedal-pusher sets, Bermuda shorts and baby doll pajamas and underwear, all brand-new and still wrapped in cellophane. There was a brand-new pair of sneakers as well, the cheap, pulled-from-a-bin kind, bound together with the same plastic thread that held their price tag, and another, even cheaper pair of brittle pale pink slip-ons studded with blue and turquoise jewels. Princess shoes. Daisy was vain about them, I could tell. She asked me immediately—she was the shy child of strict parents so most of what she said involved asking for permission—if she could take off the worn saddle shoes she had traveled in and put them on. "I won't wear them outside till Sunday," she promised. She had the pale blue, nearly translucent skin of true redheads, a plain wisp of a child under the thick hair and the large head. It made no difference to me what kind of shoes she wore, and I told her so. I was pretty sure they were meant to be bedroom slippers anyway. "Why wait for Sunday?" I said.

Kneeling among the packages that made up her wardrobe, I asked, "Didn't you bring any old clothes, Daisy Mae?" She said her mother had told her that whatever else she needed to wear she could borrow from me. I was fifteen that summer and already as tall as my father, but my entire life's wardrobe was stored in the attic, so I knew what she meant. Daisy herself had six brothers and a sister, and even at fifteen I knew that my aunt and uncle resented what they saw as the lavish time and money my parents spent on me, an only child. I knew, in the way fifteen-year-old girls know things—intuitively, in some sense; in some sense based purely on the precise and indifferent observation of a creature very much in the world but not yet of it—that Daisy's parents resented any number of things, not the least of which, of course, was Daisy. She was only one of what must have been to them a long series of unexpected children. Eight over the course of ten years, when apparently what they had been aiming for was something more like two or three.

Just the winter before I had spent a weekend with them in their tidy house in Queens Village. I had come up from East Hampton precisely to take poor Daisy (to us, she was always "poor Daisy") into Manhattan to see the Christmas show at Radio City. My Aunt Peg, my father's sister, picked me up at the Jamaica station and immediately dropped the hint that it was impolite and unfair of me not to have invited Bernadette, her twelve-year-old, to come along, too. Aunt Peg was a thin and wiry woman, only, it seemed, a good night's sleep away from being pretty. Under her freckles, her dry skin was pale, and her thick, brittle hair was a weary, sun-faded shade of auburn. Even as she drove, she had a way of constantly leaning forward, as if into a wind, which of course added to her air of determined efficiency. (I could well imagine her pushing a shopping cart through the Great Eastern Mills in Elmont, pulling shorts sets and tennis sets from the crowded bins—one, two, three, four, underwear, pajamas, shoes—dumping all of them directly from shopping bag to suitcase, toss in a hairbrush and a toothbrush, slam the case, done.) "Bernadette will have to find her own fun tomorrow" was the way she put it to me, leaning into the steering wheel as if we were all headed downhill.

Their house was at the bottom of a dead-end street: narrow, painted brick, with a long driveway and a shingled garage and a square little back yard big enough for only an umbrella clothesline and a long-disused sandbox. Upstairs there were three bedrooms, and then up another flight of stairs, hidden behind a door, a finished attic that served as a kind of dormitory for the three older boys. There was the odor of children about the place—endemic to any house I have ever visited with more than three kids living in it—a distillation of the domestic scents of milk and wet socks combined with the paper and paste and industrial-strength disinfectant of elementary-school hallways. Despite the number of people living in the small house, there was a remarkable sense of order about the rooms, most especially in my aunt and uncle's bedroom, which was at the head of the stairs. It was a small, square room with one large window that looked out into the street. It held a high four-poster bed, a tall dresser (his) and a low bureau (hers) with a mirror, two night tables, and a straight-backed chair with a tapestry seat. The curtains that crisscrossed the window were white lace. There was a crucifix above the bed, a large oil painting of the Sacred Heart on the far wall—the first thing you saw when you looked into the room from the hallway—a mostly blood-red Oriental carpet on the floor. There was only one photograph in the room: my aunt and uncle's wedding picture. No sign, in other words, of the eight children that had been conceived on the double mattress, under the eternally smooth bedspread. Explanation enough, it seemed to me, for the apparent forgetfulness on their part that had yielded all those unexpected pregnancies. With the bedroom door pulled closed, they couldn't have found it difficult to make themselves believe that they were perfectly free to begin again.

Uncle Jack was a transit cop. He had a pitted, handsome face, dark eyes, thin lips, and a thousand and one inscrutable but insurmountable rules regarding his home and his children. No one, for instance, was to walk on the front lawn. Or sit on the bumper of his car when it was parked in the driveway. No one was to call out from an upstairs window when someone was at the front door. No one was to play handball against the garage, or stoop ball against the stoop. There was no going barefoot around the house. No getting up from the dinner table without a precise answer to the precise question "May I please be excused?" No sitting on the curb or standing under the streetlight. No dishes left in the dish drainer. No phone calls from friends after 6 p.m. No playing down in the basement after eight. No sleeping on the couch—day or night, in sickness or in health—which put me in the smallest of the three bedrooms with Daisy and Bernadette, Daisy on the rickety army cot because I was the guest and because Bernadette was not going to have the wonderful day in the city that Daisy was getting the next morning, so she might as well, said Aunt Peg, at least have a good night's sleep.

I didn't much care for Bernadette—she was plain and chubby, but, more to the point, she was also extremely smart, which made her mean. It was as if she had already weighed the value of her intelligence against the value the world would assign it and knew instinctively that she would be gypped. Although I always attempted to feel sorry for her, I was more successful at feeling a smug satisfaction as I placed my overnight bag on Daisy's bed and realized that all of Bernadette's Honor Roll certificates plastering the walls could not earn her my affection, or my company. Because whatever sympathy her forlorn expression might have elicited as she watched me from her frilly, dancing-ballerinas bedspread (a bedspread meant for another kind of child altogether) was dissipated by her questions about how I tolerated living "way out at the end of Long Island" after all the interesting summer people had gone.

She refused to come along on a walk. It was too cold for walking, she said. There was nothing worth walking to, anyway, not around here—as if she alone had some experience of a better place, a place filled with worthy destinations. I understood even then that this cool disdain of hers was the last refuge of the homely (generosity and sweetness—which was what she saved for adult company—being the next to last), and was glad enough to leave her to it. There is no misanthrope like a chubby misanthrope. Daisy and I were free, then, to slip through the slight jog of space between the tall hurricane fence that ran along my cousins' property and the chain-link that ran along their neighbors', into an alleyway that no doubt had some part in Uncle Jack's listed prohibitions. It ran behind the series of dead ends that made up the neighborhood, and was broken here and there by even smaller paths that led between other narrow yards and other houses and out into other streets. We followed these smaller passageways randomly, emerging from between fenced winter gardens and storage sheds, or battered garbage cans and tangles of abandoned bicycles, onto streets neither one of us had ever seen before. I was, of course, within half an hour, totally lost, but Daisy held my hand with complete confidence, marveling, I could tell, at just how I knew where to turn.

When we came out onto a broad boulevard divided by a series of lacy, winter-bare willows, I heard her catch her breath. All the little houses here had front sunrooms, and by some wonderful neighborhood consensus every windowpane of every one of them had been decorated with a sprayed-on

8

parabola of snow. "We're in Bavaria," I said, and Daisy whispered, "We are?" as if this were a surprise, and a destination, I had planned for her. And then real snow began to fall. If you had seen the way she glanced up at the sky, you'd have thought I'd planned this, too. It accumulated first on the grass, and then, more rapidly, on the street and sidewalk. Our footprints were the first to mark it. We walked down the narrow divide, under the thin willow branches as they gathered snow, unable to tell if it was the yellow sky that was darkening above us or only the thickening canopy of coated trees. We threw back our heads and opened our mouths and stuck out our tongues and felt the snowflakes in our eyes and on our bare throats. When other children started to come out of the houses behind us, shouting, optimistically scraping sleds over sidewalks, we ran to get away from them, up to Jamaica Avenue, where the streetlights were already on. It was that odd light of early winter, afternoon turning prematurely to steel-blue night. We went into a candy store on a corner, its entrance already slick with wet footprints and its smell of newsprint and candy bars and the cold overcoats of men just up from the subway making us feel we had indeed traveled a long way.

At the counter, I bought us each a hot chocolate with the extra money I always put in my shoe when I took the Long Island Railroad. It was lovely stuff, made with hot water, not milk, and topped with whipped cream from a cold silver can. It was served in chipped and yellowing cups and saucers that smelled faintly of coffee—the warm rims of the cups delightfully dry and thick against our lips. Drinking it, we pretended to speak French—tossing the word *chocolat* back and forth between us—and hugging the cups like Europeans, our elbows on the counter. (Cup-hugging and elbows on the table being, of course, Daisy said, two more of her father's taboos.) After I paid, I asked for directions home from the man at the register, pretending I was only out to confirm what I already knew, although I'm not sure Daisy would have noticed anyway. There was a barrel of lollipops beside the newspaper rack, a handwritten sign, TWO FOR A NICKEL. Her parents had made her too polite to ask for one, so I casually bought a hundred of them, refusing a paper bag and stuffing them instead into our pockets, pant pockets and coat pockets, and then lifting the hem of her sweater to form another pocket and filling it as well.

When we got back to the house, we dumped all of them over her brothers and Bernadette, who were lying on the living-room floor watching their allotted hour of television before dinner. The lollipops in their wrappers were wet with snow, some were muddy from where we had dropped them on the walk home. "Where did you get these?" Bernadette asked, and before Daisy could answer, I said, "We found a lollipop tree. You should have come." The boys said, "Yeah, sure," but Bernadette couldn't resist grilling us on the particulars, her eyes narrowed, her thin mouth opened skeptically, showing the little blowfish teeth.

A house on the boulevard, I said. A willow tree. A huge willow tree filled with lollipops for the taking. The tree belongs to an old couple, I said, whose only child, a little boy, had dreamed of a lollipop tree in his front yard on the night he died, fifty years ago this very day. Once a year and only on this day, I said, they make his dream come true by filling their willow tree with lollipops. (And the odd thing is, I said, it was snowing in his dream, too, and it snows every year on this date the minute the old couple hangs the last lollipop on the tree.) They invite children from miles around. I'm surprised you guys have never heard about it before. The old couple serves hot chocolate out on their lawn while the children collect the lollipops from the tree. They hire tall men to help lift the smaller children high into the branches. The single rule is that you can pick only as many lollipops as you can carry home— no paper bags or suitcases, oh, and that the picking lasts for just one hour, from dusk to nightfall, to the second the first star appears. Corresponding to their son's last hour on earth, since the evening star in the dark blue winter sky was the first thing the old couple had noticed when they went to the bedroom window only a minute after the doctor had pulled a blanket up over his peaceful little face.

Although Bernadette squinted skeptically through it all, the boys had their backs to the TV set by the time I'd finished. "We'll have to go next year," Jack Jr. said softly. But Bernadette turned on Daisy. "Is this true?" she demanded. Daisy shrugged her thin shoulders. There was a remnant of hot chocolate on her upper lip and the top of her wiry hair was darkened by a little skullcap of melted snow. "You should have come," she said matter-of-factly, skirting the lie. Child of my heart.

At eight o'clock my parents called to say that in order to keep the peace, I would have to ask Bernadette to join us tomorrow, which I did, much to my aunt's grudging satisfaction. Bernadette, of course, was not the walker Daisy was and found the huge, winking tree in Rockefeller Center a meager distraction from her cold toes. She found no enchantment in the silver knobs and glass pockets of the Automat. She refused to follow a woman in pancake makeup and fur coat, clearly a Rockette, through the crowds in order to discover the Music Hall's secret stage door. She complained so vehemently about the taste of the roasted chestnuts I had bought from a stand in the park that Daisy and I could no longer pretend to enjoy them. She couldn't believe Radio City Music Hall didn't sell popcorn. She couldn't be convinced to hop on a downtown bus just to "see" Greenwich Village. She complained of a stomachache the whole train ride home and then sabotaged the day completely by asking her mother that evening to go and tell me that sometime during the course of the afternoon she had been visited by her "friend." I suppose it was an apology of sorts, for what a whiner she had been. Or maybe it was just an excuse. A plea for sympathy from a being as discouraged by herself, by the humorless personality, the unshakable intelligence, the heavy face and limbs—none of which she would have chosen had the choice been hers—as was everyone else.

I told my aunt that I understood, and smiled warmly at Bernadette in her pajamas, but when I invited Daisy into my bed that night, or back into her own bed, I curled around her little body and, while her sister slept and bled, promised a summer visit, all by herself, a week or two, or three or four— as many as her father would allow. Just the two of us, I whispered. Would she be brave enough to take the train out by herself? In the darkness she nodded. She would.

My own parents had moved out to Long Island when I was two years old. They had done so because they knew by then that I

was the only child they would ever have—they were already
in their mid-forties—and that I would be good-looking. Un-
usually so. A young Elizabeth Taylor was the immediate word.
(Later, among the East End crowd, it was a young Jackie
Kennedy.) Blue eyes and dark hair and full lips and pale skin.
A somewhat startling change from the red-haired or red-faced
relatives who leaned over my crib, speculating, as they would
continue to do until I was in my thirties, if I wasn't evidence of
some French blood in the family. But my mother claimed that
my looks were due only to the intercession of St. Theresa
of the Little Flower, my Gallic patron saint—which was
her homely and pious way of deflecting both their vanity-
provoking praise and the notion that somewhere in our Irish
heritage there had been dropped a tincture of impious blood.

Being who they were—children of immigrants, well-read
but undereducated—my parents saw my future only in terms
of how I would marry, and they saw my opportunities narrowed by the Jewish/Irish/Polish/Italian kids who swarmed
the city and the close-in neighborhoods where they could af-
ford to buy a home. They moved way out on Long Island because they knew rich people lived way out on Long Island,
even if only for the summer months, and putting me in a place
where I might be spotted by some of them was their equiva-
lent of offering me every opportunity.

It hardly mattered that we lived in a two-bedroom house
that had once been a fisherman's cottage, or that our neighbors, the Morans, piled bedsprings and car parts in their front
yard, or that both my parents had to commute to Riverhead to
work. Proximity to wealth was what they were after, and to
that end, they encouraged me to answer ads for summer

babysitter or mother's helper from the time I was ten or so, driving me to my June interviews in order to check out the size of the house and the pool and the number of servants before I accepted the job. Walking into those interviews, across high-ceilinged entryways that opened onto the sea, or around back to a pool where the lady of the house—always slim and already tanned—would remove her sunglasses at my approach, I must have fit right into the pretty summer dreams those pretty young mothers had had back on Fifth Avenue in March. I was hired immediately, first time out, although I was only ten and Mrs. Carew had been looking for a teenager. By the next summer, I was in demand—having been checked out thoroughly by the other young mothers at the Maidstone Club and the Main Beach. Pretty, intelligent, mature in speech although undeveloped physically (another plus), well immersed in my parents' old-fashioned Irish Catholic manners (inherited from their parents, who had spent their careers in service to this very breed of American rich), and, best of all, beloved by children and pets.

I don't know how to account for it, my way with small creatures. Nor did it ever occur to me to try. Because I was a child myself when I began to take care of other children, I saw them from the start as only a part of my realm, and saw my ascendance as a simple matter of hierarchy—I was the oldest (if only by a year or two) among them, and as such, I would naturally be worshipped and glorified. I really thought no more of it than that. And when they clung to me and petted me, when the boys, lovesick, put their heads in my lap and the girls begged to wear my rings or comb my hair, I simply took it as my due. I was Titania among her fairies (the summer I was thirteen I even named the Kaufman kids Cobweb and Pease-blossom, to their unending delight); and the dogs and cats and bunnies and gerbils that seemed to follow their young owners in their affection were only doing what nature, in our little realm, prescribed.

Ironically, it was my way with pets that caused me more trouble with my employers than my way with children—because while on occasion a mother would pretend to be hurt by a child's insistence on my company if a nightmare woke her from a nap or if a knee was scraped, fathers were genuinely offended by their pets' changes in loyalty. I remember in particular one young black Lab, Joker was his name, who would not leave my side, not even for a run on the beach with his down-for-the-weekend master, not even when I urged him to go ahead, pushed him to his feet, whispered into his velvet ear. He would only slowly wag his tail at the sound of my voice and then sit down again at my feet—much laughter from the children on the porch or the beach blanket, much consternation from the rejected owner. I gathered from the children the next summer that there had been some advocacy on the father's part not to have me back.

If there was any trick, any knack, to my success as a minder of children, it was, I suppose, the fact that I was as delighted with my charges as they were with me. Although I had spent my own childhood in what seemed to me a kind of leafy green contentment, I had been alone much of the time, as happens with only children of older, working parents—especially only children of older parents who live in a village filled with summer houses and temporary residents—and the time I spent with my charges was probably the longest stretch of time I had ever spent with anyone other than my parents and myself. As a result, I didn't have to devise games and entertainments for the children I watched, I had only to include them in the ongoing games and entertainments I had devised for myself long ago.

And then there were the Morans. Except for an elderly couple I saw only when my mother sent me to their house with a jar of beach-plum jelly or a basket of tomatoes from our garden or the extra bluefish my father had caught, the Morans were our only full-time neighbors. In my earliest memories, Mr. Moran lived in his house alone. I have the impression I thought then he was a retired sea captain—maybe my father had made some joke about it that I had misinterpreted (he often referred to Mr. Moran as being "three sheets to the wind"—a nautical-enough reference for a six-year-old), or maybe my Uncle Tommy, my mother's dissipated younger brother, told me the tale and I believed him (because if I inherited my way with children and animals from anyone, it must have been from Tommy). Or maybe it was just the way Mr. Moran looked—bowlegged and Popeye-thin, with a constant two-day growth of beard. His house was behind and perpendicular to ours, surrounded by a tall hedge that obscured all but the gravel driveway and a bit of his overgrown lawn. I don't recall seeing much of him then. I'd hear him singing sometimes on the other side of the hedge when I played alone in our back yard—burring, Celtic folk songs that I took to be sea chanties—and I'd sometimes see my father chatting with him over our split-rail fence or at the dock in Three Mile Harbor, where they both kept their boats. On occasion, the town police would pull into Mr. Moran's driveway—bringing him home, my father would explain, after a "bender"—and twice my parents had to summon the police for him themselves: once when he appeared at our door at dinnertime with his lip gashed open and blood pouring from his mouth; another time when they discovered him out cold on our side lawn, his face in the grass and his pants down around his ankles (too late, they had tried to shield my eyes, but not before I got a quick, bone-chilling glimpse of a mound of a pale adult backside, as gray and lonesome as a sand dune in winter). Not long after this, Sondra, Mr. Moran's daughter, and her family moved into the ramshackle house.

It was the winter before I took my first mother's helper job with Mrs. Carew. Sondra was a bleached blonde in those Marilyn Monroe/Jayne Mansfield days when being a bleached blonde made for instant glamour. She wore a black lambskin jacket and had a baby in her arms and three more toddling, towheaded children around her. On that first day, there was no sign of their father. They arrived in a wood-paneled station wagon that for the next week was left parked and unpacked by the side of the road. My mother had seen them all arrive from our kitchen window, and it wasn't an hour or two later that I stepped out our back door and found the three little ones draped over the wide wooden plank of our tree swing. Although it must have been January or February and the winter chill of the ocean was in the air, only one of them, the girl, wore a jacket and a hat. The two boys were in sweatshirts and pajama bottoms. All three wore socks on their hands but none on their feet, which became abundantly clear when one of the boys (Petey, as it turned out), not ten seconds after I'd said hello to him, leaned too far over the seat of the swing and landed headfirst on an exposed and frozen tree root.

Rivulets of blood running over a pink scalp, running through the stubble of their white-blond hair, will remain for me forever the emblem of the Moran kids.

Nobody ever paid me for minding them, but from that day forward I had only to walk out our back door to find one or more of them suddenly in my care. They'd be slumped against our fence, all four, eventually all five, of them, locked out of their own home by their raging parents, or one or the other would be sitting bereft in our yard, tears streaking dirty cheeks, blood, more often than not, coming from somewhere—a scraped elbow, a scratched mosquito bite. It got so that when I brought one of them inside to wash the cut and the dirty hands and face, I could pretty much name the date and place of every other scar I found on them as well.

Sondra's husband arrived a week or so later, a vague figure coming and going, sometimes in dark suits, sometimes in jeans, sometimes, I suspect, in the guise of another man altogether. She fought with him, and with her old father, exchanging curses and throwing things and then screeching out of the driveway in her car at any hour of the day or night, the children left in her wake seeming to settle behind her, in the road, on our lawn, across our back steps, like the detritus of some explosion.

Every once in a while the Moran kids would show up with a new pet, sometimes a cat or a dog they had found, a length of clothesline tied around its neck, sometimes a turtle or a salamander or a fledgling bird. These, too, of course, would eventually fall into my care, at least until they ran away or died or were claimed by their real owners. Two of them came and went regularly: Rags, a mangy but sweet little mutt, and Garbage, an orange tabby cat.

The summer Daisy came, I had limited my babysitting duties to Flora, the artist's child, but had also supplemented my pay with a couple of dog-walking and cat-sitting arrangements with some of the people in the neighborhood. Flora was easy enough. She was two and a half and mostly docile, and my charge was to pick her up every morning and, if the weather was good, push her in her stroller to the beach, give her lunch there, let her take her nap, and then bring her home again at four or five so the housekeeper could bathe her and put her to bed. On rainy days, I would play with her in her room or walk her back to my house, where I would have to keep her, like some delicate china vase, just slightly beyond the full grasp of the Moran kids' dirty hands. She was tiny for her age, with very little hair, and her mother dressed her always in loose white dresses, like a baby in a painting. Her mother was some kind of dancer or actress. She was thin and tall, with something severe about her face—a sharp nose and high cheekbones and a narrow mouth, a certain gray roughness to her otherwise flawless skin that would put you in mind of expertly poured concrete. She was a good thirty or forty years younger than Flora's father, the artist—maybe more. He was an unremarkable old man, glasses, khaki pants, a stoop. He had a long thatch of white hair that seemed to rise over his head like a pure white tongue of smoky fire. I don't think I ever figured out just where it took root, but it seemed to me that his hair moved constantly, like a flame—perhaps fanned by the constant stirring of his artistic brain. My parents said he was supposed to be a genius. He painted huge abstracts in a garage-sized studio beside the house, and sometimes out on the gravel driveway itself. They weren't particularly colorful or interesting pictures, but he had done some sketches of Flora and his wife that hung in Flora's bedroom, and these were good enough to make me believe he actually knew what he was doing.

The first time I babysat for Flora he gave me a bit of his work. It was an evening in the early spring, the April before Daisy came. They had called me at the last minute because their housekeeper had missed her train from the city and they had an affair to attend (or so it was put to me by my mother, who took the phone call) in Southampton. My father dropped me at the door and the cook let me in. I found him sitting at a narrow desk in their long, low living room. He was waiting for his wife and he was drawing, scrawling really, two or three charcoal lines on sketch paper. As soon as he had done one, he threw it on the floor and began another. I introduced myself and he said, still drawing, that the girls would be right out. He sat sideways at the little desk, his long legs crossed, drawing, tossing, drawing again. As I waited (sitting on the edge of what seemed a quite modern and impractical white leather couch), he must have gone through fifty pieces of paper, and from what I could see, the pattern of marks on each one was exactly the same. When Flora toddled into the room, he barely looked up, not even when she stepped on some of his strewn papers. She was in a white nightgown and her thin hair rose straight up like her father's. A pretty child in her own, odd way. I showed her the magazine I'd been paging through, and without hesitation she leaned against my knees. She was on my lap by the time her mother came in (dressed, as I recall, in something elegant and vaguely Chinese), and as I received my usual instructions about where they would be and what lights should be left on when Flora went to sleep, I noticed that he continued drawing and tossing his drawings on the floor. Then suddenly, without a word to him, his wife leaned down to kiss her daughter's head, turned her long nose toward the front door, and followed it out. I had a moment when I wondered if he was going along. I even wondered if he was the husband at all and not some visiting grandfather I'd be expected to mind as well. I kept talking to Flora about the pictures in the magazine, keeping her distracted from her mother's departure but watching him, too, from the corner of my eye. He drew a few more sketches and then, answering to no call, like a man alone in a room, he slowly stood, paused, and then, still standing, leaned over the desk to draw the pattern once more. Flora and I by this time had gone through the magazine and she now had me by the hand and was pulling me toward a basket of books beside her father's desk. He looked up and saw her and smiled distractedly, and then he looked at me. He took off his glasses. He had that delicate, almost crinkling, thin skin you see in old men. The piece of charcoal was in his hand and had dirtied his fingertips. He gave me a different kind of smile, rolling the charcoal between thumb and forefinger, taking me in. His white hair moved as if caught in a soft breeze. "I hear you're a babysitter par excellence," he said—not the way I would say it, but the way someone who really spoke French would say it. I told him I just liked children. He nodded slowly, as if this were a sad but complex piece of information, and then, putting on his glasses, he turned back to his sketch. He signed it with the charcoal and then handed it to me, over Flora's head. "Take this home and frame it, then," he said. "It'll help you put all your own kids through college." It was unremarkable enough—a loop, a line, a thing like a chicken leg—also vaguely Oriental. The paper was thick and lovely, though. After he left (strolling toward the door as if it were an arbitrary destination, although I could see when he opened it the headlights of the car where she sat, I could hear the impatient idling of the engine), I placed it between the pages of a *Life* magazine and put it on the table by the front door so I wouldn't forget it. I thought less of how it would help me to put my kids (*all* my kids) through college than of what an embarrassment it would be to him if I didn't bother to take it home. He might well have been a genius, a famous artist, a man whose signature and doodles were valuable, but I was fifteen and pretty and I didn't doubt for a moment that I was the one with the advantage here.

The next morning, Flora asked for me as soon as she woke up and then cried when she understood that I wasn't still in the house, and so her indulgent mother called me to ask if I'd like to take Flora for a walk in her stroller, and then asked if I would do the same every day after school and then full time when summer came. If summer comes, she said, with some melodrama, because it had been cold and damp and overcast for weeks, and she was, she said, bored, bored, bored to be out here so early in the season. Out here only so her husband could work. She turned her nose toward the gray studio, where you could see two single lightbulbs hanging in the window, burning into the driveway's gloom. It was a new use of the word for me: I had never before associated drawing and painting with "work." I liked the idea. And I was beginning to like their house, which was long and low and full of plate-glass windows and smelled delightfully of her Chanel and his pipe smoke. I already liked Flora.

My parents were none too pleased with the arrangement, since it didn't seem to offer as many opportunities for mingling with wealthy potential boyfriends that sitting for stockbrokers or lawyers or plastic surgeons did, but I reminded them that Daisy was coming and that spending the day with Flora would mean spending the day with Daisy, too, whereas any of my usual mother's helper jobs would leave Daisy on her own until I returned. Poor Daisy, I said, deserved a good summer for a change, and my mother—whose pity for Daisy was a marvelous vehicle for her disapproval of my father's sister—rolled her eyes and repeated, "Poor Daisy," and the course of my summer was determined.

The first thing we have to do for you, I told Daisy, is not so much unpack your clothes as unwrap them. She sat on the floor beside me, her thin legs straight out so we both could admire the hard pink shoes. I had tried to convince her not to wear them with socks, it was summer, after all, I said, but she had shyly insisted that the socks made the shoes more comfortable. There was an iridescence to them, I saw, in the sunshine of my bedroom, a bit of metallic blue beneath the pink, and when I pointed this out to her she said, delightedly, that she hadn't noticed it before. "It probably wasn't there before," I told her. Softly, she asked me what I meant. "They're changing," I said bluntly. "They're not the same shoes they were when you found them at Great Eastern. They're not even the same shoes your mother put in the suitcase this morning. They're becoming something else. I don't know what yet. We'll have to wait and see. Maybe by the time you go home, they'll be all blue, or even silver. Maybe these," I leaned over and tapped one of the turquoise gems glued to the cheap leather, "will have become real."

I sorted and stacked her outfits—four shorts sets, three tennis sets, a pedal-pusher set, underwear, pajamas—and then unwrapped them one by one, pulling out straight pins and pieces of odd-shaped cardboard. I had her try each one on and was dismayed to see that not only would each of them have to be ironed to get out the factory-sealed creases and wrinkles but that each was at least a size or two too big. Here was my Aunt Peg's logic, here was evidence that her grudging sense of life's unfairness had seeped into everything she did. She would not send her middle child out to the hoity-toity Hamptons for the summer with a suitcase full of Bernadette's hand-me-downs. Oh no. (I could hear her say it to Uncle Jack, at their kitchen table, over his favorite dessert of canned fruit salad sprinkled with tiny marshmallows.) No, siree. Daisy would go with new clothes, still in their wrappers. But neither would she want me or my parents to forget that life was not easy for a transit cop with eight kids, not nearly as easy as it was for a working couple with only a daughter, and luxuries like one-season shorts sets bought from racks, not bins, were simply not in the cards for this hardworking family. The "poor Daisy" refrain had its benefits, no doubt—a few weeks in summer with one less mouth to feed, for instance, one less child to keep track of—

but even in her harried, downhill existence, Aunt Peg would
want to mark her child with evidence of both her dignity and
her practicality.

Poor Daisy stood in my bedroom in her pink shoes and
hooked two thumbs into the drooping armholes of her sleeveless tennis dress, like Mr. Green Jeans pulling at his sus-
penders. "It's a little big," she said, laughing at herself, at the
way the pleated skirt nearly touched her knees. Beneath the
white polyester/cotton of the cheap dress, I could see her
skinny chest with its shadowy hollows and pink nipples and
nearly translucent glow. Even at eight, her skin gave off the
peculiar, new-to-the-light aura of a newborn's. "Let's save it
for Bernadette," I said, and stood. "This way, Daisy Mae," I
said.

Our house was so small that both bedrooms led directly into
the living room, and the place where the living-room ceiling
dropped down to accommodate the attic stairs delineated the
extent of the dining room. A fisherman's cottage to be sure,
built in the late 1800s, we were told, with one stone fireplace
and wide-plank floors and a walk-up attic that smelled of
cedar and mothballs and dust, and, on sunny days such as this,
the warmed breath of old wood. The stairs to it were steep and
curved a little at top and bottom, and when I reached the top
and leaned down to take Daisy's hand, I could feel she was
trembling. When she reached the last two stairs, she pulled her
hand away and kind of scrambled on all fours onto the attic
floor, getting, as she did, very little traction from the pink
shoes. When she saw that the floor was safely beneath her, and
the entrance to the attic stairs a good enough distance away,

she turned and sat, her legs spread, as if she had arrived there after a fall, not a climb. "Are you all right?" I said, laughing a bit, just to dampen her panic. She nodded, breathing heavily, the too big dress now spread around her like a gown. "I'm fine," she said softly.

This attic was my favorite place in the house—and I loved every corner of that house, even then. It was all rafters and ancient treasures and chinks of broken sunlight coming through the walls and the one tiny window. Two old iron beds that had belonged to my mother's parents were set up under one eave, covered with two ancient quilts and two somewhat wilted feather pillows—our guest suite, as my mother called it (my Uncle Tommy being the only guest it had ever accommodated). There was a faded Queen Anne chair, some old-fashioned lamps with tasseled lampshades. A dresser. A full-length standing mirror. A steamer trunk that opened sideways. My father's army footlocker, stenciled with his name and rank and the yellowed cargo tag from the *Queen Mary*. There were a number of rolled-up rugs, a couple of antique pitchers and basins. Boxes of old photographs, of Christmas decorations, of magazines and books. My disassembled crib. My black baby carriage draped with an old sheet. My pale blue teeter-totter, my rocking horse. A stage set of an attic in every way. My stage.

Under the other eave there was a long metal rod that held our winter coats in cloth wardrobes, and, for the rest of its length, my biography in clothing. My mother had all my dresses and tops and slacks and skirts and shorts arranged in chronological order down the expanse of the bar, so that behind my father's overcoat there was my Catholic school uniform skirt, abandoned just a week ago when vacation began, my uniform blouses and sweaters, my Easter dress and coat, my green St. Patrick's Day shirtwaist, my velvet Christmas dress, my fall kilts and cardigans, followed by everything I had outgrown from last summer, followed by my freshman-year uniform, another Easter dress, etc. It was all orderly enough to merit documentation, and I only had to count off velvet dress sleeves or the yellow, green, pink, or blue shoulders of my Easter coats to know exactly where I needed to look to find something for Daisy.

I pulled out the first dress I recalled, a white one with pale yellow flowers and a green velveteen sash, puffy sleeves, a sweet collar, a full skirt. Daisy was still sitting on the floor, but when I held it out to her, she rose slowly, walking carefully toward me over the warm, worn floorboards, as if she were not yet sure she trusted them. Kneeling in front of her, I unbuttoned the tennis dress and slipped it over her shoulders. "Arms up," I said, and pulled my old dress over her head. I turned her around and buttoned up the back and tied the sash. "Beautiful," I said, turning her again, and she was: the yellow and white and green and her flushed cheeks and bright red hair.

"I could wear it to church on Sunday," she said, a little breathless. And I said, once again, "Why wait till Sunday?"

I showed her my baby clothes, at the far end of the long rack. The little dresses on their hangers, the boxes on the shelf beneath them with the sweaters and the sleepers and even a handful of worn cloth diapers, all wrapped in tissue paper, weighed down with pieces of cedar. I held the box to her nose and told her to breathe in. I said, Isn't it something, how all my baby clothes smell like that? As if my parents hadn't gotten me from the hospital at all but from some old forest. Found on a bed of moss, perhaps, cradled in the roots of an ancient tree. It makes you wonder, I said mysteriously, loving her for the way she was taking me in, her mouth opened and her eyes bright. I put the lid on the box and slipped it back onto its shelf.

"Do you remember anything, Daisy Mae?" I asked. "About the time before you were born?"

She thought for a moment and said no, she didn't think she did.

"You don't remember God?" I said. "Or heaven? Or the angels? Or the other children waiting to be born?"

She frowned. "I don't think so," she said.

"You don't remember meeting Kevin" (one of her younger brothers) "or Brian or Patrick," (the others) "before you were all born?"

She shook her head.

"You should try to remember," I told her. "You're only eight. I remembered a lot of it up until just a few years ago. You should think about it more and see what you come up with."

I told her I could remember the name Robert Emmet. I said I had once asked my mother, probably when I was about your age, who Robert Emmet was, and she, after a long pause, had said he was an Irish patriot her father had been particularly fond of. I said no, he was a little baby boy, the one I was talking about. A little baby boy still in a blanket. That's the Robert Emmet I was talking about.

Later on I found out that before me, my mother had had another baby who'd died just as he was being born and who was baptized Robert Emmet by the delivery room nurse because that was the name my grandfather offered when my father was asked and had no response to give.

Clearly, I said, my brother and I had met, and exchanged names, sometime between his birth and mine. I'd had a glimpse of my grandfather, too, I was certain, but the memory was not as clear.

I walked over to the old dresser and pulled open its bottom drawer. There were a number of shoeboxes lined up inside, and in one of them my mother had her father's old shaving things: a cup wrapped in tissue paper, a brush, a long thin razor. A brown bottle of bay rum with a cork stopper and, on its label, a stained and yellowed drawing of a palm tree and a beach. I took out the bottle and showed it to Daisy. I pulled out the cork. The bottle was empty, but there was a faint whiff of the stuff still inside. Again, I told her to take a sniff.

She leaned forward and breathed deeply.

I remembered smelling this same smell, I told her, sometime before I was born. I think my grandfather and I must have passed each other, he on his way in, me on my way out— he died in March, I was born in April. I think I must have smelled it when he leaned over to pat my head as he walked past.

I put the stopper back in and returned the bottle to its box. "That is," I said, "I think I remember."

I looked at Daisy. She was nodding, her eyebrows raised, her mouth turned down, as if she were considering all this and finding it very reasonable, very likely. I loved the way she looked, in my old dress, in her pink shoes and socks, so I picked her up and turned her around a couple of times and then put her down again. Going back to the clothes rack, I told her how my Uncle Tommy slept up here whenever he visited, and how he always said, before he climbed the stairs, "If I see the ghost, I'll give him your regards."

I told her how sometimes he said the old fisherman who built this house appeared during the night, just standing over there by the window, looking out, smoking his pipe. The first time Uncle Tommy said, "Can I help you, sir?" And the man just turned around a little bit and waved his hand behind his back and said, "No, no. No, thank you," in a voice so choked with emotion that Uncle Tommy didn't ask anything else, just watched the man staring out the window and smoking until he fell back asleep again.

Once he asked him, "Can I get you a chair, sir?" And the man again waved him away, saying, "No, no." But the next morning, Uncle Tommy moved the chair over to the window anyway and was very happy to wake up during the next night to see that the man was sitting in it, his legs crossed comfortably. And oddly enough, Uncle Tommy said, there was a little boy asleep on his lap.

"Who was he?" Daisy asked.

I shrugged. "Who knows?"

I pulled out a checked sundress, red and blue, with ribbon ties at the shoulder. "This is cute, too," I said. And another of white eyelet. And a pair of pink pedal pushers that would go with her shoes. "Maybe some night we'll sleep up here," I said. "You and I."

She hesitated for a moment and then said, "Okay," looking down at the dress I held against her.

"Chances are, the only ghost we'll see is me at your age," I said. "Looking to see who's wearing my old clothes."

Before we went back down, I told her to take off the shoes if the stairs made her nervous.

She shook her head. "I'm okay," she said.

I went ahead of her, the clothes on their hangers draped over my arm, turning at each step to make sure she was all right. There was no banister, but she kept both hands flat against the wall and descended so slowly, and with such cautious trepidation, you'd have thought she was edging along some building ledge.

"Are you afraid of heights, Daisy Mae?" I asked her, halfway down.

She shook her head. She would not take her eyes from the stairs, or the hem of my old dress, or the pink shoes whose wooden heels and slippery beige soles slapped loudly against each bare step. "I'm only afraid of falling," she said.

I awoke every morning to the sound of my parents' voices coming through the wall behind my bed. They slept in twin beds with quilted leather headboards, a nightstand in between, and their voices in those first moments of the day were subdued and conversational. I imagined at one point that they simply told each other their dreams, and in much the same matter-of-fact way they might relate the details of an ordinary and unremarkable trip to the market. I don't pretend to understand it: why they never slept in the same bed but began each morning talking to each other as if they shared the same mind. The wallpaper in my bedroom, and in theirs, was full of yellow

roses, fist-sized yellow roses that became, as I stared and listened and tried to make out what they said, the fist-sized yellow faces of wrinkled babies and grinning gargoyles and
startled guardian angels, of choir boys in war paint with open,
oval mouths.

My parents got up at five, bathed and had breakfast, and
were usually out of the house by six. During the school year I
went with them, to be dropped off with the nuns at my private
school twenty miles to the west—essentially a boarding school
for the daughters of wealthy Asians and South Americans,
with only a handful of us day students squeezed in to keep the
locals agreeable—but in the summer the house was mine. This
had been the case for nearly as long as I can remember, although there was a time, before I started school, I suppose,
when old Mrs. Tuohey would be stirred into the mix before my
parents left for work, stirred like the hasty half teaspoon
of sugar my mother always added to the black tea she made
for herself and my father. Even before I was old enough
for school, Mrs. Tuohey was a gesture only, mostly a second
thought, and quickly diluted by the vast solitude of the tiny
house, and my own preference for it. The poor woman, a pale
and frail little widow who lived in the village, usually spent
the day in the first seat she had taken when my father brought
her in, not much more than a ghost herself.

I loved that house, as I've said, and I loved it especially on
those summer mornings when the sun lit the kitchen and
the bedrooms but kept the living room cool and damp and
smelling, because of the old stone fireplace, like a recently inhabited cave. I'd cross it in my bare feet and go into the
kitchen, where my parents would be having their bacon and

eggs, continuing that same back-and-forth, just-passing-the-time-of-day conversation they'd been having since they'd first regained consciousness. When they saw me, my father would pull out the third chair and my mother would stand up to get an extra plate, as if I were an unexpected guest. She would pour me some of the tea she had made for just the two of them, and scatter a bit of sugar across it while I took a piece of toast or bacon from the plate between them. They would then continue their conversation, with only an occasional word or two addressed to me, like a sidelong glance. They kept their voices low, as if I were still asleep, and their eyes, it seemed to me, were always somewhat averted.

I believe my parents had grown a little wary of me by then. Not merely wary of the physical changes, of the long, bare legs I pulled up under my chin as I bit my toast into odd shapes, or the widening shoulders under my T-shirt, the budding breasts, the way my easy-to-admire childish beauty was quickly becoming something a little thinner and sharper and certainly more complicated, but wary as well of what they must have believed was the fast-approaching time of my fulfillment of their dream for me—of my absorption into that world they had taken so much trouble to place me on the threshold of. I suppose it was one of the ironies of their ambition for me, of their upbringing and their sense of themselves, that they would not see me as fully a part of that brighter world of wealthy people and supposed geniuses if I did not at some point recognize that they were not. That the best assurance they would have that I had indeed moved into a better stratum of society would be my scorn for the lesser one to which they belonged.

They were dear people, both my parents, but the vividness of their dream of my rise, their absolute confidence in the inevitability of my success, made them resent what they saw as its consequences even that summer when I was fifteen and part of no other social set than my own. Turning away from me in anticipation of my turning away from them, they left me more alone that summer than perhaps I'd ever been.

Once they had gone to work, I took a peach from the bowl of fruit on the counter and crossed the living room again. Our front porch was short and square, its floorboards painted a glossy gray, the trim and balustrade white and wet at that hour of the morning. I sat on the steps with the newspaper and my summer reading book. There were lilac bushes on either side of the porch, my father's dahlias all along the split-rail fence. Across the narrow macadam road there was only a high hedge, a deep green dropcloth the length of the street, meant to conceal the summer house beyond it, but serving also to make our house seem the only inhabited place—or maybe the only place (and us the only family) bold enough to live within easy sight of strangers. I read the paper and ate the peach and then tossed the pit into the grass. I walked down the three steps to the lilac bush and shook the branches and caught the dew that fell in my palm and rubbed the sticky juice from my hands. Then I turned my face up and closed my eyes and shook the branches again to get the peach juice off my lips. The dew was cold, despite the sunshine that had already begun to hit the leaves, and I lifted my hair and bent under the branches to feel it on the back of my neck. I shook my head to make the bush shake and felt a drop of dew slide down my shirt and along my spine. A branch caught my hair as I straightened up, and as I reached for it, I felt it press into my scalp, a bony finger drawn along the back of my head. I moved against it, pulled away a little, and then moved back against it again, entangling the hair even more, no doubt, but enjoying the grip it had on me, the sweet pressure and scratch. I turned under it, let my head fall back, pressed my shoulders into the green leaves, arching like a cat and feeling the dampness of my T-shirt, the drops of dew scattered across my arms. I ran my fingers through my hair, from temple to crown, and met the single hard branch that had caught me. Gently, I freed myself from it and stepped away, and the words I was looking for were in the paperback book on the step: Send me great love from somewhere, else I shall die.

I shook the hem of my T-shirt, lifted and twisted it not because it was soaked but because I wanted to feel the new sun on my midriff. I would have taken it off altogether if I'd had the courage. I shook out my hair and wound it at the back of my neck. I brushed the dew from my arms and walked through the grass and the sun to the back of the house, where there was a hedge under both bedroom windows. I stepped behind it, my bare feet in the soft, damp dirt, and at my own window leaned down toward the sill. I put my mouth to the screen, at the place where the window was raised, breathed its metallic taste, and said, "Margaret Mary Daisy Mae, will you ever get up?"

Through the shadowy mesh I could see her stir in my bed, and then, after the briefest pause, sit bolt upright and look around. I pressed my lips to the screen. The taste of the peach was still at the back of my tongue. "There's work to do," I told her, and she rubbed her eyes and said, still groggy, "I'm awake."

I slipped out from behind the hedge and in through the back door. There were English muffins in the pantry and I toasted her one and spread it with butter and my mother's beach-plum jelly. I poured her some juice and was carrying both to her when she emerged from my room in the floral dress and her white socks and the pink shoes, her hair a mess and her skin so pale it seemed to be made of nothing more substantial than the cotton gauze of my mother's summer curtains. I placed the glass and the dish on the dining-room table. "You okay, Daisy Mae?" I asked her, and she nodded and obediently sat down. "Just sleepy," she said. I watched her as she ate. She ate demurely, one hand and the napkin on her lap, one bite at a time and the careful chewing with the mouth closed. Touch of napkin to her lips after each sip of orange juice. All the niceties that Uncle Jack required at his own Formica-topped table in the overcrowded kitchen in the overcrowded Queens Village house, where I had seen him preside at breakfast with the Transit Authority gun and holster he'd worn the night before still hung around his hips. I picked up the second half of the English muffin and folded it over and asked, "Don't you ever do this?"

She shook her head. Her eyes were tired. I pointed to the fold in the bread. "Bite it here," I said, and she did, and then I showed her the perfect hole she had made in the middle. I told her to raise her index finger and I placed the muffin on it like an oversized ring. "Now you can take it with you," I said. "And nibble on it all day long."

I lifted her plate and her glass and left them both on the kitchen counter as we headed out the back door. I had the Kaufmans' dog to walk first, I told her. And then the Richardsons'. And then we would feed the cats at the Clarke place on the way to pick up Flora. I took her hand as we went through the back fence. She continued to balance the English muffin on the other. The Morans' house was silent as we passed it, the shades in the front room only partially and unevenly closed, giving it that creepy, stupid look of a person sleeping with one glazed eye half open. There was the perennial rusted outboard motor on the grass, a large and battered cardboard box beside it, an abandoned garden hose beside a deflated plastic wading pool, scattered bits of toys, a few bicycles, a pair of little boy's white underpants hanging from the hedge and looking for all the world like a popped balloon. I was grateful to see that there was no sign yet of the Moran kids themselves. I wanted Daisy to be the only child this morning.

We walked down the center of the road and sang "Zip-A-Dee-Doo-Dah" together, swinging our arms back and forth until she lost her balance in the pink shoes and I had to pull her up by the arm to keep her from scraping her knees—which was not hard to do, of course; she was so light I could easily have pulled her right up over my head. A bit of yesterday's fear crossed her face as she recovered, but I got her laughing again when I said, "Have a nice trip?" The sun was fully over the trees by now, and the birds were busy in them. There was still some mist rising from the brown potato fields and the green lawns of the larger estates, and the few people who passed by in cars waved casually. There were enough rabbits still about to keep Daisy perpetually charmed.

I have until now kept out of this account and even, mostly, out of my own recollection, the fall and winter that awaited poor Daisy, because while it may well be the end point of this particular story it is not, after all, the reason I tell it, but this is the morning she mentioned on the phone back in Queens Village, in late February—the morning we saw all the rabbits, she said. The morning she wore on her finger, like a garnet ring, the English muffin spread with beach-plum jelly. Until Red Rover ate it. That morning in June.

The Kaufmans' house was fairly modest, a single-story cedar shake with a curved gravel driveway and white shutters and green flower boxes and red trim. I'd been a mother's helper here two summers ago, when I had dubbed their twins, Colby and Patricia, Cobweb and Peaseblossom. They'd spent last summer with their mother in Europe (my own mother suspected a divorce, and rightly so), and this year they would be at sleep-away camp until August. But their father was out here for the summer and he was the one who had called to ask if I could help him with the dog for the three days a week he needed to be in the city. He was a nice man, short and balding and Jewish, far friendlier than his blond Presbyterian Brooks Brothers madras (and now ex-) wife.

One afternoon when I worked there, while we were sitting around the table beside the pool, just back from the beach, he suddenly leaned over and placed his forearm next to mine. I had the twins, wrapped in beach towels, sitting sleepily in my lap, but they both struggled up to see what their father was doing. "Look at this," he said. His arm was deeply tanned, covered in thick black hair, and mine was its usual after-the-beach

pale red. "Did we spend the day under the same sun or what?"
he said. Then he leaned over me to pull the children's thin,
golden arms out of their towels, and in our efforts to line up all
eight of our arms, he knelt down in front of us, his bare chest
just brushing my knees, and took all of us into a kind of embrace. There began a debate about which of the twins was
tanner—I was immediately declared the least, their father
the most—and they called to their mother to cast the decid-
ing vote. She had just stepped out of the pool house. She had
already showered and was wearing a seersucker kimono and
striped slippers and had a Turkish towel around her head. She
walked over and bent down to add her own arm to the mix. It
was a lovely shade, lighter than the children's, darker than
mine. Her skin was slick and glistening and smelled of lemons.
She held it there for only a moment—her robe fell open for a
second and I could see the spidery white stretch marks against
her tanned breasts—and then, without declaring a winner, she
stood up and said to her husband, who was still pressed against
my knees, "Can I talk to you, please?"

Dr. Kaufman leaned across my lap to kiss the hand of each
child. "You're both beautiful," he said, and then ran his fingers
along my arm as he stood up. He touched my hair and said,
"You, too, Irish," before he followed his wife inside. The twins
immediately pulled the beach towels back over their heads and
snuggled against me again. Cobweb was still a thumbsucker
and Peaseblossom had the end of her braid in her mouth. I
hummed some Christmas hymns for them—it was what they
liked—"O Holy Night" and "What Child Is This?" and "O
Little Town of Bethlehem"—all three of us smelling of pool

water and Coppertone, delightfully warm and sun-weary in the shade of the umbrella, in the sweet offshore breeze. And then I heard their mother's voice calling through the open windows that faced the back of the house. My first impression was that she had dropped something or lost something and was saying, Oh, what happened? or Oh, where is it? Then I wondered for a second—until I remembered who she was—if she might be attempting to sing.

But the sound never formed itself into speaking or singing, and the tone and timbre, the volume, of her voice was something I had never heard before, certainly something that had never drifted through the rose-covered wall that separated my parents' bedroom from my own. I tried to look down at the children: Cobweb's wet thumb had fallen into his lap, but I sensed, although I could not see, that Patricia's eyes were wide open. Their mother's voice grew louder. Oh, what happened? Oh, where is it? But in a language I didn't know. I had only heard voices raised to such a pitch in anger—Daisy's brothers quarreling, or the worst nuns at school demanding our respect—and although I knew this wasn't anger, I wasn't surprised either, when she began to swear, or what sounded like swearing, and then, finally, to cry her husband's name—Phil, Phil, Phil. Somewhere behind all this I thought I heard him saying, Hush, hush, but then even that sound was wiped out by her voice as it veered into a kind of scream. Well before I had admitted to myself that I understood what was going on, I had an impulse to put my hands against the children's ears. The scream gave way to a recognizable moan, what seemed an endless series of them, and then—I wasn't following the logic here at all——a deep-throated laughter that, even after all the commotion of the last few minutes, seemed inappropriately, falsely, raucous——as if she were making an effort to be heard. For me to hear. There was silence, and then I heard him cry, Oh, oh, oh, as if someone were bending back his thumb.

It was some time before they emerged from the house, both of them showered and dressed now. The children had slept soundly in my lap and were just stirring again, and there were pins and needles in both my legs. She took them from me gently, led them into the house, where the cook had already begun to fix them their dinner, and then she turned back to ask me if I wanted to take one last swim before I went home, her voice its usual slightly flat and nasal drawl. I dove in, mostly to hide my own awkwardness, and when I climbed out only he was on the patio, fiddling with the grill. I pulled my T-shirt over my wet bathing suit, gathered my beach bag and my towel, and slipped into my flip-flops. "Good night, Dr. Kaufman," I said, and he turned to look over his shoulder, not really looking, only putting his face in my direction, not his eyes. He said, "Good night, sugar," the same endearment he used with the kids. They were eating toasted cheese at the table in the breakfast nook, and I kissed them good night and then unwound Cobweb from my waist at the front door with a hundred assurances that I would see him first thing in the morning. I walked home in what was fast becoming twilight, something of the encroaching blue-black sky and the lingering scarlet sunset now embedded like a dark jewel in my own vision of married life—— of my own, unformed future.

Last summer, when my mother guessed that the trip to

Europe meant the Kaufmans were divorcing, I thought that afternoon was proof positive she was wrong. I didn't realize, she argued, how easy a thing divorce had become for non-Catholics. She didn't realize (I failed to argue) what the Kaufmans were capable of doing in the waning hours of a summer afternoon.

The dog kennel was in the back, behind the pool house. The pool without the children's toys and swim rings seemed desolate, and Red Rover threw himself against the fence when he saw us as if I had orchestrated their return. He was your usual jittery Irish setter, but mostly pretty well mannered, so I wasn't prepared for the way he rushed for Daisy as soon as I opened the gate, devouring her English muffin in an instant and then nearly knocking her over with his wiggling and wagging. She was startled, but not frightened, and although she backed away, she was closer to laughter than to tears. I grabbed him by the collar and snapped on his leash, while he took a minute to lick the jelly from his chops. And then he turned his head toward me and seemed to say, "Oh, it's you!" and, nearly beside himself with joy, began to lick my face and my chin, his paws on my chest. I had to push him off me, and push him out the kennel door, Daisy all the while hanging on the fence and now laughing breathlessly.

We continued on, down toward the Coast Guard beach, where I was able to unleash him and let him run. Daisy was still a little overwhelmed, and I told her to sit on a stone and take off her shoes and socks before she walked in the sand. "Maybe tomorrow you'll want to wear your sneakers," I said. She sat down as I'd told her, but she made no move to take off the pink shoes. I had one eye on Red, who kept turning back and going forward, more or less waiting for us, but running off a little farther each time. I knew he was too much of a coward to run very far, but I didn't want to be stuck walking to Amagansett to retrieve him—I had to be at Flora's by nine.

I turned back to Daisy, but she had still made no move to take off the shoes. "The sand will ruin those, Daisy Mae," I said, and I bent down to pull them off myself. Abruptly she scooted her feet away from me, and when I looked up at her, somewhat startled, she had her nose in the air, one of those bratty, overacted poses I had seen plenty of other kids strike, but never her. "What's the matter?" I said, and to complete the picture she folded her arms across her chest, across the bodice of the sweet-collared dress, and said, stubbornly, "I don't want to take them off." The sun on her wiry, uncombed hair brought out the reds and the golds and the possibility that she did indeed, as her mother and Bernadette had assured me, have a redhead's temper.

I stood up straight and shrugged. "Suit yourself," I said and, without another word or look, kicked off my own battered Keds and ran down toward Red Rover, who saw this as his signal to take off full tilt ahead of me. I ran after him for a while, the leash in my hand, and then slowed down to a walk as he began to nose and sniff at whatever he could find along the shoreline, playing his own game of keeping me near without seeming to. When I finally turned to look back, Daisy was running toward me down the beach. It took a few minutes for me to see that she had her pink shoes in her hands and her white socks still on her feet, and that she was crying. I held my arms out to her as she grew nearer, and when she reached me, I lifted her and spun her around. When I put her down again, she sobbed into my hip. "Were you afraid someone was going to steal them?" I asked, and she waited a moment before she nodded. "Do you want to take off your socks, too?" I said, and she whispered, "No." Red came bounding toward us, and I picked up a piece of driftwood and tossed it to make him head back toward the road. "All right," I said.

Sitting on the same stone, Daisy brushed the sand off the thin socks and slipped them back into her shoes. "You still don't want to take those off?" I asked, and she shook her head. "You don't have sand between your toes?" Smiling, she shook her head again. I shrugged. With kids, you never knew. It could have been a broken toenail. It could have been that her brothers, or Bernadette, had told her she had stinky feet. It could have been that she did indeed fear that her magic slippers would be stolen. It could have been a whim.

I got the leash on Red Rover and we started walking again, toward the Richardsons'. They had two Scotties—an obvious choice for a couple of tweedy New Yorkers with vaguely British accents. The Scotties got along fine with the setter, and so to save time, we stopped to pick them up on the way to bringing Red Rover home. Their house was Tudor, naturally, and pretty grand, with lovely flower gardens and what seemed a big staff. The Richardsons walked their dogs themselves for a good hour or so every afternoon—which is when I had met them—coming home from the beach with Flora at the beginning of June. Mrs. Richardson was one of those blunt, loud, bangs-across-the-forehead women who seemed to believe that everyone else must surely be as pleased with her as she was with herself for being so no-nonsense and direct and, as she saw it, egalitarian. She and her husband were astonished at the paroxysm of stumpy tail-wagging their two little dogs launched into as we passed each other, and astonished further by the way they lowered their bellies to the ground as I bent down to scratch their ears. "They're usually terribly standoff-ish," she said in her semi-British way. Leaning over the edge of her stroller, Flora was delighted by them, too, and so a conversation began between us, and Mrs. Richardson learned by direct inquiry that I lived in that sweet cottage with the dahlias (interested) and went to the academy (more interested) and babysat for this child of the famous artist (most interested) down the road. Staring straight into my face with the divine right of a dowager queen, she said, "You're very pretty, aren't you?" She turned to her husband, who carried a pipe. "Isn't she?" Embarrassing us both. "I bet you're bright, too, and industrious, aren't you?" She could have been a black-and-white character actress in pearls, staring at me through a monocle. "You've certainly charmed my dogs," she said. Just as we parted—the Scotties digging their little gray nails into the road to express their reluctance to move on—I mentioned that I walked dogs, too, for some of our neighbors. "*Do* you?" she said. She smiled smugly at her husband—didn't I say she was industrious?—and then turned back to me. Well, then, she said, seeing how her dogs had taken to me, and seeing how they were growing rather stout, she wondered if I wouldn't like to come by the house some morning and walk them a bit while she and her husband played golf. I *would* like to, I said, as if I were correcting her (telling Flora, after we had pushed on, that if I wouldn't like to, I wouldn't, would I?). And so it was arranged.

As usual, the dogs were handed over to me at the back door

by one of the maids ("A maid?" Daisy whispered, laughing, as if I had said a leprechaun or a centaur). And since they were far more predictable than Red Rover, I handed both their leashes to Daisy and kept Red's for myself. The road the Richardsons lived on was wider and grander and lined with great oaks that were lush and fresh that time of year, bordered with green grass and dark hedges, and at one point as we walked along, I held back a bit so I could watch Daisy, with her messy red hair (I vowed to braid it later) and in my old dress and the cherished pink slippers and the sandy socks, walk regally behind the plump and pampered Scotties, who, in the same year that Daisy had been born to her baby-beleaguered parents, had been flown first-class from Edinburgh to Idlewild, to be delivered into Mrs. Richardson's waiting arms.

We put Red Rover back into his pen with fresh water and some dog biscuits and the reassurance that we would return in late afternoon, and then walked the Scotties back to my house to pick up our beach things before we got Flora. Tony and Petey Moran were already sitting on my back steps, Petey with a new quarter-moon cut under his eye that had almost blackened it. The two boys fell on the two dogs as soon as we were inside the yard with them—literally fell on them, like halfwit hillbillies chasing a greased pig, going down on them chest first, their arms spread, and then rolling in the grass as the dogs, with surprising speed and presence of mind, and even a bit of a growl, scooted away. I had to raise my voice (to the boys, not the dogs) to restore order, and then I got both boys and both dogs and Daisy to sit in a circle on the lawn. The poor Scotties were panting by then, and Petey and Tony seemed to be panting, too, with love and desire and their wild blue-eyed affection for all creatures they could pet or caress and, often in the same gesture, hurt. I let Petey sit beside one (Angus, I think; I never could tell them apart) and Tony beside the other (Rupert) and watched them gently stroke their dogs for a few minutes, the dogs quickly growing accustomed to the long, soothing strokes, if not to the little-boy faces hanging beside theirs, hovering as if to plant a kiss. At one point Tony slipped his arm around the dog and tried to pull it into his lap, but I stopped him. These were not really old dogs, I explained, but they had really old owners, and if the boys were not calm they might very well end up with a nose bitten off. I guided their hands over the tops of the dogs' heads and down their backs. "Nice and calm," I said. Then I introduced Daisy, and the two boys gazed at her out of their trance of affection. "My cousin. She's here to help me for the summer."

"Hi," they said, and then Petey added, "I like your shoes," something of both larceny and lechery in his voice, a tone aided and abetted no doubt by the pirate patch of a black eye. Petey was maybe nine or ten that summer, and had only recently gotten over his habit of asking me, at constant three-minute intervals, "Do you like me?" "Do you like my brother?" "Do you like my mom?" "Do you like me?" He was the neediest of the Moran kids, and they were a needy lot. Twice in the past year he had spent the night under the hedge outside my bedroom window, and twice my parents had considered calling Child Services about him. But he was well fed and went to school and his cuts and scrapes and bruises were no different from any of the cuts and scrapes and bruises of his siblings, all of which seemed to be the product of bad luck and ill timing, accident and fate. When I asked Petey what he'd done to his eye, Tony explained for him that he had been running around with two juice glasses on his face, pretending they were binoculars, and had smashed right into a doorjamb.

"You must have been going pretty fast," I said.

"He said he was chasing the last remaining looney bird on earth," Tony said.

"And who was the looney bird?" I asked Petey.

He bowed his head. "Baby June," he said, and then, abashed, buried his face in Angus's (or Rupert's) neck. Surprisingly enough, the dog, still panting, tolerated it, even thumped his tail a bit and raised one paw as if to stay balanced. Perhaps he realized that in all his eight years at the Richardsons', he'd never been quite so necessary. I leaned across the grass and put a hand on Petey's prickly head. "Perfectly understandable," I said, hoping it would mean, "I like you, Petey."

When boys and dogs seemed properly subdued, I gave the ends of the leashes to Daisy and, standing slowly, walked back into the house. I gathered our beach things and made our sandwiches—all the while glancing out the window to make sure everything was all right, because with the Moran kids, you could never be sure. But the dogs were lying in the grass by now, the boys still stroking their coats, and it seemed Petey and Tony and Daisy were actually having some kind of conversation. Daisy was idly braiding the leashes together, nodding, and Tony was slowly pulling at the grass as he talked. I wondered if they were commiserating—about too many siblings and harried parents and a family in which you were loved, but perhaps not well enough. About houses that smelled of wet wool and old socks and hastily applied industrial cleaner, where parents sometimes stumbled on your name or slapped you without meaning to or looked at you as if you were everything they'd ever wanted going down the drain—and then closed a door and forgot you completely, crying, Oh, where is it? Oh, what happened? Oh, oh, oh—in misery and happiness and anger and laughter and pain.

I made two extra sandwiches for the Moran kids, but just as I brought them outside, two of the girls showed up, Judy, who was about eleven, and baby June, whose drooping diaper was so wet it seemed to leave a kind of damp slug's trail on the grass. I sent Judy back to their house for a new one and changed the baby right there on the lawn, Tony and Petey standing over me, eating their sandwiches and offering casual bits of guidance ("There's a piece of grass on her tush"), like construction workers on coffee break. I tossed the wet diaper into my mother's empty laundry basket at the side of the house and let the boys walk the Scotties to the corner, Judy and the baby coming along, too, where I told them all I really had to get to work. They turned back readily enough, but a few minutes later Tony and Petey came zooming by on their banana bikes, slowing beside us and circling around us and then zooming up again. They were waiting there when we emerged from the Richardsons' driveway after dropping off the dogs and followed us most of the way to the Clarkes' as well, until they were distracted by a red convertible with a wide and startlingly white interior that passed by on an intersecting road. Standing straight up on their pedals, they headed off to see if they could chase it down and find out if it belonged to a movie star. "We'll let you know," Petey shouted back over his shoulder, his voice deep and serious, full of comic-book urgency. It was clear that there were two of us now whom he wanted to impress.

"He likes you," I said to Daisy, and she smirked and shrugged and said the requisite "Eeww," and then, when I said it again, the pro forma "Does not."

I stopped and bent down and took hold of her skinny leg. I lifted her foot, and she leaned against me, hopping on the other to keep her balance. I pretended to inspect her shoe. I could see how the white socks were still peppered with grains of sand. There was a shiny scar on her knee and a series of black-and-blue marks down her freckled calf. A girl with brothers. "Your shoes are getting pinker," I said, dropping one leg and picking up the other one. "You must be in love."

The Clarkes' house was vaguely Victorian, with a nice big front porch and a back patio that looked out on a wide sloping lawn and a little pond surrounded by cattails and dragonflies. Mr. and Mrs. Clarke were friends of my parents who shared the same city background and middle-class income, the house itself being an inheritance from a bachelor uncle of Mr. Clarke's who had done well in the garment industry. In my childhood I had been enchanted by the house, not only because of its pond and porch, the diamond-shaped panes in its bay windows, or its turret and widow's watch, but also because I believed for many years that it actually had been given to Mr. Clarke by a fairy——by his fairy uncle, as I'd heard him say, or, his uncle the fairy. In the wonderland that was my solitary childhood, such a bequest—a wave of a cattail wand, a flash of sunlight on a beveled pane of glass, a flutter of dragonfly wings——seemed both credible and marvelous. Had I not learned the truth of the matter in my freshman year at the academy (it was, I'm afraid, more of a slow, disappointed dawning than a flash of illuminating light), I might, on this pretty June morning now full of bee sound and birdsong and the scent of mown grass, have told Daisy the same.

The Clarkes spent every summer in an apartment on the North Shore so they could rent their house to a wealthy Westchester family, the Swansons, from June to September. The cats belonged to the Clarkes, but the Westchester family liked the idea of renting the cats as well, so their children could have the experience of pets without the year-long obligation. I was part of the bargain, too. I took care of the cats on weekdays when the Swansons went home (unlike so many of the summer mothers whose husbands worked in the city, Mrs. Swanson would not spend five nights a week out here alone), and I sometimes babysat for the kids as well on Saturday nights. My parents wouldn't let me take any money from the Clarkes, since they were friends and apparently struggling to keep the old house in good repair, but the Swansons always drank too much at dinner and paid me twice what I asked when they came home.

The Clarkes and their tenants had one of those odd, long-term relationships that seemed more like a custody deal than a summer rental. Although they had no children themselves (they had cats, and the fact that they were willing to rent out their cats as well as their house probably tells you all you need to know about them), the Clarkes had allowed the Swansons to install a basketball hoop over the garage and a small swing set in the side yard. They'd also let the Swansons put an extra refrigerator in the basement and an awning over the patio. When the Swansons offered to replace all the kitchen appliances and repaint most of the rooms, the Clarkes had complied. They'd also let them buy the wicker furniture for the porch and tear up the fairly new wall-to-wall carpeting and refinish the wood floors. In another summer or two, the Swansons would offer to install an in-ground pool, a real coup for the Clarkes (my parents thought), who got both a boost to their property value and further insurance that their faithful and generous renters would indeed return for many more summers. Later still, long after I'd moved away and in the midst of outlandish interest rates and a depressed real estate market, the Swansons would offer the Clarkes a princely sum for their house—enough for them to buy another on the North Shore as well as a condo in Florida—a cause for much discussion among my parents and the Clarkes, who urged us to talk to a real estate agent ourselves. But, my parents said, the offer was a fluke, a stroke of tremendous luck for the Clarkes, a purely emotional gesture by the Swansons. Never mind that in another decade the Clarkes' house would be worth more than ten times what the Swansons had paid them, for a while it seemed that the electrician and the housekeeper from Woodside had trumped the Wall Street guy from Westchester, who, the joke went, had more dollars than sense.

In the kitchen, Daisy and I changed the water and the litter box and put out the three bowls of fresh food for Moe, Larry, and Curly—who circled our legs and purred with their yours-for-the-asking love and allegiance. She sat on the floor with them and laughed when they stepped across the skirt of her dress, which she had stretched taut between her two knees, or when Curly rubbed his face on the hard sides of her pink shoes. "They're so friendly," she said, and I told her, "That's how they get fed."

As I went around opening the windows for a few minutes (an extra service Mrs. Clarke had asked me to provide), I gave Daisy a tour of the place, which even that early in the season was more Swanson than Clarke, what with the grass-cloth mats on the floors, and the elaborate vases of fading wildflowers on each table, and the children's rooms. The Swansons had two kids, a boy and a girl (millionaire's choice, my mother called it), Debbie and Donald, and because of them, the two guest rooms that during the Clarkes' reign were as plain and serviceable as convent cells—unadorned beige walls, white chenille spreads, single mahogany dressers—were now colorful and chaotic, with construction-paper artwork and garish stuffed animals and painted seashells and bedspreads and curtains in bright blue and hot pink. The cats—named by Mr. Clarke, of course, who was a short-armed man with a round, pugnacious face, a hybrid of all three of the Stooges himself—followed us in and out of every room with their tails and noses in the air, evidence of their feline assurance that no matter the decor, the place was theirs alone. I wondered if it was because of them that Daisy, peeking into one room and then the next, felt obliged to whisper.

On the third floor, which was part guest room, part unfinished attic, I showed her the short door to the widow's watch. In the old days, I explained, with no telephones or even telegraph, the only way a wife would know if her husband was coming home from the sea was by looking at the horizon—the straight, uninterrupted blue by day, and at night, when there was a moon, the nearly indecipherable line of inky black. She would have to look and look until his ship appeared, and at first it would be just the slightest dot, or the tiniest light, at the edge of the world, nothing more. Being able to see the ocean, I explained, was as important to the wives of sailors and ships' captains as having a telephone or a radio, or even a mailbox, was to us, because otherwise, if you couldn't look out and check the horizon for his boat, you'd be forced just to wait in your living room until he came through the front door. You wouldn't know if your husband, or your son, or your father, was coming back till he walked in the front door.

Listening politely, Daisy nodded and pushed her wild hair behind her goofy ears—the obedient child who knows she's supposed to be learning something. "Sometimes," Daisy said, "I sit up with my mother when my father works late."

"Yeah," I said. "But, see, he can always call. If he's going to be late. He can call and say he's on his way home. But sailors, in those days, couldn't call."

"She gets really worried," Daisy said, indicating with a roll of her eyes that this was a "really" to be reckoned with. "Whenever he's late."

"Well, sure," I said. "She gets nervous." As if Aunt Peg ever stopped being nervous. "Imagine what it would be like if you had to go up on the roof every night to look for his car—if there was no other way to know he was coming. Imagine what that would be like."

She shuddered, laughing. "That'd be funny," she said. But still, I couldn't convince her to step outside for a glimpse of the ocean.

Going through the rooms again to pull the windows closed, I started to sing a song my father sang—one of a hundred mournful tunes he knew—about a ship that never (ne'er) returned, and I wasn't halfway through the refrain when Daisy joined in: "No, they ne'er returned, they ne'er returned, and their fate is still unlearned. / And from that day to this, fond hearts are watching for the ship that ne'er returned." Hearing the words in her thin little voice, as opposed to my father's baritone, it suddenly struck me that they weren't delightfully melancholy and noble, as I had always thought, but wrenchingly, even cruelly sentimental. ("Said the feeble lad to his aged mother, as he kissed his weeping wife / Just one more trip, let me cross the ocean, and I'll settle down for life . . . But he ne'er returned.")

"How do you know that song?" I asked her, interrupting, and she said her mother sang it—which revealed it to me, for the first time, as something my father must have learned in childhood. It struck me, too, for the first time, and on Daisy's behalf, not my own, that it was a terrible song to sing to a child, and even though I was the one who had begun to sing it—and who had broached the whole idea with my social-studies lesson in sailors' wives—it was Aunt Peg I blamed for teaching it to poor Daisy.

"I've never heard your mother sing," I said, and Daisy nodded. "She does. Mostly at night, to get us to sleep."

I had an instant vision of Aunt Peg standing in the upstairs hallway (the Sacred Heart peering over her shoulder)—hands on her hips, her toe impatiently tapping—getting through the song as if it were yet another task to complete: "Ne'er returned, still at sea, fond hearts, still watching, life is short, life

is cruel (don't I know it) there you go, off to bed, done"—and
I began to do an imitation of her as Daisy and I marched down
the stairs to shut the remaining windows. Daisy joined in, and
by the time we'd locked the kitchen door again and returned
the key to the flowerpot under the porch step, we were singing
at the top of our lungs, fast and furious, clipping off the
words—"that-day-to-this"—until, on about the twelfth repeti-
tion, I shouted, instead of "fond hearts," "hard farts," and
Daisy, face red, her hands flying to her mouth (check off another of Uncle Jack's no-no's), doubled over in shame and
delight. Shame and delight being, it seemed to me, a fine antidote for the song's dreary message about the cruelty of time
and fate, and the useless longings of all of us who get left behind. On to Flora's.

The side gate for Flora's house was easy to miss, which made it
a better alternative to the more obvious driveway entrance another quarter mile down the road. "Here we are," I said to
Daisy, suddenly pausing in the middle of the street, and the
lovely thing was that she looked up first, into the trees, before
her eyes fell on the narrow wrought-iron gate that had been
placed across what was essentially a child-sized hole in the
thick and brambly hedge. "Here?" she said, and I said, "Here."
The hedge was so high and overgrown that there was, of
course, no evidence of anything that lay beyond it, which no
doubt made her hesitate after we crossed the little berm of
grass and I began to pull against the stubborn hinges. "Go
ahead," I said, holding the gate, but she paused. "It's okay?"

she asked. "It's fine," I told her. "Just a back door." Still, she
looked at me warily until I put my hand on her shoulder and
scooted her along. "They put this gate here just for us," I said.
"They call it the caretaker's gate. It's just for us." Still cautious,
she went ahead, passing rather elegantly under the low and
tangled bower that I had to stoop (brush of leaf and branch
against my hair) in order to clear.

Inside, the path was mostly grown over—only a sprinkling
of tiny rocks and sand here and there among the weeds and
the fallen branches. The path ran through a pretty substantial
wood, this whole side of the property was heavily wooded, and
because the sunlight came in stripes—thick shafts of it, ahead
of us and to either side—the undergrowth still felt damp and
the air a little musty. Suddenly the sun, which had been growing progressively, appropriately, warmer on our heads through-
out the morning, seemed to have lost its pace, or its rhythm
—its certainty, anyway—and for a moment I felt we could
have been passing through any time of day at all, early morning, late afternoon, and nearly any season. I mentioned this to
Daisy and she said, "It's nice." There was the scurry of salamanders or field mice near our feet, and the crossing shadows
of birds high up in the leaves. I stopped to break a stalk of
milkweed for Daisy, and she nodded earnestly, as she did at
everything I had to show her. I took her hand. Cathedral light,
to be sure, and the smell of damp earth and wet wood and, as I
began to see the shape of Flora's house through the trees, the
faint whiff of paint or turpentine, or whatever it was that
Flora's father was using—something to do with art, anyway.

He was out on the driveway, standing behind an old door

set across two sawhorses and stirring a small can of paint. There was a canvas placed upright against the garage wall. It was about the width and the length of a man's arms, and there were already a few dribbles of black and gray paint scattered across it. There were four more cans on the makeshift table, each with its collar of spilled color—white, gray, black, and even, I was happy to see, bright red. He had some sketches on the table as well, and he was studying these as he stirred, staring at them in that same vaguely disinterested way he had looked at his work the first night I came here—assessing it by some criteria I couldn't begin to imagine or understand. There was a cigarette in the corner of his mouth, and when Daisy's hard shoes hit the gravel drive, he looked up for a moment, squinting through the smoke just long enough to determine what it was that had emerged into the sunshine from the path through the woods, and then—he may have laughed a little—going back to his work. I waved, just to be polite, and edged Daisy back onto the grass to quiet her footsteps.

"Is that the artist?" she whispered. I told her it was, and then I told her not to stare.

"He's very old," she said, turning back.

"He's Flora's father," I answered, as if to contradict her.

The housekeeper met us at the front door and said in her agitated and accented English that the lady went into the village for a few minutes with the baby but would be back right away, we should wait. I put our beach bag down beside the door and then crossed the porch and sat on the step, Daisy beside me. The front porch was long and low, with a few white canvas chairs scattered across it and a pair of ashtrays on tall white pedestals placed in between them. The front lawn was wide and planted with three small weeping-cherry trees, which I told Daisy we would someday hang with lollipops and maybe candy necklaces or strings of licorice, to give Flora a treat. We leaned over our knees. The tips of her pink shoes were darkened with dew and I touched the little jewels to see if the dampness had loosened them. It hadn't. I drew a tic-tac-toe in the sandy dirt at our feet and was just letting her win the second game when we heard him say, "Excuse me, ladies." And then he was stepping between us, his canvas shoes and khaki pants speckled with paint, his ankles bare, an unearthly shade of yellowish white and deep pink. There was a whiff of cigarette smoke and turpentine in his clothes. As soon as he went into the house, Daisy stood and walked to the end of the path, leaning out so she could see the canvas against the garage wall. She turned and looked at me. "What is it?" she whispered.

"It's a painting," I said.

"What's it of?"

I shrugged. "I don't know. Something in his head."

Impressed, she looked at it again. "But what?" I heard her say. Behind me, the door opened, and I moved my knees aside to let him pass. Pant legs and strange, soft shoes (I'd never seen a man wear such shoes) and in his hand, held low by his thigh, a short glass with ice and some brownish alcohol in it—the sudden scent of Uncle Tommy in the air. His fingers and the back of his wrist were sinewy and old and flecked with dark paint. Daisy turned to look at him, her mouth open and her eyes wide—he might have been a dragon passing by—and as he passed her, he lightly touched his hand to her head, the way you would just idly touch a fence post or a garden statue.

Quickly Daisy came back to the steps to sit beside me, her pink shoes drawn up under the floral skirt. He did not return to the table with the paints, or to his sketches, but went instead through the side door of the garage—we saw the bare lightbulb come on in the far window—and was still there when his wife's car pulled into the drive.

Flora was in the back seat, crying. Her mother got out immediately, her face severe, and said to me, without pause or greeting, "Would you get her out, please?" And then walked into the house, her sandals flapping against her bare heels, spitting up bits of gravel as she went. In the car, Flora was pinned to the upholstery by an elaborate harness made of her mother's silk scarves, one across her waist, two tied bandolier style across her chest, and each secured to the black cloth seat by huge diaper pins. I said, "Hi, there, Flora Dora," and she kicked her feet and pulled at the scarves across her chest and whined, but in a halfhearted way that made it clear her tears were subsiding. "You look like you've been kidnapped by Gypsies," I said. She had been crying for quite some time. Her little face was swollen with it, her already unremarkable features further diminished by the crying she had done. I knelt beside her on the car seat, brushed some thin hair from her wet forehead, and, as I unpinned the scarves one at a time, began to tell her about Daisy, who was just behind me on the driveway. Still sniffling, Flora leaned forward to see her. Daisy came all the way from New York on the train, I told her, all by herself, and Daisy has six brothers, three big ones and three little ones, a matching set, and a sister named Bernadette, named after another little girl who once saw the Blessed Virgin Mary, the most beautiful woman anyone has ever seen, while she was out playing with her friends, in a grotto by a stream in another country far away, the same country where Paris is, and the Eiffel Tower. And now when sick people go to France and drink the water from that stream, they get better, and when old people drink it, they get young again, and when crying babies drink it in their bottles, they begin to smile, and all their tears turn into lovely jewels that their mothers pluck from their cheeks and put into rings and necklaces and bracelets, some even glue them to their shoes, the way Daisy's mother did.

The scarves—black and gold and white and turquoise blue—were beautiful and expensive and had the lovely, faded smell of perfume not recently applied. I folded each one as I unpinned it, and placed it on the ledge behind the back seat with the closed-up diaper pins. Then I lifted Flora out and put her on the driveway next to Daisy. Together, both girls bent to examine the pretty shoes. As I reached back in for the scarves and the pins, I heard Daisy say, "Jewels."

Flora's mother was in the kitchen speaking French to the housekeeper, and when I handed her the scarves she shrugged and said, with a laugh, "There's no other way to keep her from rolling down the windows," and then put the scarves on top of the refrigerator. She asked me to give Flora some crackers and a cup of milk—she'd eaten nothing for breakfast, she said—and then she and the housekeeper both left the room. I'd had no chance to introduce Daisy, but Flora's mother had hardly seemed to notice her. I poured both girls some milk and put a plate of digestive biscuits on the table between them. Flora took only a sip of the milk and then slipped off her chair and climbed into my lap and wearily put her head on my chest. She was wearing another shapeless white dress, her white baby shoes, and white socks trimmed with lace. Her bare legs were dimpled and chubby and rosy pink, and I saw that Daisy was studying them, too, perhaps recalling, as I was, her old father's thin white skin. "Somebody wore herself out this morning," I said, to Daisy and to Flora as well. "Crying's hard work, isn't it?" And both girls agreed.

When her mother came into the kitchen again, she was wearing a beige dress and high heels and there was a white cardigan draped over her shoulders. Her dark hair was pulled back smoothly, giving more prominence, and power, to her long, determined nose. Her lipstick was freshly applied, more bright red. "Listen," she said, her eyes just momentarily falling, indifferently, on Daisy, "I need to go up to the city, I don't know how long I'll be. You keep coming, as always. Ana will be here. And the cook. Keep Flora out for as long as you can if the weather's good. She sleeps better when she's been out all day." She turned to Ana as if we had all left the room. "It's going to be as hot as hell in Manhattan," she said. Despite the curse word, she was smiling under her long nose, anticipating something delightful—perhaps what a fine time she would have in Manhattan while we were all back here trying to wear Flora out. I thought of my own summer visits to the city with my parents, the stifling streets, the gritty air, the hot smell of the subway blowing up from those heel-catching grates. Women in short white gloves and sleeveless dresses, touching shoulders, sweating, waiting in crowds at corners for the light to change. And that moment of disorientation and fear when we left the Music Hall or the Museum of Natural History or the restaurant (Patricia Murphy's) where we'd gone for dinner, and saw that the sky above the city was now pitch dark—that the city had become a city at night. I was pretty certain that it was this particular city, the city at night, that Flora's mother was bound for—and delighted to be bound for—while we, the caretakers, stayed behind. "I must be out of my mind," she said, turning away from us, clearly pleased with herself but still annoyed with Flora, because she did not give her a kiss goodbye, although Flora, weary from weeping, didn't seem much to mind.

From the kitchen window, I saw her cross the driveway, Ana scurrying behind with a small valise that she stopped to put into the back seat of the car while Flora's mother went on, through the side door of her husband's workshop. I didn't recall ever seeing her go in there, and she wasn't inside for more than a few minutes when she came out again, her face harder and tighter than before, the white sweater buttoned at her throat and thrown over her shoulders like a little Superman cape of resolve and indignation. She gestured to Ana, and Ana quickly got into the car. Then she turned on her heels once again and came back into the house. I heard her shoes on the wooden floor, across the hallway, through the living room, back into the carpeted bedrooms, and then, a few minutes later, out again. I looked at Daisy, who was used to the permutations in the weather of a house with people in it. She shrugged and smiled. Then Flora's mother once again appeared in the kitchen door. "My scarves," she said, and I pointed to the top of the refrigerator, where she had placed them. She reached up and took them down, sorted through them, and then chose the turquoise-and-white one, placing the others on the kitchen table right in front of me. I took the moment to introduce Daisy, and although she seemed hardly to hear, she did say, as she shook out the scarf, pausing to examine a small hole the diaper pin had made, "What a pretty dress. I had one just like it." She then folded the scarf into a triangle and placed it over her hair, leaning her head back as she did, her eyes half closed. She tied it under her chin and then wrapped the ends around her neck and tied them again. "You might also want to come by a little earlier while I'm gone," she said. "Eight or eight-thirty or so, to give Ana a hand." I said that I would. She leaned down to look at her reflection in the side of the toaster. On my lap, Flora said, "Bye-bye, Mommy," and Mommy said, "Bye-bye, dear."

She straightened up. In the scarf she seemed very tall and very elegant, but homely, too, without her dark hair to soften the hard lines of her face and that gray, precise skin. "If my husband tries to fuck you while I'm gone," she said softly, "don't be frightened. He's an old man and he drinks. Chances are it will be brief." She cupped her fingers to the back of Flora's head, which put her hand right under my chin. "You can always send him to Ana, if you want," she said, and then bent down, the fragrant scarf right at my nose, and kissed Flora on the head, leaving lipstick and the scent of her face powder on the child's pale scalp.

I sat for a few minutes after she had gone, waiting for the heat to leave my cheeks before I looked at Daisy. I had one arm around Flora, but my right hand was on the table and I was surprised to see that my fingers were trembling. I was embarrassed and angry and surprised—I would have thought the housekeeper was too old to be included in such talk, just as, a few minutes ago, I might have presumed I was too young and Flora's mother too elegant to speak such a word. I heard the car pull out of the driveway, and then waited a few minutes more before I slowly raised my eyes to Daisy. She was looking at me with more expectation than caution, certainly with no fear. I wondered if she'd missed the word, or if she recognized its sound only when it was shouted in anger or used as an adjective, as her father tended to do. I blew some air through my lips and Daisy did the same: even if she didn't know the word when used in its proper context, she knew a marital spat when she saw one, and she nodded a little, wisely, when I said, "Oh, what fools these mortals be."

"She's falling asleep," Daisy whispered, pointing at Flora in my lap, whose eyelids were indeed fluttering closed. I hoisted her to my shoulder and stood, pushing my chair back with the back of my knees. I told Daisy to go out to the porch to fetch the beach bag and then carried Flora to her bedroom. I fully expected her to revive when I placed her on the changing table, but she only whined and cried and did not open her eyes, so when I was finished, I lifted her into her crib and covered her with a thin blanket. She smiled sleepily. She seemed grateful to be out of the fray. I wondered what had gone on in the village this morning, and whether it was her daughter's tantrum or her husband's familiarity (my parents' word) with the maid that had sent Flora's mother off to New York. I smoothed Flora's hair. Either way, the door had been shut on the child.

On the wall above the crib were the three simple pencil

sketches of Flora and her mother—sweet enough to be hung in a church. Good drawings, I thought. But in the living room I had just passed through there was also a large canvas of what seemed to me to be only smashed images, perhaps of a woman—an ear, a breast, some lips. And another, smaller painting that was simply color, and not even particularly pretty color, dark paints that had merely been dropped or spilled or smeared. I pulled the blanket up to Flora's cheek.

It suddenly occurred to me that Ana was not too old and I was not too young, because he was both this baby's father and an old, old man. Because he could draw sweet Madonnas and dismembered faces and pictures of nothing, nothing at all. I wondered if it took an act of will or just a long, long life to achieve this—to exceed or to outlive or simply to escape the limits of time and age, of what could or couldn't be done, should or shouldn't be done. To use no other criteria but your own, straight out of your head.

I turned away from the crib and saw Daisy coming along the narrow hallway that led from the living room, the beach bag over her arm. She seemed to be favoring her right leg as she walked. I put my finger to my lips and touched her on the small of her back to lead her out again, and as soon as we had passed through the front door I asked if she was getting a blister from her shoes. She said no, her foot was just asleep, but not without a bit of a flush rising to her cheeks.

"If they're hurting you," I said, "you might want to take them off for a while." But she shook her head and handed me the beach bag and changed the subject by asking, "Now what are we supposed to do?"

"Sit and wait," I said. "Until she wakes up." And seeing

that was unsatisfactory, I offered, "We can read." I moved two of the canvas chairs under Flora's window and then told Daisy to go inside to pick out some books from the basket beside the desk. I took my own book from the beach bag and sat with it, pulling my legs up into the sway-bottomed chair, my paperback on my raised knees. And then I watched him from over the top of it as he left his studio and walked to the house. He climbed the three steps slowly, shuffling on the balls of his feet, his head down, not to avoid me, I think, but in a real failure to notice I was there. He went into the house and I listened. I heard the rattle of an ice tray in the kitchen, and then, a few minutes later, he came through the door again with a new drink in his hand and said, as if we'd already spoken, "The little redhead inside says you'll know where the Saint Joseph's is kept."

I put my book down, and my legs. I had some unformed and disconcerting image of old St. Joseph and the young Virgin Mary before I even managed to say, "I beg your pardon?" He was smiling, about the eyes mostly, as if it had pleased him to discover a little redhead in his house, or to see me so puzzled. "The children's aspirin," he said again. "The St. Joseph's children's aspirin. The little girl inside said you would know where we keep it."

"In Flora's room," I said. "The shoebox in her closet." And then, suddenly understanding his expectation, I stood and told him I'd get it. I met Daisy at the door, a pile of picture books in her arms. I told her I'd be back in a minute.

When I returned, he was in the other canvas chair and Daisy was on the porch floor, the books spread around her. I handed him the bottle and then had to step between her and him, over the books and his feet, between her shoulder and his knees, to get back to where I'd been sitting. I could feel the heat rise in my cheeks, and I put my book on my lap, afraid if I held it up I would see my fingers trembling again. I was only beginning to fully understand the full, rotten effect of Flora's mother's last-minute instructions for the babysitter.

I couldn't look at his face. He placed his drink in the smoked-glass ashtray, then opened the bottle and handed it to Daisy. "See if your clever little fingers can get that cotton out for me," he said.

Solemnly, she took it from him, pulled the cotton out, and handed the bottle back. With her mouth open, she gazed up at him, the cotton ball still in her hand, and I reached down to relieve her of it. He shook a few of the aspirins into his palm and then, picking them off one by one, put them in his mouth and began to chew. I felt him looking at me as he did. I looked up. Behind his thick glasses, his eyes still seemed to be on the verge of laughter. His white shock of hair might have stirred.

"Never get old," he said. He was chewing all on one side. "Or, better yet, never get old teeth." He reached for his glass, took a sip, swished it around in his mouth, and swallowed. He returned the glass to the ashtray and shook a few more aspirins into his palm. "Nothing better to remind you of your mortality than your teeth rotting in your gums." He looked down at Daisy, lifted his brows. "I really have no idea if these things will do any good," he said, as if she alone would understand his dilemma. "But they're chewable, they're orange-flavored. They go directly to the source of the pain." He shrugged. "They can't hurt, right?"

"They're good," Daisy offered. "I love them." And he gallantly held his palm out to her. "Would you like one?"

She looked up at me.

"You're not sick," I said. But he moved his outstretched arm to knock me on my knee. "Oh come on," he said, his thumb against my skin. "She can have one."

"My leg does hurt a little," Daisy said; and she touched the leg that was drawn up under her skirt.

"Your foot's asleep," I told her, more harshly than I intended. "You said so yourself." And then I added, "They're not candy, Daisy. They're medicine." They looked at me, both of them, surprised and disappointed. There was a tightness in my stomach and in my chest, and I felt as constricted by my own prim, close-fisted humorlessness as Flora had been by her mother's silk scarves. It was, I suppose, a learned response, how one behaved in the face of potential lechery. If I was not the most popular girl at school, I was, perhaps, the most attentive, especially when the talk turned, delicately, to sex. I could hear Sister Alphonse Marie: "Stand fast, girls."

He shrugged and closed his hand, pulling it away. Daisy slumped at my feet, returning quietly to her books. Then I said, into the silence, "Okay, just one," which made him suddenly throw his head back with laughter, a shout of laughter that I feared for a moment would wake Flora—although Flora waking would be the very thing that would allow us to leave.

He leaned forward again and Daisy took one of the aspirins from his palm and put it in her mouth. "I can tell what kind of mother you're going to be," he said, smiling at me—fondly, it seemed. "A dozen kids who can get away with anything." His eyes went to my hair, which at that hour of a summer day was probably as wild as Daisy's, then to somewhere around my mouth, and then my throat. He wore a thin white shirt, open at the collar. I thought he was about to tell me I was pretty—I knew the look, a gift about to be delivered—but instead he leaned over and took the book from my lap. He pushed his glasses to the top of his head to read the title, and suddenly I saw in his face little Flora's features, worn out by tears.

"Hardy," he said, turning the pages, his nose raised so his eyes could focus. An old, old man after all. "Egdon Heath. Lovely Eustacia." I told him it was for school, and he nodded, of course it was. "At least it's not *Jane Eyre*," he said. But I told him, "I like *Jane Eyre*, too," as if I had missed his irony. He handed the book back to me, over Daisy's head, and I did not look away. There was black paint under his fingernails, splatters of gray and white on the back of his hand. He plucked the glasses from the top of his head, placed them on his knee, and then ran his hands up over his face, through the tongue of smoky white hair. "Twelve children," he said, as if to himself. "And a clam digger for a husband." He reached for his drink and took a sip and once again swished it around in his mouth. "Pain," he said as he swallowed. "Someone should write a history of the world according to the toothache. What kingdoms lost because of a toothache. What romances gone unconsummated. Ships sunk. Masterpieces left unfinished."

Daisy was looking up at him with quiet concern, and noticing this, he reached down and touched her hair. "Never get old," he said again. "Sell your soul if you have to." He looked at me, Flora's face, worn out, receding, the skin grown yellowish and paper thin. But the weak eyes were his. "What I wouldn't give to have the time you've still got, kiddo," he said. "Kids, clam digger, and all."

I lowered my eyes and shrugged, as I might have had he delivered the prize of admitting I was pretty. I'd lost my fear of him, I knew, the knot of it in my stomach and chest, its ricochet in my fingertips. There was a trace of Uncle Tommy's third-drink philosophy in what he said, and it reminded me once again of my own capacity to embarrass him, to feel sorry for him. The advantage I had of youth and beauty and time left. I wasn't even startled when he slowly, maybe a little drunkenly, leaned toward me once more and took my wrist and gently insinuated his paint-spattered finger into my closed fist, prying it apart. In my palm was the bit of cotton from the aspirin bottle. He took it from me, dipped it quickly into his drink, and then pressed it into his mouth, into the corner he had favored as he'd chewed the aspirin. He moved his tongue around a bit, tasting—his eyes let me know—not just the whiskey but the warm salt of my skin.

I shrugged again and reached back to lift my hair off my neck, twisting it, as I had done this morning, into a loose bun. The day was growing warmer. "Flora's worn out," I said, and Daisy at my feet murmured, "I'll say. We'll never get to the beach." She put her chin on her hand and idly turned a page. I could tell she was familiar with this kind of disappointment, the disappointment brought about by the endless and inevitable accommodation of younger children. "Sure we will," I said. Now he was simply watching me, sunk back in the canvas chair, his fingers on the side of his head, watching but no longer smiling. Even as Ana pulled the car into the drive, his eyes were still on me.

Ana climbed the steps and looked at the three of us, surprised and not pleased to see us there, her hands on her hips.
"Baby asleep?" she asked me, and I said yes. She gestured toward the house. "Inside?" I resisted saying, Where else? "Yes,"
I said. "In her crib." She shook her head and clucked her
tongue and looked at her watch. "No good," she said. "Too
early. She'll be too tired for her dinner tonight." She was a
nice-looking woman, although I had never thought to notice
before. She had olive skin and softly permed hair and large,
dark eyes, a small gold cross on her neck. Plump in her pale
blue servant's dress, an ample figure, I suppose it would be
called. I was under the impression that she had a husband in
the city. "You should wake her up," she said, gesturing toward
the street; she might even have been angry at me. "Go for your
walk."

Flora's father said, "Nonsense," from his chair. He put on
his glasses and then stood up slowly, wearily, a tall, thin man
getting back to work. His drink was still in his hand. "Let her
sleep," he said to me, and then, as he walked past her, something in French to Ana. She stood there for a few minutes as
he walked down the steps and back to his studio, her head
turned over her shoulder but her eyes on the floor, her mouth
pensive, her hands still on her hips. Even if she wasn't French,
and despite her middle-aged figure, you'd have to call the pose
coquettish.

She threw a final glance at me and went into the house. I
wondered what last-minute instructions Flora's mother had
left for her before she boarded the train. Or what Ana herself
had planned on, with the wife safely on her way and the child
and the babysitter and her redheaded shadow off to the beach

for the day. The French maid and the aging artist frolicking under the weeping-cherry trees.

"Jeepers creepers," I said to Daisy after the screen door had slammed, and Daisy rolled her eyes and said, "What's she so mad about?"

"Beats me," I said. I sat with her on the floor of the porch. Flora's books were mostly new, and, Daisy pointed out, many of the pages were scratched over with crayons, an infraction Uncle Jack would never have allowed, which seemed to take Daisy's breath away. "She's spoiled," I explained. "Only children like us usually are." Daisy considered this for a moment and then, afraid, I think, that she had given some offense, said, "Well, her dad is an artist, after all. Maybe she can't help it."

I laughed and leaned forward and kissed her forehead, which was warm. Then I scooted around behind her and drew her between my legs and began to braid her tangled, heavy hair. Ana appeared behind the screen door once or twice to see what we were doing—I wondered if she was going to go in and shake Flora awake—and then came out with a lunch tray held high between her hands. She crossed the porch with it and went down the steps and the path and then into the side door of the garage.

While she was still inside, Daisy and I moved out to the lawn, where we ate our own lunches in the scattered shade of one of the small cherry trees. The day had grown warm, but it was perfect June warmth, soft as water on our skin, and with the low house and the woods and the high green hedge, the blue sky was just a lovely canopy over us alone. Lying on the grass together, Daisy's head on my thigh, we were quiet enough to hear the ocean.

My advantage, I realized, was not only that I could embarrass him or pity him, or recognize his foolishness—a supposed genius, a rich man with a young wife—not even the years I had left while his were spent. My advantage was that I knew what he was trying to do, here in his kingdom by the sea, where art was what he said it was and the limits of time and age were banished and everything was possible because everything that mattered was inside his head. My advantage was that I knew what he was trying to do—and I was better at it.

When Flora finally woke, she was hot and sweaty but happy to see me, and Daisy with her shoes, so I gave her a quick lunch and packed up her towel and her bathing suit and plopped her into her stroller. "Should I put my suit on?" Daisy asked, and then looked at me warily when I said we'd change on the beach. "You don't want to walk all that way in a tight bathing suit," I said. And then, by way of further explanation, "Under a towel, Daisy Mae. It'll be fine. You'll see."

Ana was back in the kitchen by then, more pleasant, perhaps, but mostly because she was ignoring us. I stuck a sun hat on Flora's head and borrowed another one for Daisy. And then, on a whim, because I usually, wisely, never borrowed anything from the people I worked for, I plucked Flora's mother's straw hat from its hook by the door and stuck it on the back of my head. I'd only seen her wearing it once, when I brought Flora home one afternoon and she was having drinks out on the lawn with another old guy (a Broadway person, the cook was pleased to tell me) and his also-too-young wife. It was on one of those cool and overcast days she had been so miserable about when I first started, and so the hat was mere costume, worn, perhaps, for the benefit of her theatrical friends. I saw

Ana glance at me over my shoulder as I took it. I realized I wouldn't mind in the least if she told; I might even want her to. Daisy looked up at me. "You look nice," she said.

I laughed. "I look like Huckleberry Finn," I told her.

She smiled wryly. "Huckleberry Hound, you mean."

I paused. In the shadow of her sun hat, her eyes were rimmed in pale blue. She was grinning with all her crooked little teeth. "You're getting there, Daisy Mae," I said admiringly. "You're getting there."

Flora's habit, a trick I'd taught her, when I pushed her stroller down the gravel drive, was to hum in a monotone, open-mouthed, so her voice would tremble and shake with the vibration of the wheels against the stones. Daisy thought this deliriously funny, and her laughter made Flora more pleased with herself than ever. Her bumpy song grew louder and Daisy's laughter more uncontrollable as we passed the dribbled canvas, the burning lightbulb in the window, the scent of paint, and headed toward the road.

Daisy walked beside the stroller—Flora had reached up and taken her hand—and although she still favored one foot, it did not seem as prominent a limp as before. Testing her, I paused, put my hand to the road, and then announced that I was taking off my sneakers. I tied them together and put them over my shoulder. The tar was warm, but not too hot beneath my feet. I elaborately wiggled my toes. "Feels real good," I said in a fake Southern accent. "Better than being civilized." But Daisy did not follow suit.

There were already a few scattered bathers on the beach. I pushed the stroller into our regular corner of the parking lot, and Flora, accustomed to our routine, immediately scooted out

and headed, with Daisy, into the sand. "There go your shoes,"
I called, and then decided not to puzzle over it anymore. In my
own childhood, my mother often told me, I had once worn a
flamboyant red Gypsy skirt, the remnant of my Halloween
costume, from October 31 to Thanksgiving, night and day, over
church clothes and play clothes and pajamas, with no other explanation for why I kept it on (or why I finally took it off) than
that I wanted to. She told the story without ever once questioning why she had indulged me in this, questioning only what it
was that had possessed me to insist that I not be parted from
the gaudy skirt, with its swirls of gold and black and its itchy
red net ruffles—the very skirt that hung at this moment in my
attic wardrobe, just to the right of a row of blue-and-green
uniform jumpers, size 7.

On the beach, I spread out the soft blue quilt Flora's
mother had provided and then pulled our towels and our
suntan lotion from the beach bag. I opened the thermos of
lemonade and gave each of them a drink. I told them I just remembered a story one of the nuns at my school had told us, a
story about a little girl—this was years and years ago—who
was given a beautiful white slip, hand-embroidered and made
of the softest, finest cotton in the whole world. It was made by
some nuns who lived upstate and came out of their convents
only once a year, when they traveled around to churches to sell
the things they made after Mass—children's clothes and altar
cloths and doilies. The slip was pure white, and the little girl
was meant to save it to wear on her First Communion, in May,
but one cold night in February, just as she was getting ready
for bed, she opened up her bottom drawer and took the slip out

of its tissue paper and put it on. The next morning, when her mother saw what she had slept in, she was really angry, but the little girl said, "But, Mommy, I wanted to show it to the angels." Her mother said, The angels will see it on your First Communion, and took the slip and ironed out all the wrinkles and put it back in its tissue paper. Well, the next morning her mother went in to wake her up and there was the little girl sleeping in the white slip again (Daisy laughed, as if to say, I like this kid), and her mother was just about to scold her when she realized that the little girl wasn't asleep at all but dead. She really had worn the slip to show it to the angels.

Daisy frowned and pulled back her chin, squinting at me in the sun. A wave crashed with what sounded like a clap of thunder.

I laughed. "I don't believe it, either," I said. Flora, impatient, began to raise her white dress over her head, showing her plump thighs and her belly button and her ruffled diaper cover. "I want to swim," she said. I reached up and pulled her into my lap to unlace her shoes.

Carefully, thoughtfully, perhaps, Daisy sat down beside us. "Bernadette knows another story like that," she said. "She told me once. Only it wasn't a slip, it was something else. White Communion shoes, I think."

"It must be a story they teach them in nun school," I said. I pulled off Flora's shoes and socks and stood her up again. "If I had been the little girl," I said, "I'd have shown up in heaven in a red Gypsy skirt from Halloween. Not exactly angelic." I tapped the toe of Daisy's pink shoe. "And I suppose you'd be wearing these."

"Jewels," Flora said, leaning to put her finger on them, too. "Daisy has jewels on her shoes."

I lifted one of the beach towels and draped it over Flora's head—it was our routine—and then joined her under it to slip off her dress and her diaper and pull her skirted bathing suit up over her chubby legs and baby belly while her hands gripped my hair so she could keep her balance. When we emerged, I pulled Daisy's suit out of the bag and told her she was next. But she looked around shyly and shook her head. "Someone might see me," she whispered. I noticed that she had taken off the pink shoes but still had her white socks on. There was a faint blush rising into her cheeks. "No, they won't," I said. I picked up another beach towel and held both of them together. "I'll make an envelope, see," I told her, holding out the length of the two towels. "You scoot under and come up inside."

This she did, laughing, her head popping up just over the towels, between my arms. I closed my eyes and turned my head away. "Now no one can see you but the seagulls." I felt her moving against the blanket, pulling the dress up over her head, bending to step into her suit. Cautiously, I looked to see how she was doing. Her bare back was bent, I could see the sharp thin line of her spine as if it had been picked out by the sun, but there was a place, too, low on her back, just over her hip that because of the sun or my half-shut eyes or the shadow of the beach towels seemed bruised or mottled. I might have asked her about it then, but as soon as she stepped out from be-hind the towel—she did it with a flourish, like a diva taking a curtain call—we saw Tony and Petey heading toward us, their bikes thrown into the sand just behind them like some useless and discarded things. "Where've you been?" Tony demanded as Petey said, in the same tone, "What took you so long?"

As they squinted up at me, skeptically, it seemed, I explained that Flora had taken an early nap and we'd had to wait for her. I sat down on the quilt. "Did you find the movie star?" I asked, and they shook their heads no, falling on their knees in the sand beside us.

"We saw what house they went into, though," Tony offered. "We were going to do a stakeout, but baby June wouldn't be quiet."

The two brothers exchanged a look from under their pale white brows, and then Petey of the blackened eye said, "Rags is back. We tied him up to your fence so my grandpa won't see him." He turned to Daisy. "My grandpa shoots stray dogs," he said.

And I said, "No, he doesn't," although, given Mr. Moran's personality, it didn't seem unlikely.

"He said he'd shoot Rags," Tony argued. "He said Rags tried to bite him."

"Rags doesn't bite," I said, and took away the sandy Popsicle stick Petey had just handed Flora. "Where's baby June now?" I asked, because the look the two brothers had exchanged had had a kind of snag in it. They exchanged the same look again.

"At home, I guess," Tony said into the sand.

"With Judy?" I asked.

"Judy and Janey got to go horseback riding with their dad," Petey said with some indignation. "Is this your hat?" He picked up Flora's mother's hat from the quilt where I'd placed it and stuck it on the back of his head. Then he pulled the brim down over his ears and said in a high voice, "Ain't I pretty."

"Is your mother home?" I said, and with the hat still pulled down and his two palms against his cheeks, Petey shook his head.

"So who's minding June?" I asked them. Hands on his knees, Tony sat up a bit to look back over his shoulder toward the parking lot. Petey said, from under the shadow of the hat, "She's coming. She was right behind us."

I lifted Flora and the beach bag and the towel and slipped my dress over Daisy's suit. I asked her to pick up the quilt and her shoes. Walking up the beach behind us, Tony and Petey promised that baby June would probably be here any minute, she was just really, really slow. She was right behind them the last time they looked.

I put a startled Flora into the stroller, and with Daisy scraping along in her pink shoes, trying to keep up, and Petey and Tony protesting at my side, I walked quickly down to the road. No sign of baby June. "Which way did you come?" I asked them, and squinting up at me, they pointed left, toward home. "When was the last time you saw her?"

Tony pointed again. "Just past the movie star's house," he said. "What's the big deal?"

We came upon her a few minutes later, sitting, like a baby in a fairy tale, at the edge of a brown potato field, her face streaked with tears and dirt, her hands filthy, her clothes—a pilly and too tight cotton sunsuit—dirtier still. I walked over the cool, lumpy dirt in my bare feet and snatched her up. She smelled like the earth, like a freshly dug potato, as if she had just rolled up out of the jumbled ground. "You guys," I said, turning to the two boys, who seemed nonplussed by the whole ordeal—she had been, after all, pretty much where they'd expected, just behind them. "You guys should never leave her like that. Do you know what could have happened to her?"

"Well, she's too slow," Petey said.

And I said, my voice growing louder, "She could have been hit by a car, Petey. She could have been kidnapped. Stolen."

"No one would steal *her*," Tony said, and the two of them laughed at the joke.

"She could have been run over," I said again, louder this time. "I can't believe you guys did this—you're idiots. Perfect idiots."

Suddenly Petey's face changed. He stepped closer, his fists clenched. "Well, we kept looking for you," he said, squinting, matching his angry voice to mine.

"Yeah," Tony said indignantly. "Where the hell were you?"

Petey stepped forward again. "Yeah, where were you?" He was right under my nose and his dirty baby sister was staring down at him from my arms. He was all open mouth under Flora's mother's wide straw hat, and his blackened eye was half closed. His voice was loud enough to hurt my ears. "We kept going back to the beach and you weren't there." He gestured wildly, like an adult. There was spit forming at the corners of his mouth. "You weren't where you were supposed to be." He jabbed a finger at me. "You're the idiot."

Softly, staring him down, I said, "You two left your baby sister alone in the road. It's about the stupidest thing you've ever done."

First I saw the tears come into his pale eyes and then I saw his fist. I turned to protect baby June's knee and he hit me solidly on the forearm. "Well, to hell with you," he cried, sounding for all the world like his grandpa. And then he turned, skidding down the incline of dirt that separated the road and the field, and, as if for good measure, punched Daisy, too, on the shoulder, hard enough to make her step back, her face filled with surprise and pain. Then he ran, Tony at his heels.

With June still in my arms, I went to Daisy, who was holding her shoulder and whispering, "Ow, ow, ow," but not crying. A girl with brothers. I put my free arm around her. "Go get your bikes, idiots," I called after the boys. "And bring me back that hat." But Tony just turned and thumbed his nose, and stuck out his tongue, and the two of them kept running.

I held Daisy tighter, and little June reached down to pat her head. In her stroller Flora began to cry, but I hushed her. "Daisy's okay," I told her. "You're okay, aren't you, Daisy Mae?"

She nodded, being brave. "It's okay, Flora Dora," she said. "I'm all right."

I told them we would forget the beach for today. I gave Daisy one more pat on the head and then with my free hand turned Flora's stroller around. "Margaret Mary," I said, "do you think you can push the stroller while I carry baby June? Something tells me she's done enough walking."

Daisy said sure, and then had some trouble keeping the stroller straight. I put my hand on it briefly to guide her, and then let her go on her own. It took some effort, I could tell, the smooth soles of her pink shoes slipping and sliding against the macadam, but she put all her legs and her sore shoulder into it, all of that tiny body, muscle and bone.

"What would I do without you, Daisy Mae?" I said. "One day here and already you're indispensable."

Back at my house, Rags was tied to the side fence with a short bit of clothesline. He barked viciously as we approached, even growled—as if the few hours he'd spent on the property had made him responsible for the security of the house. I told the girls to stay where they were—I could see them drawing back anyway, and then I approached him and said, "What are you growling at, you silly dog?" At the sound of my voice he immediately cowered a bit and thumped his tail, whining an apology. He was a sweet but odd mutt, mostly collie, I think, by turns skittish and friendly and shy, schizophrenic, I supposed. And stupid. He came and went, a stray for the most part, proba- bly left behind by some summer people who didn't want the year-round responsibility of a pet; occasionally—those times when we didn't see him for weeks—adopted by another summer family who made him theirs for whatever time they were out here. The Moran kids weren't allowed to keep him, but they dragged him back to me whenever he came around. Rags, being stupid, tolerated them for the most part, although I'd seen him nip their fingers once or twice. Now he rolled over in joyful sub- mission as I petted him and talked him into calming down. I then let the girls bring him some water and dog biscuits.

With Rags still tied to the fence but happily subdued, I stripped off baby June's dirty clothes in the yard and washed her off with my father's garden hose. Then I wrapped her in a

beach towel and carried her into the bathroom, where I filled
the tub with water and shampoo and let June and Flora both
play in the bubbles. Daisy laughed, watching them, but didn't
want to join in, not even in her bathing suit. Out on the lawn
again, in what were now the long shadows of the afternoon, I
gave everybody cookies and fruit punch. Judy and Janey wandered over to take Rags for a walk, but there was no sign of the
boys. I turned baby June over to her sisters and asked Daisy if
she might possibly want to get out of her bathing suit, and
maybe even change her shoes for the afternoon walk. To my
surprise, she nodded and went into the house, coming out a
few minutes later not in her new sneakers but in the old saddle
shoes she had worn on the train. "They look comfortable," I
said, mostly because she seemed so disappointed to be wearing
them again.

We got Flora into her stroller and walked her home,
singing loudly most of the way——"Barnacle Bill the Sailor," a
song that came to me as we passed Mr. Moran, standing, sway-
ing, shirtless in his driveway, mumbling to himself. We were
trying to keep Flora from falling asleep before she had her dinner. The lights were still on in her father's painting place, but
there was no sign of him, or Ana either, which was just as well,
since I didn't have the straw hat. Inside, there was the familiar
smell of the place: her perfume, his cigar, something new
and complicated riding on the scent now. The cook was in the
kitchen, just taking a single baked potato out of the oven, and
when I told her Flora had already been bathed, back at my
house, she reached up and ran her hand over my hair. She
was a lady who went to our church, a vague friend of my
mother's, fat and grandmotherly but not, I now realized, un-

aware. "Thank you, dear," she said. "That helps." As if she knew, and I knew, that Ana's duties would fall to her tonight.

As tired as she was, and perhaps because she was tired, Flora cried when Daisy and I said goodbye. She didn't cling, or even run after us, she was too exhausted for that. But she sat at the kitchen table in the terrycloth bib the cook had tied around her neck and simply sobbed. On the plate in front of her were the steaming baked potato, a few peas, some cut-up bits of poached chicken. She sat on a couple of phone books, but still her chin was only just above the food. She cried with her mouth open, the tears streaming down her cheeks. The cook sat at the table with her, wiping away the tears with her thumb. Under her fat elbow were Flora's mother's scarves, all but the turquoise-and-white one, just where she had left them.

Daisy and I backed out of the room, waving. The house behind us seemed empty. I took her hand as soon as we got outside. The spattered canvas was still against the wall of the garage, and I thought about what he had said, about masterpieces unfinished. I told Daisy, as we walked to the Kaufmans' to give Red Rover his evening walk, that maybe tonight we could sleep in the attic, in the two old beds. We could push one of the chairs over to the window, and maybe, I said, if we wake up and see the ghost Uncle Tommy always saw, we could ask him his name, and the name of the little boy in his lap. "What do you think their story is, Daisy Mae?" I asked her. She thought awhile and then she said, "The ghost is the little boy's father. And he was waiting by the window for him to come back. And then the little boy came back and sat on his father's lap, in the chair."

I nodded. "Reasonable enough," I told her. "Now we just have to figure out where the little boy had been."

"On a ship," she said without hesitation. "That finally returned."

I laughed. The sun was lower now, and the grackles were going crazy in the trees, preparing for night. Somewhere from behind one of the high hedges we heard children's voices calling, laughter and a shout. From somewhere else came the sound of a tennis ball. There was the lovely scent of fading summer afternoon in the air——maybe a hint of the unseen children's suntan lotion. I began to sing, "And it finally returned, it finally returned, it came back from the sea. And from that day to this"——I glanced down at her and she looked up at me, expectantly. "Fond hearts," I said clearly, "are happy"——she seemed relieved: the air was too lovely for more bad words——"because the ship had finally returned."

We heard Red Rover whining and yelping even before we reached the house. Clearly, he'd had a miserably lonely day, and I let him lick my face, and Daisy's, to make it up to him. We walked him back to the beach, and sure enough, Petey's and Tony's bicycles were still in the sand. Daisy and I picked them up and rested them against the garbage cans while Red Rover explored the shoreline, then we brought him back to his pen. A light was on in the Kaufmans' front window, as was the side porch light, but this house, too, was empty. Dr. Kaufman had not returned from the city yet. I hoped he would remember to visit Red when he did.

Going back to the beach to fetch the boys' bicycles, we ran into the Richardsons with their Scotties. Mrs. Richardson looked Daisy up and down as I introduced her, and I feared for a moment that she would actually say—the word was all over her mannish face—pitiful. Poor Daisy did indeed look like a waif. Her braid was coming undone and her sash was limp and there were streaks of dirt, baby June's handprints, Red Rover's paws, on the skirt of her white-and-yellow (and now, suddenly, under Mrs. Richardson's all but monocled eye, outdated) hand-me-down dress. And then the unpolished saddle shoes, merely two shades of gray, rather than black and white. I had the notion that the shoes alone had transformed her from the charming sprite she'd been this morning, walking the Scotties under the tall green trees, that those cheap pink things had some magic in them after all. "And where in the city do you live?" Mrs. Richardson asked her, and Daisy, mumbling, shy under her scrutiny, bowed her head and said, "Two Hundred and Seventh Place."

Mrs. Richardson put her big face into mine. "What did she say?" (The implication being, of course, that the child should really be taught to speak up.)

I smiled, pushing Daisy along. "She lives on Sutton Place," I said. "Shall I come by for the dogs in the morning?"

Mrs. Richardson glanced at her husband, who had his pipe stem in his mouth. "Yes, of course," she said. "Nice meeting you, Daisy," and Daisy, even in the worn-out shoes and the dirty dress, did a splendid curtsy and said, "Nice meeting you, too."

"Can you imagine living with that woman?" I asked her as we went on, and Daisy shook her head. "Poor dogs," she said.

We rode the wobbling bicycles back to the house, leaving them both in the Morans' battered yard. My parents weren't home yet, so I went into the kitchen and peeled some potatoes and put them on to boil. Daisy was sitting on the couch in the living room, looking at some magazines, but when I went in to join her, I saw that she was crying quietly, the tears just rolling out of her eyes. I pushed the magazines onto the floor and sat down beside her. I put my arm around her, drawing her close.

"What is it, Daisy Mae?" I asked, and she sniffed and said softly, "I miss my mother."

This surprised me a bit, and immediately I regretted having made fun of Aunt Peg, back at the Clarkes' house this morning. Of course, of course, it seemed perfectly sensible now—crazed Aunt Peg was, after all, Daisy's only mother. "I miss my house," she added.

I kissed the top of her head. "You can go home whenever you want," I said softly, into her hair, the sweet odor of her warm scalp. Although the very notion of it made me realize, perhaps for the first time in my life, that I would be lonely without her, here in my own house, where I had always been alone. "I can take you home on the train tomorrow, or whenever you want. Just say the word." But she quickly shook her head, and then turned to look at me earnestly. "Oh, I don't want to leave," she said. "I love it here. I could stay forever." Tears came into her eyes again. "I just miss them," she said.

I told her I understood. "It's hard when you're used to people," I said, and she nodded. "You can miss them but not necessarily want to be with them."

She nodded again.

"You sort of wish you could be two places at once. With them, because you love them and you're used to them, but also away from them, so you can be just yourself."

"That's right," Daisy said, leaning against me, her skinny elbow pressing into my thigh.

"You wish you could appear and disappear, like a little ghost. Be around them, but not be stuck with them." She nodded again. "It's the mystery of families," I said.

She rested her head on my shoulder. Her face was drawn and tired. I could hear the boiling potatoes drilling in their pot, and knew they should probably be turned down, but I didn't want to leave Daisy to get up and do it. I told her to put her feet up, instead, to take a rest, and when she did, I said, thinking more of my mother's love of the rose-colored slipcover than of all the nonsense we'd gone through today over the pink shoes, "You'd better take off your shoes." Obediently, wearily, she leaned down and untied the worn-out saddle shoes, no argument here, of course, because the shoes, ordinary school shoes, contained no magic. "And those sandy socks," I said. With only the slightest, saddest nod, a mere remnant of her earlier hesitation, she slipped off each of the thin white socks and placed them into her shoes. She drew her feet up on the couch again, her knees pulled up into the generous skirt of my old Sunday dress, and put her head in my lap. On the wall next to the fireplace was the sketch Flora's father had given me back in April, now carefully matted and framed. Framed in what my parents had called a museum-quality frame—"a small fortune"—they'd said. But the man in the frame shop had offered them one hundred dollars for the drawing, which pleased and surprised them no end. When they brought it home, they hung it up with great ceremony. Although they still thought the drawing itself looked "like nothing," it was, nevertheless, the first real evidence of my success by association, the very reason they'd moved out here. I saw Daisy looking at the picture, her hands under her cheek, and I said, "Flora's father drew that."

She nodded. "I thought so."

"I don't know what it's supposed to be," I said. "He drew about fifty of them and gave one to me." I moved my arm down the length of her little body, stroking her side.

"It's a picture of something broken," she said matter-offactly, not as sleepy as she had been, revived, it seemed, by her own thoughts. "Something you sort of expected to break, but you still wish it hadn't. You still think maybe it won't."

I moved the hem of the dress off her thin ankles. The sun was coming through the living-room window in that heavy red gold of near-dusk, but it did not hit the couch and so there was no glare to blind me and no real shadow to convince me I was mistaken in what I saw. I leaned over her a bit. "Daisy," I said. And then I touched her shoulder and asked her to sit up again. She seemed for a moment to hold her breath. I slipped off the couch and knelt down among the magazines. Gently, I took both of her feet into my hands. Across each instep, tracing, it seemed, the outline of her old saddle shoes, an unmistakable bruise—I licked my finger and rubbed it a bit, just to make sure—a black-and-blue crescent that reached nearly to her toes. I touched it softly, and then with some pressure, but she did not flinch.

"Does this hurt?" I said, and she shook her head sheepishly. "Not really," she said.

"What is it, then?" I whispered.

She shrugged, her two hands politely folded together in the

lap of her skirt. "Just a black-and-blue mark," she said cautiously, raising her chin and turning her head away from me just a little.

"How did you get it? Your brothers?"

Now there were tears in her eyes again and her voice was very soft, nearly inaudible. "No," she whispered. She met my eye and nodded as if to admit that here, then, was the thing she had worked so hard to conceal. "I don't know how I got it," she said. "It was just there one day, a little while ago. I don't know why."

I looked at it more closely. It was a mottled bruise, yellowish in spots, in some spots almost black. "Did you tell anyone?" I asked her. "Did you show your mother?"

Daisy shook her head again, and now her mouth was trembling. "I was afraid they wouldn't let me come," she said softly. "I was afraid they'd make me go to the doctor and then I wouldn't be able to come." A tear slipped over the brim of her eye and ran down her face and hit the pretty collar of her dirty dress. "I really don't want to go home," she said earnestly. "I was just missing my mother, but I don't want to go home." I moved back onto the couch and again took her into my arms. Like a baby, she put her open mouth to my shoulder.

"I thought it was because of the shoes," she said. "My school shoes. I thought the pink ones would make it go away. But I wore them all day. It's not going away." She moved a hand up to my face. "I don't want to go home already," she said.

I held her for a while, stroking her arm, patting her back, hushing her, hushing her. I thought of the discoloration I had seen on her hip as she changed. The pale wash of her skin this morning, the heat of her scalp and her forehead when I leaned to kiss her. All the things Aunt Peg and Uncle Jack, in their busy, child-infested lives, could have missed, could have been missing for quite some time. Poor Daisy. Poor Daisy, we all said. Poor Daisy, the jolly family story went, poor Daisy doesn't get much attention, what with her noisy brothers and fat, fragile Bernadette, and the house to keep orderly, the rules to enforce, the long, dangerous nights her father has to work (not to mention all the busy, closed-door nights he was at home). Poor Daisy's a good little thing, the family story went: obedient, polite, wonderfully independent—getting herself her own bath, putting on her own pajamas, coming down for school in the morning all ready to go. She's a quiet little thing, poor Daisy, but around here, she doesn't have much chance to be anything else, does she? (This from Uncle Jack in his gun and holster, his dish of fruit salad with tiny marshmallows placed on the Formica table before him, and Aunt Peg hovering, touching his shoulder, his scarred cheek, all the children in bed but me. The kitchen window behind him sprayed with false snow. "Poor Daisy," he said, and swallowed a bright spoonful. Uncle Jack at one in the morning, in his own kitchen, finally returned. "She's a quiet little thing, but I guess we'll keep her.")

I don't know that I made any decision. I don't know that I understood what the bruises might mean, or forebode, although I think Daisy and I both had a sense of something menacing about them, something making its way into her life, and mine. Something that had broken. Something you sort of expected to break. But still hope it won't.

"One day isn't very long," I said to her, eventually, when

she was ready to hear me. "You never know. You haven't really given those pink shoes much time."

She sat up, her arms still around my neck, our faces just inches apart. "You only put them on yesterday," I said. "They only got out here yesterday. They were perfectly ordinary shoes until then." I heard my parents' car pull into the driveway, the crunch of their tires on the gravel. "We have to give them a chance, right? We have to wait and see." I wiped my thumbs over her flushed cheeks, which were still wet with tears. There was the screech of the old car's handbrake.

Gently, I leaned across Daisy's lap to pick up her socks. "You know what they say about magic, and ghosts, and good luck, too," I told her. "They say first you have to believe, right?"

I unrolled the socks. They were warm and damp, still sandy. I shook them out elaborately, first one, then the other. I slapped them against the inside of my wrist. Then I brushed off Daisy's discolored feet, running my fingers between her toes, tickling her a bit. I heard the car doors slam, my parents talking to each other as they made their way across the path between the garage and the porch, their voices ordinary and gentle, the same conversation they had begun on first waking.

"Point your toes like a ballerina, Daisy Mae," I whispered. And I slipped the socks over her feet, and then held them both, concealed in my hands, as my parents came through the screen door.

They might have been visitors from another, darker planet, my father in his rumpled navy suit, my mother in her skirt and stockings and heels, a newspaper, a briefcase, under their arms.

The smoky smell of the office and the car in their clothes. "Well, here they are!" my father exclaimed, as if he was indeed surprised to see us. And my mother asked, "How did you girls get along today? Did you wear poor Daisy out? Are the potatoes on?"

I gave Daisy's two feet a single shake, as if to seal our agreement, and then pulled her off the couch. "Oh my gosh, the potatoes!" I said, pretending, just to welcome them home, that I didn't always know what I was doing.

After dinner, Daisy and I went out to catch fireflies. She had put the pink shoes on again, giving them time, and they did indeed make her seem brighter. We sat together on the tree swing, facing each other, Daisy's legs around my waist, our hands together on the thick rope, and when I had pumped us too high and I began to feel her tremble with each upward swing, I scraped my bare feet along the grass to slow us down a bit. We were sitting like that, in the darkness, only our back-porch light and the light from the kitchen where my parents still sat, talking and smoking, reaching into the yard, when Petey and Tony came along, through the gate this time, although they were accustomed to merely hopping the fence.

"Have you seen Rags?" Petey asked softly as he approached, barely raising his head to look at us.

"Judy and Janey took him," I said. "Just before I walked Flora home."

"Well, he's gone again," he said into the ground. "They haven't seen him."

"I haven't seen him, either," I said. I continued to push the swing back and forth, slowly, the sound of the rope creaking against the high branch the only sound among us for a while.

In the darkness, I could really make out only the boys' bright eyes and the white stubble of their hair. Their bodies seemed to have vanished.

Finally I said, "You need to tell Daisy you're sorry, Petey," and as if he'd only been waiting for my cue, he said, "I'm sorry, Daisy."

She glanced at me, and then turned to him to say, "It's all right."

I moved the swing slowly, back and forth. "You might want to say it to me, too," I added, and once again, without hesitation, Petey said, "I'm sorry."

Tony stepped forward, drawing the straw hat from behind his back. "Here," he said, handing it to me with some formality. It was somewhat the worse for wear, and although I couldn't examine it thoroughly in this light, I could tell it had been bent out of shape, perhaps even chewed on here and there.

"I'm going to give Daisy something, too," Petey said shyly. "I just don't have it yet. But she's really going to like it when I get it."

Daisy and I exchanged a glance at this news, and then Daisy said, somewhat regally, "That's very nice of you."

Now added to our silence in the darkness was the hollow and faraway sound of old Mr. Moran yelling at someone inside their house, and then his daughter's shouted answer. I let Daisy slide off my lap and we all caught fireflies for a while— Petey and Tony more often than not having to peel the broken, still-illuminated things from the heels of their palms, where they had caught them just a second too late and with just a touch too much violence and enthusiasm. Judy wandered over eventually. She was carrying Garbage, the stray cat, up under her chin, and she cursed softly when he struggled out of her arms and disappeared into the bushes. Then Janey followed, as the volume of the argument inside their house ebbed and flowed and doors slammed. I made popcorn for us all, and then let them come in to eat it at the kitchen table, since the mosquitoes were getting bad. I sent them all home at about ten o'clock, when my parents called in from the living room to say that Daisy really should get to bed.

We slept in the attic that night, putting the old wing chair in front of the little window just as Uncle Tommy had done. I could tell by a certain texture in her voice, a certain terseness in her words, by the way she glanced now and then at the back of the chair as she pulled down the bedspread and arranged her pillows, that Daisy was beginning to worry a bit that the ghost would indeed appear, and so I showed her how it said in my novel that ghosts appear only to single people who sleep alone. This seemed to reassure her a bit, although still she asked me to lie down with her until she went to sleep. I did, whispering Hail Marys as my mother used to do for me, one after the other, monotonously. We said no more about the bruises, although as she dressed I had noticed a new one, on her shoulder, small and round, from Petey's fist. I had showed her that I had a smaller, matching version on my forearm. In only a few minutes she was sound asleep. I got up, drew the blanket over her shoulder, and got into the other bed.

I looked at the window, at the dark silhouette of the high-backed chair in front of it. Of course Uncle Tommy, lying alone, would have seen the ghost. Ghosts, as the story said, didn't appear to married couples. I thought of Uncle Tommy

lying alone in this very bed, Uncle Tommy, past fifty, unmar-
ried, childless. A small boyish body, a large, handsome face,
also boyish in its way, his thinning hair still fair, his cheeks
baby-smooth until they met the web of deep lines around his
smiling eyes. Uncle Tommy, always alone, always smiling. Always, even past fifty, going through jobs and girlfriends. He
lived in an apartment I had never seen, on the Upper West
Side, and my entire experience of him was merely a series of
unexpected visits and unexpected departures. Here and then
not here. I liked him because he called my mother Sis or Sissy,
and whenever she begged him to be serious he said, winking at
me, "Nothing's serious." He said, laughing, that he wanted no
part of marriage "and, while you're at it," no part of the
Church. He said he didn't much like the sound of till death do
us part—a shudder of his shoulders and a shake of his head.
He didn't like the notion of deferred joy in heaven, either. "I'd
rather be joyful now." He liked children and he liked dogs, he
said (although he had neither of his own), because they were
the only creatures who truly understood what now is. If I'd inherited my own talent from anyone, it must have been from
him.

"Being happy," Uncle Tommy liked to say, "takes a great
deal of work." He said he had no time for anything else.

But the ghost who appeared to him here in our attic had
been watching and waiting, wanting something, a ghost so
choked with emotion, Uncle Tommy had said, that he could
barely speak. A mournful ghost, until Uncle Tommy gave him
a chair, and a little boy to hold in his arms. Finally returned.

I stayed awake for as long as I could, lying in Uncle
Tommy's bed, listening to Daisy's soft breath and being some-

what afraid of it, afraid of her unconsciousness, I guess, until I heard her giggle in her sleep. The ghost and his boy never did appear, not that night anyway, although I learned in the morning that Petey was there, sleeping in the dirt beneath the window of my empty room.

He was at the kitchen table with my parents the next morning. My mother had draped a crocheted blanket over his shoulders and there was a milky cup of the black tea and a plate of toast on the table in front of him. My parents were pretending they didn't know he had slept out there, telling me when I came into the room that Petey was up extra early today because he had hoped to catch a rabbit in our yard. My father was showing him how to go about it, demonstrating with a matchbox and a toothpick the kind of trap he could build, and my mother was leaning into the refrigerator, getting some carrots for him to use as bait. Since Petey was in my seat, I stood against the counter, watching him. There must have been a hundred mosquito bites on his face and arms and his bare brown legs, I could even see a few of them on his pink scalp. His right shoulder and arm, the right side of his face and head were dirty, still caked with mulch from the way he had slept under the bushes. He didn't touch the tea, but ate the whole plate of toast and then, with my mother's carrots in hand, stood up and said thank you and headed out, like a rabbit himself, through the back door.

My mother returned to her chair wearily, as if Petey were her own wayward child. She asked me if I'd heard the police car last night, at the Morans' house again, and when I said no, she shook her head. "Your father didn't hear it either," she said. "Or all the shouting."

"I heard the shouting earlier," my father said, but my mother shook her head. "No," she said. "Late into the night." And he shrugged, sheepishly acknowledging that he had slept while she hadn't.

When they were gone, I climbed up the attic stairs to wake Daisy, bringing with me as I did one of the new outfits her mother had sent along. My own gesture of reconciliation and regret toward Aunt Peg, whom Daisy loved. Who loved Daisy. It was the smallest of all the outfits she had brought—a pink-and-blue-plaid shorts set that went nicely with her pink shoes. I had already ironed out the creases, and planned to pin the elastic waist if it was too loose. But Daisy pouted a bit when she saw it. She already had her heart set on the red-and-blue-checked sundress from my own eight-year-old wardrobe. She liked the ribbon ties at the shoulders. Downstairs in my own room, I held her between my knees and brushed out her hair, tying it up on the top of her head with a rubber band and another thick red ribbon. Her face was suddenly narrower, with her hair pulled off it, and her ears stood out like the handles on a teacup. Her skin, the bones of her bare shoulders seemed teacup thin, pale blue and fragile.

That morning, over my own shorts and T-shirt, I had put on an old white dress shirt of my father's, and on an impulse I lifted the tail of it over my head and then swooped down on Daisy, pulling us both onto the bed. She laughed and squealed, and then, remembering, put her hand to her hair and said, "Don't mess up my bun." "Oh, it's your bun, is it?" I asked, tickling her. "I thought it was *my* bun." I loved her little crooked and missing teeth, and her tiny nose and the pale red arcs of her brows. Catching our breath, we lay together for a moment on my chenille spread, the tail of the worn shirt covering both our faces, blotting out everything but the morning light. And then she whispered, "You won't tell?" I shook my head, almost imperceptibly, and only to reassure her. "Don't think about it anymore," I told her, and then pulled the shirt-tail off our faces. I told her we had work to do.

Last night I'd placed Flora's mother's straw hat on the hook by the back door, and this morning I saw more clearly that it had been twisted and broken, definitely chewed on around the brim. I slapped it on the back of my head anyway. I had money enough to buy her a new one.

Petey and Tony and Janey were in our yard with a cardboard box and Rags's clothesline leash and the limp carrots. Petey stepped in front of the box as soon as we came out the back door, the carrots behind his back, and Tony gave me one of those scooting gestures that meant Daisy was not supposed to see. Janey's eyes went from the red ribbon in Daisy's hair to the checked sundress to the jeweled shoes. Like all the Moran kids that morning, she was dressed in the same clothes she'd had on yesterday, and perhaps the day before, the same blouse and pedal pushers she'd gone riding in with a father Petey and Tony didn't share. She was a striking little girl, despite the dirty face and the stringy white-blond hair, one of those little girls whose adult beauty was apparent even at this age, and she was only about six, apparent in the sharpness of her features and the curve of her spine and the hard blue of her eyes. "Where you going?" she asked, and then followed with, before I had quite said where, "Can I come?"

Tony shouted, "Janey, no," his chest inflated with authority, and then told her in the same rough and loud voice a dog trainer—or perhaps his own father—would use, "Stay here. Mommy said."

"I guess you're supposed to stay here," I told her, and Tony added, "The police will pick her up if she leaves this street. My mother said."

Janey looked disappointed for just a moment, and then she turned to him, her blue eyes narrowed, and what she had hoped for was suddenly erased from her face by her scorn. I could see a shin kick coming on, so I took Flora's mother's battered hat from the back of my head and placed it on Janey. "You want this?" I asked. "It looks good on you."

She looked up into the shadow of the brim and her face changed once more. She was a six-year-old again. "You look like a movie star," I said. "Sandra Dee." I shot Tony a look that said, Don't you dare contradict me. And Janey slowly smiled, touching the brim all around. "Can I have it?" she said. I said, "Sure," as if it were mine to give. I told her to come by after dinner tonight and I'd find her some colored ribbons to decorate it with.

Now Petey, still trying to block the overturned box, made the same scooting motion with his free hand, the carrots held behind his back. "Go," he mouthed. "Will you guys go?"

Although Dr. Kaufman was supposed to be home today, Daisy asked if we could stop by Red Rover's pen just to say hello. It wasn't much out of the way, so I agreed. The car was parked in front of the house when we got there, but the window shades were all pulled down, so I told her we'd just go quickly around the back, give Red Rover a pat and a biscuit, and then get going. But when we went around the house, Dr. Kaufman himself was on his patio, his back to us, looking out over his empty pool and pool house. He was barefoot and wore only boxer shorts and a polo shirt, and I would have turned around and disappeared if he hadn't heard Daisy's hard foot-step on the concrete and turned around himself. His thinning, wiry hair was mussed from sleep and he needed a shave. Everything about him, as a matter of fact, arms, legs, even the backs of his hands, everything but the crown of his head, seemed muted by curly dark hair. He had a cup of coffee in his hand. "Well, hey," he said slowly. "You coming to walk Red? Did I tell you today?"

I shook my head and introduced Daisy and said we were just stopping by to say good morning to the dog.

"Oh, hey," he said again softly, as if he were searching for words. He might still have been half asleep. "Isn't that nice?" He suddenly moved to pull out one of the patio chairs. His hairy legs were bowed and he was not as tan as he would be by August. "You want to sit down?" he said, gesturing with the coffee cup. "You want some juice?" He looked at me, trying to gauge something. "You don't drink coffee, do you? I brought some rolls back from the city. You want a roll?" I said no, thank you and no, thank you. I told him I was just on my way to my other jobs.

"Oh sure," he said, nodding, his voice soft and vague once again. Behind him, the water in the pool was beautifully blue and still, reflecting only the small clouds that had begun to move into the sky. The pool house was closed up. It seemed never to have been opened. I heard Red Rover whine once or twice, not much hope in it.

Daisy took my hand, as if to say, Let's go, but Dr. Kaufman seemed to want to keep us there. "You having a nice summer?" he said, leaning against the patio table, as if we would have a long chat. "Yes, thank you," I told him. "Busy." Although we had spoken on the phone a number of times to make our arrangement, this was the first time I'd seen him this year. He was broad-shouldered but about my height, a little stooped, maybe a little heavier than I'd remembered. He always had a kind, unhappy face. "You look good," he said. "You're taller," and because he looked at me for what seemed just a second or two too long—his dark brown eyes sad and assessing at the same time—he turned to Daisy and asked, "Where in the city are you from, sweetheart?"

Without missing a beat Daisy said, "Sutton Place."

I laughed out loud, I couldn't help it, and Dr. Kaufman turned to me, smiling and puzzled—the first he had smiled since we arrived—and said, "What? What's funny?" His eyes kept slipping from my face to my legs. Daisy was smiling, too.

I grabbed the bun on Daisy's head and shook it. "Well, Queens Village, actually," I said, and she giggled and shrugged, and Dr. Kaufman, siding with her, said, "So she's got a good imagination." Now he looked her over, too. "And some nice shoes," he said.

Red Rover was whining with more vigor now, punctuating each whine with a mournful bark, so I said we'd just go down to the pen and then be on our way. Still leaning against the table, Dr. Kaufman waved his coffee mug. "Go right ahead," he said. "He'll love you for it."

We fed the dog some of the biscuits I carried in my beach bag and scratched him behind his ears. We were just getting ready to lock the gate again when Dr. Kaufman joined us. He had pulled on a pair of shorts over his boxers and was wearing boat shoes. He looked as if he had just, hastily, shaved. He had Red Rover's leash in his hand and he said he and Red would just walk us to our next "assignment." I glanced at Daisy. I knew she would be happy to have the dog's company but perhaps a little disappointed to have to share the morning with a grown-up. But her face was expressionless. Disappointment of one sort or another was nothing new. He walked next to me, his arm brushing mine as Red Rover pulled ahead. I asked about the twins and when they would be down here, noticing as he answered, that Mrs. Kaufman had now become "their mother," whereas two years ago, when I'd worked for them, I'd never heard him refer to her in any way other than "my wife." He asked me if I'd thought about colleges yet. I told him I hadn't. Their mother, he said, had gone to Smith. "Don't go to Smith."

"You might want to think about modeling," he said, and when I told him I didn't think so, he said, "Oh no, you could. You really could." He asked Daisy, "Don't you think your cousin could be in magazines?" Daisy looked at me to see what it was I wanted her to say—perhaps sensing my distaste for such talk. "If she wanted to," she said softly.

"You could," he insisted, warming up to his own idea. His voice, his whole manner seemed to be changing, some kind of transformation I didn't quite understand yet but knew to be somehow akin to the transformation that had made "my wife" into "their mother." "I know some people in the business," he said. "Some of my patients. I could introduce you. Point you in the right direction. I'm telling you, you could be in magazines.

Like *Seventeen*. You read *Seventeen*, don't you? Even my daughter reads *Seventeen*, and she's only six." He laughed. It occurred to me to remind him that I knew his daughter, I was her babysitter. "I know some of these models," he said. He laughed again. "I'm a bachelor now, you know," by way of explanation. "They all started very young, and what are you now, almost eighteen?"

"Fifteen," I said, although I was tempted to say twelve.

He looked at me over his shoulder, Red pulling at the leash. There was still the smell of sleep on his polo shirt, the faint odor of perspiration. "Is that all?" he said. "I thought you were older." Then he said, "You were a real baby then, when you worked for us. Boy, I didn't realize it." He seemed, slowly, to remember something. "Wow," he said. "You were thirteen. Did their mother know you were thirteen?"

I shrugged. "I suppose so," I said. He continued to shake his head. "Wow," he said again. After we had walked awhile in silence, only the sounds of the birds and Red Rover's rapid panting, Daisy's hard shoes against the street, he said, "I'm not going to tell you what went through that woman's head."

I might have thanked him for that, but instead I said, "This is where the Scotties live."

We had finally reached the Richardsons' driveway, and when we paused there, he looked so bereft, I thought for a minute he would burst into tears. Whoever he was trying to be just a few minutes ago, with all his energetic talk about modeling, and how gorgeous I was, and how old I was, seemed to have vanished, and he was once again as soft-spoken and disoriented as he had seemed when we came upon him this morning. Still holding Red on the leash, he suddenly cupped his free hand over the back of my neck, over my hair and the collar of my father's old white shirt, and gently leaned to kiss me on the cheek. Then he ran his hand over the shirt to grip my shoulder softly before he let go and stepped away. He turned to Daisy. "Can I give you a little kiss, too?" he said. "I've got a daughter just about your age who's way up in Maine this morning." Daisy simply said, "Yes," and I suppose I saw a mirror image of myself in the way she leaned forward, her cheek proffered, demurely accepting his sad affection. He touched her shoulder, too, and, seeing the bruise Petey had left there, put a finger to it for a moment and said, "How'd you get this?"

"A little boy," Daisy said, with no further explanation required, as if she had said a wasp or a mosquito.

"An angry little boy," I added.

He pursed his lips and nodded. "Watch out for those," he said, and then added, "us." But he also ran his fingers from her shoulder down behind her arm, lifting her hand when he got to it, her palm in his fingertips. I saw him study, for just a second or two, her fingernails. It occurred to me that I wasn't exactly sure what kind of doctor Dr. Kaufman was. A Park Avenue doctor was all I could recall. Something that required him to be in the city only three days a week. Someone my mother was quite pleased to have me work for.

"You girls come take a swim sometime," he said as he left us, walking backward as Red pulled him along, calling out, "That pool's just going to sit there till the kids come down in August. It breaks my heart. You girls come use it. Really. You'll be doing me a favor."

After we had walked the Scotties and fed Moe, Larry, and Curly—finding a note on the kitchen table that said the Swansons would be down tomorrow—we double-timed it to Flora's, walking quickly for the first half and then, when Daisy became too breathless with walking and swinging her arms and laughing, I lifted her onto my shoulder and carried her—"Tiny Tim–style," I said—the rest of the way.

Flora was already strapped into her stroller, and the stroller was on the front porch with the beach quilt folded into its basket and the lunch bag hung from the handle. She had been given a baby bottle full of Hawaiian Punch, although her mother had prohibited all bottles just last month, and although she was sucking at it contentedly when we climbed the steps, I could tell immediately that she had shed some tears this morning, too. The vacuum cleaner was running inside the house. I gathered I was to take the child and disappear for the day, and although this was pretty much what I had always done, I suddenly felt a bolt of black anger cross my eyes and my chest. I turned around and bent down to help Daisy slip off my shoulders, trying not to grip her ankles or her wrists with too much pressure. I thought at first that I would pull open the screen door and find Ana and pull the plug on the vacuum cleaner and tell her in no uncertain terms (my mother's phrase again) that Flora was not supposed to have any more bottles and should never be left alone on the porch like a sack of potatoes, but I knew, too, that Ana would just pretend she didn't understand and speak a stream of French until I went away, which was pretty much what she did to the cook every time they had an encounter.

I looked at Daisy. "I wonder how long this poor kid's been sitting out here," I said. She shrugged. Her red ribbon had come undone, and so I retied it, slowly, and then brushed back some of the wisps of hair that had fallen around her face. She was warm, sweating a little, although, with the clouds gathering, the morning was cooler than it had been. She was paler than she should have been, too. I looked over my shoulder to Flora. "How long have you been out here, Flora Dora?" And Flora pulled the nipple from her mouth and said, "I have a bottle," pointing to the three fingers of bright red juice still left in it.

"That's right," I said. "And your mother doesn't want you to, does she?"

"Ana gave it to me," she said, and then quickly stuck the thing back into her mouth in case anyone entertained any notions of trying to get it away from her.

Daisy laughed, leaning against me. "Is it good, Flora?" she asked, and Flora nodded and then pulled out the bottle again, with a smack. "It's good," she said, and plugged it in again. Swinging her baby shoes and her fat, dimpled legs, content with the world.

"Take a rest for a minute," I told Daisy, and I moved one of the canvas chairs next to Flora's stroller. I went into the house. The vacuum was back in the master bedroom now. I walked down the hall to Flora's room, checked the shoebox in her closet, and, seeing that the bottle of aspirin had not been returned, walked into the kitchen. The can of punch, just opened, was on the counter, and I poured a glass for Daisy, to cool her off. There was a dimpled bottle of Scotch on the counter as well, also opened. I put some ice into another juice

glass and poured some Scotch into it, and then carried both
outside. I gave Daisy the punch. Flora assessed the situation
with her unremarkable brown eyes, and then was moved to
take the bottle out of her mouth once again. "Red juice," she
said to Daisy. She had already dribbled some of her own onto
the front of her white baby dress. "It's good," she added, as if
urging Daisy to drink. She might have said, Skoal.

I told the girls I'd be back in a minute. The clouds had
grown a bit darker, a bit thicker, and it occurred to me that if I
delayed our start just a few minutes longer we might end up
spending the day in the house. Poor Ana. The painting was no
longer leaning against the outside wall of his studio, although
there was a line in the grass that marked where it had been.
Seeing for an instant Flora's mother with her little white
sweater marching through this door, and then Ana, with her
lunch tray and her wide blue hips, I almost said forget it and
turned around, but I didn't, and stepped over the threshold,
onto the concrete floor. The place was much more stark than
I'd imagined, really just a converted garage or storage shed
with a skylight carved into its roof, something I had never seen
from the outside. The light it cast into the room was milky
gray. There were a few piles of canvases leaning against the
walls, and a couple of sawhorses and old door tables, a single
tall shelf with a jumble of paints and cloths and papers and
brushes, the two bare lightbulbs on long wires, neither one of
them turned on. There was paint spattered on the floor, as I
might have expected, and in the far corner a single bed (something I never expected) draped with what looked like heavy
silk. He was lying on it, posed, it seemed—and if he'd been a
different kind of painter, I would have said it was a bed meant

exactly for that purpose—one arm hanging off the edge (I saw where he had dropped his glasses on the floor), the other thrown across his face, a knee raised, the other leg stretched out. There was a small stool beside the bed, a glass already on it, and another, larger, bottle of St. Joseph's aspirin. I wondered if he had spent the night out here or if this was just an early-morning nap. I said, Excuse me, twice, until he moved his head just a little and asked, "Who's there?" An old man brought back from sleep.

"Theresa," I said.

An old man brought back with some reluctance and confusion. He lay there for a moment, not moving, and then turned his head more fully and raised his arm from his face. "Theresa," he said, moving his mouth, tasting the word. "Theresa," as if to himself.

"The babysitter," I said.

He sat up slowly, with some effort, but smiling, too. "I know who you are," he said as he swung his feet over the side. "I'm not that senile."

He reached between his knees to retrieve his glasses from the concrete floor, and then slowly put them on. He ran his hand over his head, but the white hair simply rose up again. "Was I snoring?" he asked. I said I didn't know, I just got here.

I crossed the room to hand him the glass of Scotch. "Ana told me to bring this to you," I said. Now he looked up at me, his eyebrows raised and his forehead wrinkled, and said, with a laugh, "I doubt that."

But he reached out and took the glass from me anyway. He raised it before he took a sip. I imagined that if the light were better he'd be able to see me blushing. This was not my kind of lying.

"Your wife," I went on, "doesn't want Flora to have any more bottles. She's trying to train her. But Ana gave her one this morning when she set her out on the porch. I know she did it to keep her quiet, so she could vacuum, but she really shouldn't."

He had turned his head and was looking toward the window, his elbows on his knees, the glass I had handed him between his legs. It was, I understood, another pose, a real one this time, one that was meant to convey to me that he had no interest at all in anything I was saying. So I stopped. It was not silk that was draped on the hard bed but some kind of heavy damask. For a different kind of artist it might have served as background for a pale nude. A painted one. But he didn't paint such things.

"My cousin's with me again today," I said softly. "Daisy."

Now he turned back to look at me. "The little redhead?"

I nodded. "She loved it," I said. "Yesterday, when you let her have an aspirin."

He was looking up at me from the bed, or the bier, or whatever it was, his eyes, through his glasses, seeming bemused, as if I were telling him something he was surprised to hear. "She's in awe of you," I said. "You've captured her imagination."

He was still looking at me, both surprised and skeptical, when he reached out his hand and ran the back of his thumb down the side of my leg, a single stroke from just above my knee to just below it. Then he turned his palm and simply held the back of my knee in his hand. His fingertips were cold and wet from the glass. His sleeves were rolled back and the hair on his arms was white. His skin was pink, a little raw-looking, as if it had recently been scrubbed. Still, the thought crossed my mind that in not too many more years, it would be dust. It was a thought that let me look right at him as he touched me. With his eyebrows raised, questioning something, he looked right back. The light in the place was just a shade grayer than it had been, which was better still, because now I knew there was color in my cheeks, and I wondered for a minute if he could feel the tremor in my knee. But I said anyway, "I appreciated your being so nice to her, she's had kind of a rough time."

He placed the slightest pressure against my leg, as if to draw me closer, but when I stepped back, away from him, he simply let go. He pursed his lips a bit, only one corner of his mouth smiling. "I'll say something to Ana," he said softly. "About baby bottles." He raised the glass. "And about sending out drinks with the babysitter."

"Okay," I said. "Thanks." Walking out, I pulled my hair back and twisted it behind me, making wings of my father's white shirt.

When I got outside, the clouds seemed ready to do something, but I pushed the stroller down the three steps and across the gravel anyway, Daisy helping and Flora too tightly attached to her empty bottle to hum. We had just reached the road when big drops of rain began to fall, and we went scurrying back to the porch, past the studio, where both lights were now on. I put the beach quilt on the floor of the porch and went inside for Flora's box of crayons and glue and construction paper. We were going to make a city, I said. Just like the one Flora's mother had gone to. The Empire State Building would be red, I told them, and St. Patrick's blue and Saks Fifth Avenue would be bright green. We'd make Central Park and the Metropolitan Museum of Art, and we'd put Flora's father's paintings inside. And then Flora's mother would ride the elevator to the top of the Empire State Building, where she'd stand out on the Observation Deck and wave her turquoise scarf until, standing on my shoulders, on the beach, Flora saw just a glimpse of it flashing up and down on the western horizon. (And Flora stood up, went to the edge of the porch— Daisy following, hovering, worried that she might fall—and called out into the rain, "Hello, Mommy.") And then, I said, Flora's mother would walk up to Saks (following with our fingers the seams of the beach quilt) to find another white dress for Flora. (No, red, Flora said, eyeing Daisy.) A red dress for Flora, with red ribbons at the shoulders and red ribbons for her hair. She'd stop at St. Patrick's, Our Lady's Chapel, and say a prayer that Flora Dora doesn't miss her too much, and then she'd walk up Fifth Avenue to visit the old polar bear at the zoo. ("Hello, Polar Bear," Flora said into the pale blue quilt, "Hello there," her hands on her plump knees, her little rear in the air, and Daisy, leaning into my lap, her head on my shoulder, said, only a little self-consciously, "Hello, Polar Bear," too.)

And then Flora's mother would walk up the steps of the Metropolitan Museum of Art and through the hushed marble rooms until she came to the special place where Flora's father's painting was. And a guard would unhook the thick velvet rope, and she would walk into the beautiful room, all marble and gold and as quiet as a church, and there would be Flora, in a painting as long and as wide as her father's arms. Flora in a white dress, framed in gold. And Flora's mother would stand there looking at it for so long that when she finally walked back down the steps of the Metropolitan Museum of Art, the sky would be black and the stars would be out and all the buildings would be lit, and she would hold up her hand—like this—(Flora and Daisy followed) and say, Taxi! (Flora said, Taxi!). And as soon she got into the taxi, she'd say, "Oh, for heaven's sake, what in the world am I doing here? Take me home to my little girl."

The rain lasted only a short time that morning, and the sun came out again while the cherry trees were still dripping water onto the grass. We were on the quilt, amid the squashed and battered and scribbled-on remnants of our construction-paper city when Flora's father came up the path. He said, "Ladies," as he crossed the porch, and then, just before he went inside, he bent down to Daisy and without a word opened his palm. Furtively, she took the two aspirins and slipped them into her mouth. He only glanced at me, but he winked as he did, and over Flora's fair head I smiled at him. By the time we were ready for the beach, whatever bit of fever Daisy might have had seemed to be gone.

At the beach I changed Flora into her bathing suit under the fragrant towel, and then Flora and I made our envelope for Daisy to slip into. I caught another glimpse of the bruise on her back and thought it seemed lighter today, the yellowish green of something on its way to healing. She took off her shoes and socks without much prompting. In the beach light the discoloration on her insteps seemed far more severe, and even Flora leaned down and looked at them with a short and sympathetic intake of breath. Daisy immediately buried her feet in the warm sand, but I distracted them both by saying it was now my turn to change. Usually, when I had just Flora with me, I would slip under a beach towel and pull off my clothes and pull on my suit in an instant, but since I had the two of them to help, I gave them each a towel and asked if they would make an envelope for me as well. I sat on the blanket and the two girls stood on either side of me, the towels outstretched in their little arms and the sun warm on my head and my shoulders. I slipped out of my father's shirt and then pulled the T-shirt over my head, my arms rising above the curtain of the beach blankets, and then pulled off my shorts and my underwear. I leaned down to work my suit up over my feet and my legs, calling out, "Stay with me now, girls," as I shifted my weight and rose up onto my knees, to pull the suit over my waist. I could see Flora's side beginning to fold and I said, "One more minute, Flora Dora," as I slipped my right arm into the suit. But I fumbled with the twisted strap on the left side and Flora fell plop backward as I did, beach towel and all, and whoever might have been watching us among the half dozen or so groups scattered on the beach would have had a good bright white glimpse of whatever little bit I had. Daisy's mouth dropped open and she raised her beach towel to her face, as if to shield her eyes. Flora simply began to cry. I covered myself with the edge of the suit, but my arm was bare and there was no modest way to get it into the strap short of wrapping myself in a towel again, which suddenly struck me as excessive. I realized I had hunched my shoulders, too, instinctively, I supposed, and cupped my hands over my chest. This also struck me as excessive. So I raised myself up fully on my knees and then stood, straightening my spine. "No one's looking," I said to Daisy as she took the beach towel from her own eyes. And I said, "Don't cry, Flora Dora," to Flora on the quilt. Making myself as tall as I could, I pulled my right arm out of the suit, pulled the suit to my waist, straightened the fabric at my hips and over my stomach and then, leisurely, drew the suit up again, one strap over my left arm and one over my right.

Daisy's mouth was wide open, the beach towel bunched in her hands. Flora was still whining on the quilt. I bent down and scooped her up and, holding her on my hip, turned to Daisy. I could see I'd become something else in her eyes, as if I had indeed made everyone on the beach disappear. "Come on, Daisy Mae," I said, holding my hand out to her. "Now let's take care of you."

We began that afternoon a peculiar therapy. I had Daisy stand at the shoreline, where the waves could swirl around her feet, but not so far in that they could upset her balance. I told her to stand in one place while the water rushed around her ankles and her feet sank into the sand, and then, when the wave went out again, to pull her feet out, move a bit to the left or the right, and then let them sink in again. It was nothing more than the usual game I had played all my life, that every child standing at the shoreline must surely play, but the precision of my instructions gave it a new meaning, or purpose, and although I said nothing about the water or the sand or the movement of the waves as a cure for whatever it was that had discolored her skin, Daisy obeyed with absolute seriousness and stood there, watching her feet sink into the wet sand, stepping to the left and to the right, while I took Flora out into the ocean in my arms.

She was fearless in the ocean, as long as she had her arms around my neck. I had already taught her how to hold her breath and shut her eyes when we went under together, and how to raise her chin and shut her eyes against the spray when we bobbed over a wave. Once, in a trough between waves, I pointed toward the city and said, "There's your Mommy, Flora," and she raised her hand and waved at the sun (gold sun in a white-and-turquoise sky, I told her, Mommy's scarf, after all). Once, diving under with her, in the rush of bubbles and green water and the sudden underwater silence, I looked at her to see that she was looking at me, eyes wide open, face serene, pale hair floating, looking for all the world like something not yet born but fully formed, something plump and otherworldly, angelic and human, iridescent, milky white, the unlikely miraculous flesh conjured out of a stooped old man and his hard and narrow young wife. In the sun again, sound again (of ocean and seagulls and children calling), and with her wet arms around my neck and her heart beating rapidly against my chest, I planted a kiss on her salty cheek and said, Let's go help Daisy.

We stood with her at the shoreline, all three of us watching our feet sink into the swirling water and sand. And then, suddenly, there was a fourth presence at my elbow and I turned to see Petey panting beside me. He was soaking wet and looked as if he had been rolled in sand. His too large bathing suit was down around his bony hips and his concave stomach, and three or four of his mosquito bites were running with blood as well as seawater. Even in a place as elemental as the shore, Petey could manage to look both besieged and neglected. He said a shy "Hi" to Daisy and then pulled me by the elbow, whispering something. I had to ask him twice what he was trying to say, and finally had to lean over to put my ear to his mouth. As I did, he took a handful of my wet and matted hair and held it over his lips. "I've got Daisy's present," he whispered. "When are you coming back?"

I told him we'd be back around dinnertime. I looked over his head. The beach was more crowded by now, the beginning of an extended summer weekend. "Are you by yourself?" I asked him. "Where's baby June?" He did not let go of my hair. He kept it still entangled in his fingers and against his lips. "I'm with my mom," he said, and pointed, and sure enough, just down the beach, there was Sondra in a black bathing suit and a large black hat, baby June and Janey digging in the sand at her feet. Janey was still wearing Flora's mother's straw hat, and her own mother was sitting like a movie star on her blanket, her back arched, one knee raised, her hands cupped around it. Suddenly she waved to us, and we both waved back. Petey still had his hand in my hair, and he tugged at it a little to say, "She's with the police."

Although I recalled what my mother had said this morning about the police being at the Morans' again, I had no idea what he was talking about. I remembered Tony telling Janey that the cops would pick her up if she left the street and wondered for a minute if this unusual family excursion to the shore wasn't part of some sentence that had been doled out by the local criminal justice system. I actually felt heartened by the notion until I saw a burly young man come out of the water and

head for Mrs. Moran's blanket, with Tony, as exuberant as a
puppy, high-stepping it through the sand behind him, and
then Judy, also wet and buoyant, running to catch up with
them both. The young man threw himself on the blanket beside Sondra, and the two children, as if uncertain about how
far they should follow, stood a short distance away from it, like
puppies waiting for the stick to be tossed once more. The man
spoke to them while drying his broad chest with a small towel,
and then sank back behind their mother, who suddenly leaned
back, too, on her elbows, in the shade of their umbrella. Judy
and Tony, rebuffed, I supposed, but showing no indication of it,
simply dropped to their knees beside their two sisters and began to throw sand into the hole they had just dug.

I looked once again at Petey, who had taken full possession
of that handful of my hair, touching it idly to his lips. "Your
mother's here with a policeman?" I asked.

He nodded. His black eye had faded to a gray shadow,
nearly healed. "He took Grandpa to jail last night," Petey said.
"And then he brought him back this morning. And then we
met him here." He shrugged, as if none of it concerned him.
"Don't tell Daisy about her present."

I took hold of his wrist and gently slipped my tangled hair
from between his fingers. "I have nothing to tell," I whispered.

Later that afternoon, when I carried our lunch wrappers to
the garbage cans at the top of the parking lot, I saw Dr. Kaufman, a beach chair and a newspaper under his arm, walking to
his car. He waved to me and I waved back, and then he turned
on his heel, as if he had just thought of something, and gestured that I should wait. Now he was wearing a bathing suit
under that same dark tennis shirt, and black leather sandals.

"Sugar," he said, squinting in the sun although his sunglasses were on top of his head, "I'd tell this to my own daughter. You're lovely to look at, but you can get fined for baring your breasts like that on this beach. A couple of Village Improvement Society matrons by me went apoplectic. If there'd been a cop nearby, they'd have had you arrested."

I lowered my eyes and said, "There was," but he didn't seem to hear me. He stepped closer. "Come use our pool if you want an all-over tan," he said. "It's perfectly private."

I looked up at him, I had to, but I didn't say anything, and I didn't say anything for long enough to make it seem purposeful. I knew my cheeks were red, but I felt I was looking at him from behind them somehow, that my face was only something I had placed between us, like a fan. His smile faltered a bit and then he said, "I don't mean to embarrass you. Just thought you should know." He began to turn away and then turned back again. "Also," he said. It occurred to me that he was going home to Red Rover and an empty summer house, a solitary summer evening. "The little girl, your cousin."

"Daisy," I said.

He nodded. "Daisy. Is she all right?"

I looked over my shoulder as if to check on her. She and Flora both were lying on the quilt, under their beach towels. "Yes," I said. "She's all right."

"Has she been sick recently?" he asked. "Had any surgery, accidents?" There was suddenly something solid and reliable in his manner, something I had seen before, when he was with his own children, but had missed in him today. If I hadn't already been sunburned and blushing, I might have blushed again.

I shook my head. "She's always pale," I said, to show him I understood his concern.

"She looks anemic," he said. "She may well be. You might want to mention it to her parents. A blood test might be a good idea. And sooner rather than later."

"She's fine," I said.

"I'm sure she is," he told me. "But you should mention it to her parents. Tell them it's my suggestion, as a friend of the family." He smiled, a nicer smile than before. "So that's enough advice out of me. I'm gone Monday through Wednesday again next week," he said. "But I might come back early if it's real hot in the city. Red will be looking for you."

I nodded. "We'll be there," I said. "Daisy and I."

He turned again. "Use the pool," he said over his shoulder.

When we brought Flora home that afternoon, there was no sign of the cook, and Ana, dressed in slacks and a silky blue shirt that showed her cleavage, was cooking something in the kitchen. Something in a big pot that smelled oniony and thick. Without a word to Ana, Daisy and I gave Flora her bath and put her in her pajamas and then sat with her while she ate. Then we put her in her stroller again and walked her up and down the street until her head began to droop. I lifted her out at the end of the driveway, and Daisy pushed her empty stroller over the gravel while I carried Flora inside and put her in her crib. I put a light blanket over her shoulders. The pictures on the wall seemed to have very little to do with the actual child sleeping here or her missing mother. Flora, for one thing, was no longer an infant. I stopped into the kitchen to tell Ana that Flora was asleep and she cried, "Merci, merci," in a sweet voice that was straight out of a movie. "Good night, girls," she added, in English, waving her fingers over her shoulders. "Have a pleasant evening."

He was on the porch in one of the canvas chairs, with his pipe and a glass of red wine, but he let us pass without a word. Halfway down the drive, I found myself thinking of excuses to turn back, maybe to ask Ana if I should come earlier tomorrow, maybe to thank him for telling her not to give Flora any more bottles—although I suspected he'd done no such thing. Holding Daisy's hand, walking quietly toward home—we were both weary—I felt a tremendous reluctance I didn't quite understand. Part of it, I supposed, was a reluctance to leave Flora—which one of them, I wondered, would go to her if she woke up in the middle of the night? Part of it was my disappointment that he had let us leave without saying a word. After this morning, we were complicit in something, he and I, something that had little to do with my having found him asleep or with the way he had touched my knee, that had more to do with the way he had bent down to Daisy and opened his palm, just as I had hoped he would. Part of it, perhaps, was the quiet house and what was for them, I imagined, the dark jewel of the approaching evening.

I lifted Daisy's hand and swung it. "I love having you here, Daisy Mae," I said. And she smiled. "I love it, too." I kissed the back of her hand and put my arm under hers. She was just a little sunburned. I had slathered her with lotion, but only after the first half hour, so she could get some color in her cheeks. "We'll put some cold cream on this tonight," I said. I ran my fingers down the back of her arm, to tickle her. She raised her shoulders and giggled. "Last night you giggled in your sleep," I told her, and she said she knew. "I always do," she said.

"Bernadette always tells me. She gets mad when I can't remember what I was dreaming about. She says if a dream was good enough to make me laugh in my sleep, then it was good enough to remember." She paused. She might have been favoring that right leg again. "Sometimes I do remember," she said, "but I don't always tell her."

"Good for you," I said.

"Last night I dreamt about the lollipop tree," she said. "The one we're going to make for Flora."

I nodded. She seemed a little breathless as she spoke, and her shoes were scraping along the street. I slowed my pace. I said, "I bet Bernadette is missing you like crazy."

Daisy shook her head. "I don't think so."

I reached down and pulled the hem of my father's shirt across her shoulders. "I'm sure she wakes up in the middle of the night and listens and can't understand why she doesn't hear you. I'm sure she even thinks you're there, when she's first falling asleep. I bet she even says something to you, as she's drifting off. And then she remembers your bed is empty and she's there all alone."

Streaks of white clouds across the lovely sky, and the sun, deep gold again and at moments blinding, just behind the thick black leaves of the trees. Bernadette alone in that tiny room with her Honor Roll certificates, four for each year she has been in school, and space left on the wall for what was to come. "I bet two big fat tears pop right out of her eyes as she's lying there. I bet they roll right into her ears."

Daisy laughed and slipped her arm around my waist. I pressed her against my hip, holding the shirt across her shoulders, her pink shoes scraping against the road. We both felt, for just a moment, I think, the loneliness of that imagined scene. I felt, only briefly, only until I banished it from my mind, my own terrible prescience.

"Do you want me to carry you?" I asked her, and she shook her head. "Do you feel all right?" I said, and my heart sank when she shook her head again. "Not too good," she said.

Petey's rabbit trap was still on our lawn when we got home, moved now to another corner of the yard, and we weren't in the house more than a few minutes when he rattled our back door. I had just put Daisy in the shower and would have told him through the screen to come back later except that his face was a mask of sorrow, his mouth open wide, tears streaming down his cheeks. I opened the door and he said, trying to whisper but with his voice hoarse from crying, "It ran away."

He put his arms around my waist and pressed his head against my shirt, digging his fingers into my flesh. "The present I had for Daisy," he sobbed. "It's gone."

I touched his head. I could feel the sand still caked on his scalp. The tips of his ears were sunburned, although the rest of his skin was a solid brown. "What was it?" I said. And he shook his head. "I don't want to tell you," he said. And then, as if against his own intentions, he said, "I caught one. It was in the box when we went to the beach. I thought it would be safe. I didn't think it could get out. But when we got back, the box was tipped over and it was gone. It took all the carrots."

"You caught something?" I asked. "In that box?"

He nodded into my shirt. "But it ran away."

"Are you sure you caught one?" I asked him. I understood that we had entered into some kind of agreement not to say the actual word.

He nodded again, but with less certainty this time.

"You saw it in the trap?"

He looked up at me, the tears spread all over his face. "It was in the box," he said. "I checked the box before we went to the beach and it was turned over. The stick had fallen. It was in there. I caught it."

I pushed him away, my hands on his shoulders. "Did you see it in there?" I asked, and he shook his head. "Did you hear it moving?" He shook his head again, his sobs becoming only a slight groan at the back of his throat.

"Maybe the box just fell over," I said. "Maybe the stick broke. Maybe it was the wind."

He considered this for a minute, sniffling. "But all the carrots are gone," he said. We both looked over at the cardboard box propped on its thin stick, the replica of my father's matchbox this morning.

"Has Rags been around today?" I asked.

He stood there for a moment, and then I felt his shoulders slump, as if all the bones within them had just shattered, fallen to the ground. He stepped away from me, the extent of his disappointment displacing even the need he had felt, just a few seconds ago, to bury his head in my chest. He looked at the box again and said, "Shit," and didn't even glance at me for a reprimand. "I'll never catch one," he said.

I heard Daisy calling me from the shower, and I called back that I'd be right there. I held up a finger to Petey and then went to the refrigerator and found some lettuce. I brought it out to him. I didn't say that my father had given me the same instructions some years ago, and that I had spent the better part of a summer trying to catch a wild rabbit with just such a trap. I said, "Bugs Bunny is probably the only rabbit that really eats carrots (and Rags may well be the only dog). Lettuce might do better."

He softened, thinking this over, wiping his nose on the back of his arm.

"Twilight's the best time for rabbits, anyway," I whispered. "You're not likely to catch one in the middle of the day."

He sucked in some air. "Yeah?" he said.

"And you're not going to catch one while you're watching," I added. "They can smell you if you're nearby. They can smell you even when you're asleep, Petey, even if you're hidden under the bushes."

He nodded, as if this might be a legitimate bit of impersonal information. Admitting nothing. I rubbed his head again. "Good luck," I said.

Daisy was sitting on my bed when I went back. She was wrapped in a towel and there was an opened package of new underwear and an opened package of ankle socks on the bed beside her. Her hair was wet and dark and Petey's bruise was a dark brooch on her shoulder. Against my white bedspread her little feet seemed blackened. I took the jar of Noxzema from my dresser and before I smoothed any of it over her arms or her shoulders or her red nose, I covered her feet, gently, with the cool stuff. She sat back, against my pillows, watching me through half-closed eyes, something fond and sympathetic in her expression. And then I pulled on the new socks. She wanted to wear the red-checked sundress again, but I said I'd run upstairs and find her a cleaner outfit. I chose a pair of pink-and-white-striped pedal pushers and a white shirt with pink pockets and short sleeves that would cover her shoulder.

The chair was still in front of the attic window, catching the setting sunlight. It was a light that swarmed with dust motes, and I knew that if I stood there for just a minute, alone as I was, and willed my eyes to see, I could conjure Uncle Tommy's sea captain ghost, or his little boy, or even Uncle Tommy himself, with his wink and his laugh.

When I got back to my room, it seemed Daisy had been doing her own bit of conjuring. She was still sitting on the bed, in her towel and her socks, but Judy and Janey were leaning across the mattress on either side of her and baby June was on the floor. Remarkably enough, all three of the Moran kids had been showered and changed, baby June even had a thin ribbon in her wet hair, and the entire rose-covered room smelled of their shampoo and their soap and the hours they had spent outside. A bit of sun had caught the cut-glass base of my bedside lamp and scattered itself across the floor, and baby June was playing with these pieces of light while the other three girls leaned over the mattress, studying Flora's mother's hat on the bed between them. It looked a bit more battered than it had this morning. I gave them my ribbon box and then went to take a shower myself, thinking only briefly—it was like a glance thrown over my shoulder—of how Ana's plump body might compare with my own. I returned to the girls and dressed quickly. Then I climbed onto the bed with all four of them and one by one combed out their wet hair and braided each with a ribbon of their choosing. I was just doing my own, baby June and Janey still sitting between my legs and Judy and Daisy stretched out on either side of me, my ribbons scattered all over the floor and the white spread, when I heard my parents come in, calling for us. I called back to say we were in here, and when they came to the doorway in their dark clothes, my father's usual expression of surprise and delight struck me, for the first time perhaps, as authentic.

We didn't sleep in the attic that night. We stayed awake a long time, Daisy and I, to listen for Petey beneath the bushes. But the Moran house was quiet, and I wondered if the police hadn't finally found an effective way to keep them all subdued by sending in a full-time cop to be Mrs. Moran's boyfriend. I held Daisy's hand under the thin summer blanket and instead of reciting Hail Marys began a long list of "God blesses," starting with my parents, who were talking quietly in the twin beds on the other side of the wall, then each of the Morans (plus the policeman), then Rags, wherever he might be tonight, and Red Rover and Dr. Kaufman, and then Angus and Rupert and the Richardsons, Moe, Larry, and Curly, and the Clarkes and the Swansons, and Flora, of course, and her mother and her father and Ana (why not?) and the fat cook, and then all the conductors on the Long Island Railroad—we could hear the whistle of the last train to Montauk (Daisy was not asleep yet, but I could tell by the way she laughed that she was heading that way)—and all the workers in every station I could remember between here and Jamaica. And Daisy's father, who might well be among them if he was not already sound asleep in his own room under the sad brown eyes of the Sacred Heart. And Daisy's mother beside him. And each of her brothers, and Bernadette, of course, lying in the dark, the tears in her ears making her dream about swimming in the ocean with Daisy, eyes wide open and hair floating, right by her side—no response from Daisy this time, only her soft breath— and Uncle Tommy in his apartment on the Upper West Side, all alone after more than fifty years of living, all alone, talking to ghosts, determined to be happy. And you, Daisy Mae, I whispered to put an end to it. I leaned over to kiss her cheek and then turned to sleep. And me, I might have added—God bless me—but I didn't. No doubt it was because I had begun to suspect that God and I, as Uncle Tommy would have put it, weren't seeing eye to eye.

Flora was back out on the porch again the next morning, another bottle of red juice tucked tightly between her teeth, and no sign of Ana anywhere, although the door to the master bedroom was closed. Both lights were on in his studio, but I didn't go in again. I wasn't exactly certain that I'd find him there. I told the girls I'd had enough of the beach and thought we might instead take a nature walk through the woods and look for salamanders and wildflowers, and then maybe, after lunch, walk to the shore.

Daisy said that would be fine, and Flora told me, pulling the bottle from her mouth, that her mommy was coming home tomorrow. "Tomorrow," she repeated. She said it with great firmness, frowning as she spoke, and I recognized the word as something she had been told emphatically by someone, sternly perhaps. Mommy will be home tomorrow. Even hearing the word secondhand from a toddler, I had a sense it was a lie.

"Tomorrow," I repeated. "Tomorrow is tomorrow." I touched her nose to erase that furrow between her brows. I wondered which of them had told her the lie, which of them had spoken to my Flora so harshly. Ana, I suspected. "Tomorrow and tomorrow and tomorrow," I said, and kissed her head.

"Tomorrow, and tomorrow, and tomorrow, creeps in this petty pace from day to day . . ." I unhooked the strap from around Flora's waist and helped her out of the stroller, pulling her up by her one free hand. Then I held my other hand out for Daisy and we walked down the steps together. "And all our yesterdays," I went on, Flora pulling at the bottle as she walked, her head thrown back and her elbow raised, like a trumpeter in some New Orleans funeral parade. Daisy kicking up the gravel with her pink shoes. "And all our yesterdays have lighted fools the way to dusty death." We passed the door of his studio. I could tell by the sharp smell of the paint that he was indeed inside and "working." "Out, out, brief candle!" I called as we passed (and congratulated myself on my timing—he might have at least told Ana not to let me see Flora with a bottle). "Life's but a walking shadow, a poor player that struts and frets his hour upon the stage and then is heard no more."

"What's 'struts'?" Daisy asked, and I showed her. And we strutted together, all three of us across the grass and onto the path through the woods. We wandered a bit, picking up sticks and rocks and trying unsuccessfully to catch the darting shadows of salamanders. When we got to the caretaker's gate, I tried giving them both a ride, but the hinges were too old and the grass beneath the gate too high to make it much fun. We stopped for a while in the grass beside the road to make clover chains, and as we did I tried telling them the story of *Macbeth*. But Flora wandered, and while Daisy let her eyes grow wide at the witches and the murder of the king and the appearance of Banquo's ghost, she didn't like the bit about Lady Macbeth scrubbing at the stain on her poor little hand and suddenly, as I spoke, leaned over to put her fingers to my lips. I held her wrist. "It's all right, Daisy Mae," I whispered. I told her it was not something she would have to hear about again until high school.

Walking back through the woods, she said, "Why wouldn't the stain come off her hand, even after she washed it a lot?"

I smiled at her. I had placed bluebells and buttercups into the pigtails I had made for her this morning, and one of the clover chains dipped down over her forehead. "It was only her imagination," I told her. "It wasn't really there. It was all in her mind."

She thought about this for a while, walking with Flora, who still clutched the empty bottle in her hand. "Everything's in your mind," she said. And I said no. I touched the bark of a tree, picked up a fallen branch. "This is real," I said. "And this." I touched her arm. "You are."

"But it's all in my mind, too," she said. She was wearing one of my tennis dresses today, a much better fit than the cheap ones bought by her mother. Her pink shoes were dusty from the gravel and the trail. "If it wasn't in my mind, how would I know about it?"

I tugged at her hair. "You're an old soul, Daisy Mae," I said.

She thought about this for a second. "Is that good?" she said.

"It's what my mother says people always used to say about me."

She smiled, clearly pleased. And then she said, "Yeah, but you remembered more. You remembered heaven from before you were even born."

I laughed. I could see she was rehearsing the stories she would tell her brothers, and maybe even Bernadette, when she got home, if anyone would listen to her. Stories about me.

"You're the one who seems to remember everything, little friend," I said, and then added, "Sutton Place."

She let out a pink, open-mouthed laugh. "I don't even know where that is," she said, as if this made her hubris more delightful. "I don't even know why you told the Scotties' mother that's where I live."

I lifted my hair off my neck, it was soft and thick from the humidity, and then ran my fingers through it, making it look a little wild, making Flora laugh. One of the clover chains I wore broke and floated to the ground. "I was playing tricks with her mind," I told Daisy, sweeping my wild hair back off my shoulders. "Just like the witches with Macbeth."

I picked up the broken chain and draped it over Flora's head. She was already covered in them—bracelets and necklaces and three wreaths around her hair. In her free hand she clutched several sticks and a few orange and white pebbles and a long stalk of milkweed and one of Queen Anne's lace.

"I don't remember heaven, though," Daisy said, after a while. "Like you do."

I scooped Flora up to lift her over a fallen tree trunk. "It's just like this," I told her.

Had she been the child of a different father, I would have sent Flora through the door of his studio to show him how she looked draped in clover and dandelions and bits of milkweed and buttercups. But given the father she had, I knew I would be sending her in only as a lure to draw him out, only to see what was on his face when he looked at me.

We ate our lunch under the weeping-cherry trees again, and then brought Flora inside to read to her for a while in her shaded room. She was only half awake when I put her in her crib, but she stood up and started to whine each time Daisy and I attempted to leave. So we both stretched out on the pale carpet beside her bed, and soon enough both Flora and Daisy were breathing softly. I may have fallen asleep myself, because I heard Ana's voice and saw her standing in the doorway, had a conversation with her even, all without opening my eyes. When I did open them, no one was there and the house was quiet. I sat up. Daisy was beside me, her hands beneath her cheek, her head resting on one of Flora's stuffed dogs, and her lips parted, moving with each breath. The clover chains were still on her head, the fading flowers still stuck into her hair, and I resisted the urge to shake her awake, just to see her green eyes. Instead, I put the back of my hand to her cheek and then to her forehead. She was warm, but comfortably so. It occurred to me that I was beginning to know the difference, the difference between the warmth of healthy blood beneath the skin and the odd heat of a fever. As a child, I had thought my mother's ability to determine this with just the touch of her hand utterly magical, mysterious. Now I could do it, too. I stood, checked on Flora, who was also still in her full forest regalia, and then walked down the hall into the living room.

An eye, a jaw, the curve of a breast, all of it disproportionate and ugly, somehow, all of it laid on with thick paint. As if he wanted there to be no doubt that he knew what he was doing. As if he wanted there to be no doubt that he could transform what might otherwise be arbitrary and unskilled into something intentional, something of value. His alone. His work.

I turned to look at the other painting, which had no images at all, a blur of paint. Scribble out the world since it was not to your liking and make up a new one, something better.

I went into the kitchen to get a glass of water. I wondered if Ana had left, since there were still cups and dishes in the sink and the floor needed sweeping. I went through the screen door and sat on the steps of the porch. The car was still there. The lights were still on in his studio. I stood up and walked, as Daisy had done, toward the path, leaning a bit to see if the canvas was against the wall. It wasn't. I walked a little farther. I could smell the paint, but I heard no voices. Keeping my footsteps light, I passed by the side door and saw he was in there, standing over the same canvas, which was now lying on the concrete floor. His legs spread, his hands on his hips, staring down at his work in his white shirt and his khaki pants like some old colossus. I couldn't see the bed in the far corner, but I had the impression that someone else was in there with him, and I walked on by, toward the caretaker's path, as if that had been my destination all along. But then I thought I heard my name called and I stopped. I listened for a minute, sure I was mistaken, and then I heard him say, "You can come in."

I walked back toward the door, uncertain but curious. He was still standing in the same place, in the same pose, a large cloth in one of the hands he held against his hip, what looked like a putty knife in the other. The light from the skylight was clearer today, a lovely bleached light that seemed to make his hair and his skin and his clothes and the cloth he held—it was a diaper, actually, stained with paint—all seem the same shade. He said, "We thought the three of you were napping," and standing on the threshold, I saw that Ana was indeed in there with him, sitting on the hard bed. She was wearing a sleeveless sweater and a black skirt, and her plump, bare legs were crossed. Her chin was lowered and thus had multiplied itself by three. She looked unhappy and her expression did not change as she watched me.

"Come on in," he said again. And I crossed the threshold, into the bleached light. I stood on the other side of his painting, which, I supposed, was progressing. There was more paint on it, anyway. He turned to look at Ana over his shoulder, said something to her in French, and then turned back to me. "The wood nymph," he said, translating, I assumed, what he had told her. I realized I still had the clover chains in my hair, too. I touched one of them. "A Thomas Hardy–reading, Shakespeare-quoting, drink-pouring wood nymph." He walked around the painting toward me, but then veered off to the shelves of paints and clutter, throwing the diaper and the knife onto one of them. I smiled politely.

"Flora," I said, "told me her mother is coming home tomorrow, so I wondered if you needed me to come so early——or at all."

He turned, laughing, as if he had caught me in another lie. He rested an elbow on a shelf above him, put his other hand on his hip. Only my experience with Uncle Tommy led me to know he had been, or still was, drinking. There was no lack of steadiness about him, no weaving or slurring, but an odd deliberateness in each gesture, a determination in his focus. "No," he said. "No. Flora's mother won't be here tomorrow. Or the next day, I imagine." He pulled off his glasses and pinched the space between his eyes. "Flora's mother is in the city," he said. "And Flora's mother is an ardent practitioner of out of sight, out of mind. There's really no telling when she'll return." He put his glasses on again, moving away from the shelves. "So your services will continue to be needed."

He walked toward me again. He reached out and touched my hair, lifting it from my shoulder with one hand and plucking out of it one of the clover flowers with the other. He spun the flower in his fingers. "And the little redhead, too," he said, looking at me from over his glasses. "What was her name?"

"Daisy," I said. There was the scent of Uncle Tommy as well, tinged, it seemed to me, with the orange aspirins. He raised his chin, getting a better look. "Daisy," he said. "Who's having a rough time."

I nodded, but then added, "At home. Not now."

He nodded, too. "I see," he said. "You've rescued her." He was placing my hair behind my shoulder now, gently, as if to put it back where it belonged. He took another clover flower from the back of my head. His neck was sinewy, full of hollows, that pale, papery skin.

"And home is . . ." he asked, his eyes searching my hair. "Brooklyn?"

"Queens Village," I said.

He nodded, as if he should have known. "Father a fireman?" He smoothed some of my hair behind my ear, his fingertips brushing the side of my face and my scalp. And then he lifted it again, as if measuring its weight. I could smell the paint on his palm.

"Policeman," I said.

He nodded in the same way. "Ten kids?" he said.

"Eight," I answered.

He smiled. There was something odd about the way his

small teeth met his gums on one side. Dentures, I supposed. A partial plate, as my parents might say. Nothing better to remind you of your mortality, he had said. His own mortality in his mouth.

He kept his one hand in my hair and took off his glasses with the other, a gesture so swift and so casual he might have done it only to see something better, maybe to read some fine print, and bending into what was his natural stoop, he leaned down and kissed me on the lips, softly, but long enough to make me have to take a breath through my nose before he was finished. And when he was finished—the taste of the alcohol on my own lips—he simply slipped his hand from my hair to my waist, brushing the backs of his fingers past my shoulder and my breast, slipped his glasses on again, and guided me to the door. We stepped over the threshold together, into the sunshine, onto the gravel path. Walking toward the house, he said, casually, "So Daisy is the eighth child of an exhausted mother," and I said—imitating his tone as well as I could, aware of the pulse in my throat—no, the fifth child. Smack in the middle of them all, I said. Three boys older and three boys younger and one older sister, Bernadette.

It was like reciting lines on a stage, pretending to be calm despite the throbbing of your own blood in your ears.

He asked what Bernadette was like.

Very smart and chubby, I said. Homely enough, I said, to keep her parents constantly apologizing.

Reaching for the screen door, he threw his head back and laughed. He put his hand to the small of my back. "In here first," he said, pointing toward the kitchen. And we both turned right, into the messy kitchen, where the Scotch was already on the table and Flora's mother's scarves were now on a high shelf by the window. He took his hand from my back in order to pour himself a drink, and as he did I stepped away, leaning against the doorframe. He looked at me from over the rim of his glass, just the slightest trace of worry, or doubt, coming briefly into his eyes.

"And you've rescued poor Daisy from Queens Village and her harried parents," he said. "To give her a few summer days out here in the country."

I nodded.

"And to teach her Shakespeare."

I shrugged.

"And let her feast on St. Joseph's aspirin."

Behind me I could hear Flora calling softly from her crib.

"You gave her the aspirin," I said.

He drank again. Now he heard her, too, his daughter; I saw his eyes register the sound. I heard Daisy sleepily responding. I thought of the surprised look she always wore when she first woke up, her features not yet fully her own.

He looked me up and down again, his head once more drawn back. Up and down from my ankles to my waist to my chest and neck and hair, the corners of his mouth drawn a little and that little bit of fear crossing his face. "You're some kid," he said finally. And then he raised his chin toward the hallway and his daughter's bedroom. "Your charges are calling," he said.

To my surprise, he went with me, walking just behind me down the narrow hallway to the bedrooms, following me right up to Flora's crib, where Daisy was standing, stroking Flora's plump wrist and saying, "Here she is. And here's your daddy."

Flora held her arms out to me, of course, and I lifted her onto the changing table. Behind me, he said to Daisy, "Come with me, won't you?" And when I looked over my shoulder, he was walking hand in hand with her down the hallway. I heard the screen door close and followed with Flora as soon as I had changed her. They were both standing at the bottom of the steps when we got outside, both of them chewing aspirin between their back teeth. He was pointing out something to her in one of the high branches of the far trees—a jay's nest, he said—and she was looking up, following his arm, still holding his hand.

I put Flora in her stroller, and she began to cry, asking for a bottle of red juice. I said, "No more bottles, Flora. You don't want a bottle." But she was cranky, still not fully awake, and her voice began to get shrill. I leaned over her. "Mommy doesn't want you to have a bottle, Flora," I said softly. "You're such a big girl now, you don't need a bottle." She kicked her feet against the bars of the stroller, crying in earnest now. I put my hand on her arm. "Oh, Flora," I whispered.

That's when he turned to us, still holding Daisy's hand, and said, "Go ahead and give her one."

I stood up straight, tossing my hair over my shoulder. Looking down at the two of them from the shade of the porch, I saw that they were both sun-washed and faded, Daisy still blurred from her nap, he, perhaps, blurred from the need for one. I was about to say either "your wife" or "her mother," had probably hesitated simply to decide which was best, when he held up a hand. "We've vanished," he said.

He said it softly, under Flora's crying, and so it was the word itself that made me start.

"We're gone," he said. He glanced down at Daisy for a moment, pleasantly, including her in the conversation. "All my life I've known women who could do this. Turn their backs and make things disappear. It's a wonderful talent." He smiled up at me. His white hair stood straight up over his head, and while Uncle Tommy's focus went awry when he drank, fell slightly to the left or right of whatever he seemed to be seeing, his was direct and thorough. "Although a bit much for a man my age. A bit too much irony." Daisy was looking up at him in her polite, attentive way. Mournfully, Flora said, "Red juice, please. Please." He looked at me. "Don't worry about my wife. Let the poor kid have a bottle."

I shrugged. "All right," I said to him, and to his daughter, "Hold on, Flora Dora." As I pulled open the screen door to go back into the kitchen, he said, "And pour something for her old man while you're at it."

I filled Flora's bottle with punch and refilled his glass as well. When I came out, he had pulled the stroller to the edge of the steps and was sitting beside it, with Daisy at his feet. Flora took the bottle with both hands, eagerly, and even smiled around the nipple when her father said, "Ah, the pleasures of the flesh." He winked at me. "What a teenager she's going to make."

He raised the glass to the three of us. "Three beauties," he said, and drank, and winced when the cold hit his bad tooth. He rubbed his jaw. "How many years would it earn me," he said, "if I swallowed each one of you whole?" Daisy, with her pink shoes tucked up under her knees and the hem of my old white tennis dress, said simply, "I don't know."

He laughed, one of his deep shouts of real laughter, and

leaning forward, reached down to pat her head. "Neither do I," he said. "But it would be worth finding out."

With his drink in his hand, he stood cautiously, the other hand gripping the wood banister, pulling himself up with it. He turned from us, walking down the gravel path a little stiffly, perhaps a little more stooped, and went into his studio, where Ana, as far as I could tell, was still waiting for him.

I convinced the girls to spend the rest of the afternoon at home, in the house and on the lawn, playing blindman's bluff and paper dolls and perfecting our cartwheels and somersaults on the grass. About mid-afternoon, Ana came out of his studio and went into the house, looking much as she always did, acting much the same as well—ignoring us in her Frenchified way. I heard the vacuum go on inside, and a few minutes later saw her come to the door to shake out a small rug. She was in her blue uniform again, although she had one of Flora's mother's scarves tied around her hair. She no longer seemed particularly unhappy, and although she was the only one who had witnessed what had happened in his studio this morning, I wasn't particularly embarrassed by her glance. It was as if I had somehow taken to heart his startling phrase, as if we had vanished, the girls and I, and this house and lawn, the studio, the gravel path, the woods up to the caretaker's gate, was the last place we lingered. Like little ghosts.

It wasn't until just before dinner that we finally walked down to the beach, and that was only so Daisy could take her therapy at the edge of the ocean. Her skin did not seem to be improving, nor was it getting any worse, although the seriousness with which she watched her feet sink into the sand as the foamy water spread around them made me think that she, too, could erase the bruises, and whatever it was the bruises indicated—perhaps anemia (I had looked it up, and had asked my mother to make liver and onions)—by an act of will.

Walking back, we ran into the Richardsons again, with Rupert and Angus and another couple, a thinner and authentically British version of themselves, a Mr. and Mrs. Hyphenated Name, down for the weekend. Mrs. Richardson introduced Flora as the daughter of "one of our better known artists"—the thin couple gave a satisfying exclamation at his name—and Daisy as a "little visitor" who lived on Sutton Place, and me as the girl who had stolen her puppies' hearts (poor Rupert and Angus beating their stumpy tails and panting as if to say, It's true, it's true), who lived in that charming cottage with the dahlias. "The village beauty," she said, as if this were merrie olde England and I were Eustacia Vye herself.

The thin couple—gaunt, really, and dressed for fall—shook hands with us all and smiled broadly, and actually said, Enchanting, enchanting, as they looked at us in the dusk. The tall trees were full now of birdsong and setting sunlight. We chatted for a while, although the conversation quickly ran its course and we needed to get Flora home. We spoke about the weather and the weekend and the fireworks at the Main Beach, and Mrs. Richardson's preference for June over July, September over August. ("Of course you schoolchildren dread it," she said, taking us all in with a warm Beatrix Potter kind of glance, "but September is really the best month of the summer. The crowds are gone. We have those warm days and those glorious cool nights." "Sleeping weather," her husband said, taking the pipe from his mouth, and the British woman exclaimed, "Oh, indeed, sleeping weather," as if it were something out of King Arthur.) With Angus and Rupert panting contentedly at my feet, absorbing into their bellies the warmth of my sneakers and whatever heat was left in the road, we lingered. We lingered although it was growing late and Flora was nodding off in her stroller and Daisy was sighing quietly, shifting from foot to foot. We discussed the fragrant air, the stars at night, the soothing sound of the ocean. Mrs. Richardson was beaming, at us, and at her thin and shadowy friends, as if we were all her own creation, and I paused longer than I should have to let her enjoy it, this fairy tale she had made of us, her own England, under the thick trees, on the quiet road that ran between a deep green lawn lit by fireflies and the brown potato field where just yesterday afternoon baby June had tumbled up out of the ground.

There was still no cook that night. When we finally got Flora into bed, it was later than usual, almost dark, and the light from his studio cast shapes on the gravel drive. As we passed the open door I could see him stretched out on the bed, in that same fallen-warrior pose, one leg up and his arm over his eyes, the painting still on the floor. At home, my mother turned from the stove as we walked in and said over her shoulder, "I was beginning to worry."

As usual, the Clarkes came over for dinner on Sunday. They liked to drive down from their summer apartment on the North Shore during the day, have dinner with us, and then stop off at the house later in the evening, once they could be sure the Swansons had left for Westchester, just to check on things, on the cats in particular, before heading back to their temporary quarters on the lesser shore.

My parents enjoyed their company. Although they had not known one another in childhood, had only met since they'd all moved out here, they had grown up in close proximity and knew many of the same people and places, and these reminiscences made up the bulk of their conversation. It was odd, I suppose, that even though they had both ended up here in this beautiful place—my parents through conscious effort to put me in the way of good fortune, the Clarkes through the good fortune delivered to them by his fairy uncle—all their interest and enthusiasm were reserved for the places they had left. Like exiles, their delight was not in where they now found themselves but in whatever they could remember about the place, and the time, they had abandoned. Even after twelve years of friendship, they were still discovering, weekly it seemed, places where their paths had crossed or their histories had merged—a familiar candy store in Brooklyn, a friend of a friend's sister whom one of them used to date, another GI who also was on the *Queen Mary*, an office mate who'd once held a job that was also once held by a friend from high school. Circuitous, circumstantial lineages that seemed to encompass all the years of their youth and the breadth of the five boroughs, and were always linked—even then I thought there was something medieval about it—to the names of Catholic parishes, as if no identity of friend or cousin or co-worker could be truly established without first determining where he or she had been baptized or schooled or married or (their phrase again) buried from—no landmark of their histories truly confirmed without the name of the nearest church to authenticate it.

Daisy's presence, of course, proved great fodder for this, their favorite kind of conversation, and over dinner in our corner dining room, under the slanting ceiling that accommodated the attic stairs, the pursuit began when Mr. Clarke pointed his fork toward Daisy and said to my father, "I wonder if my brother Bill might have known her mother. She's your younger sister, right? And she graduated from St. Xavier's, right?" There followed the usual testing of names and dates and parish dances and high school teams—the names of saints and of all the familiar hopeful, holy phrases (Incarnation, Redemption, Perpetual Help)—passing over the white tablecloth and the liver and onions and mashed potatoes and fresh peas, over Daisy's head and mine, until they struck pay dirt with a link, tentative at first, between Daisy's father's older brother (St. Peter's parish), who had briefly distinguished himself as a bandleader at a series of Knights of Columbus dances, and Mrs. Clarke's sister (Holy Name), whose best friend, for a good year or so, had been his girl.

Isn't that something? they all said in amazement and quiet satisfaction. Small world—forgetting, it seemed, the tremendous effort they had just gone through to establish this link. They all ate quietly for a while, shaking their heads at the pleasure of it—lives connected and bound, the world made small, parish-sized, and logical. Inevitable, somehow. Mrs. Clarke said to Daisy, "My goodness, we're nearly related, I might have been your aunt's best friend's little sister, if they hadn't parted ways. I certainly would have known your father, and your mother, too."

Daisy made a polite attempt at looking impressed and surprised (I noticed she was more interested in hiding her liver under her mashed potatoes), until the conversation took off again in pursuit of further connections.

Now Peg, my father went on, graduated from St. Xavier's, and Jack, as far as he knew, was the only boy she had ever dated. He played basketball at St. Peter's and lived with his brother, the bandleader, and another, younger sister who was now a Dominican nun on Long Island, having lost both his parents fairly early. Jack's father had been a beat cop in Harlem, you see, until some no-goods toppled a chimney on him, killing him in an instant, right there on the street, and as far as anyone could tell, just for the fun of it. The mother, Jack's mother, had a kind of nervous breakdown—she was expecting what would have been her fourth child, and neither one of them made it through the birth. The three kids were split up for a while, and then Jack's brother, Frank, got out of high school and got this orchestra started, and with his day job was doing well enough to bring the three of them together again, just when Jack was starting high school himself.

"I guess Jack," my father said, "was a pretty sad case in those days—he tells some stories" (glancing at Daisy and me, indicating by his look the stories were not for our ears). A real little hoodlum himself—but then the good Fathers knocked him around a bit and got him playing basketball every spare minute of the day, and then Peggy showed up at one of the games. And the rest is history. Eight kids—little Daisy here our particular favorite—a nice house in Queens Village. Jack didn't make it into the police academy, but the transit authority took him. He needed to be a cop, he said. Because of his father, no doubt. He sometimes says he got into so much trouble as a kid just so he could spend time in police stations. You know, around men in his father's uniform. He needed that.

I thought of Petey and Tony and the cop on the beach.

Not wanting to lose her connection, Mrs. Clarke said, "That was some nice orchestra his brother had." She turned to Daisy. "This would be your uncle."

Daisy smiled politely, her hand in her lap.

"Wasn't it, though?" my mother said.

"I guess Frank was some musician," my father went on. "Jack says his brother could play anything—piano, drums, clarinet. He said he could walk into a room and pick up an instrument he'd never seen before—trombone, flute, you name it—and play it for all it was worth. And he never had a lesson."

"No kidding," Mrs. Clarke said.

"Never," my father said, equally astonished. "According to Jack, it just came to him naturally."

"That's a gift," Mrs. Clarke said.

"That's what got him through his troubles, Jack said." My father seemed to withdraw a little, picturing it. "Jack said all Frank would have to do is close his eyes and play something, and it would be like everything else that was happening to him—his mother, his father, even the stomach cancer that eventually killed him at, what was he—"

And my mother said sadly, "Forty-three."

"—at forty-three," my father went on, "everything that was happening to him just vanished and he was without a care in the world. Just his music."

"That's a gift," Mrs. Clarke said again, but my father had begun to chuckle.

"At Frank's wake," he said, glancing at my mother, who had lowered her head and was chuckling, too, knowing, of course, what he was recalling, knowing as always what he would say, "which was at Fagin's, we walk in and here the room is completely filled with colored people. Packed with them. And we're both thinking that we're in the wrong place and we're just starting to back out—and we're saying, Sorry for your trouble, sorry for your trouble, to all these colored people squeezed in there—when along comes Jack, from the lobby, and he's mad as anything and he whispers to me from between his teeth, 'Doesn't this look like the' "—pause, glance at us minors—" 'the GD darktown strutters' ball?' " My parents both laughed, recalling it, in complete synchronization. "Turns out Frank had been playing in clubs up in Harlem for years, years. And never told Jack about it. Harlem, where his father had been killed. And a whole contingent of them, there must have been eighty of them, I guess they were other musicians and fans and club owners, you know, hep cats and zoot suits, the whole scene, had come out to Brooklyn together to pay their respects. And here's Jack, all red-faced and furious, and surrounded by his cop friends, in this Irish Catholic funeral parlor, having to shake hands and get hugged by every one of them."

Now all four adults were laughing and shaking their heads, and my parents said together, somewhat wistfully, "Only in New York, right?" as if New York were long lost to them all.

"But see," my father said. "It was just the way Jack had always told it. When Frank played music, everything else, for him, just vanished. He probably didn't know what color anybody was."

Mr. Clarke reached his short arm across the table to lift his water glass, shaking his head, laughing. And then he asked, one eyebrow cocked a bit in a way that would indicate, if he were indeed one of the Three Stooges, something up a sleeve. "You folks ever know Jimmy Fagin? Not the old man, the younger one. From St. Cyril's?"

"Oh sure," my mother said. "He and my brother Tommy worked together right after the war. At Brooklyn Union. They were great pals for a while there."

Mr. Clarke chuckled, rolled his tongue into his cheek. "Well, he was my cousin Marty's best man!"

"No kidding," my parents said together, and took up anew the pursuit of these vague connections.

Since our television was in a corner of the living room, and since the adults were still lingering over their coffee at the dining-room table, Daisy and I went up to the attic together after dinner. I had a deck of cards with me, and my book, and the jar of Noxzema for Daisy's feet. The light was low up there, one of the ceiling lights had burned out and I had only the bedside lamp turned on. We could hear a gentle rain falling overhead. We sat on one of the beds and played rummy for a while, and when we grew bored with that, we went to my old clothes and picked out another outfit for tomorrow——a seersucker shorts set in yellow and white stripes. I told Daisy that it seemed I could recall the entire summer I had worn it just by touching the cloth. The summer I was Daisy's size, if not her age. Not so very long ago, and yet a time as lost as my parents' days of basketball games and the service and first jobs, when the world was divided into parishes named for saints who had lived and died, or for the intricate stories that made up our faith—Incarnation, Holy Redeemer, Queen of Heaven, Most Holy Innocents.

I laid the shorts set out on the bed and then took the jar from the nightstand and smoothed some of the cold cream over Daisy's thin arms. I asked her if she had known that story about her father's father, the policeman, and she said yes. She said she knew he had fallen off a roof and died, and although that wasn't quite the way I'd heard it, I didn't contradict her. I asked if that was why she always worried about falling, but she shook her head and shrugged. She said she didn't think that was why—she said she didn't remember meeting her father's father in heaven before she was born. She suddenly brightened. But maybe she had, she said, an idea dawning, and maybe he had told her to be careful.

I laughed and she grinned up at me, and then I said, "Give me your leg," and smoothed some Noxzema onto her calf. I slipped her sock off and examined her instep in the dim light. "See, it's going away," I said. And it was, or it appeared to be. "Those shoes are doing the trick." I looked at the other one. It, too, seemed to have faded. "I wonder what could have caused it," I said, as if whatever it was had already passed—vanished. "You should have eaten more of that liver," I said, and she made a face. "Seriously," I said. "And we have to get some spinach into you, too. Anything with iron."

She folded her arms across her chest. "I only eat creamed spinach," she said haughtily. And I said, "All right, Miss Sutton Place, creamed spinach. Spinach soufflé. Spinach with caviar, for all I care." I rubbed the cold cream carefully into her instep, holding her foot in my hands. The light that obscured the odd bruises also brought out the pale blue hollows beneath her eyes. "I don't want you to have to go back home too soon, Daisy Mae," I said. "I want to keep you with me."

When my mother called up the attic stairs, I saw Daisy start and I quickly reached for her socks. But my mother climbed only halfway up to ask if we wanted to take a walk with my father and Mr. Clarke over to the house, to check on the cats. Daisy considered this for a minute, I knew she loved the cats, but then shook her head. "Too tired," she whispered.

I called back that we would probably just stay here. We went downstairs to get ready for bed. My mother and Mrs. Clarke were doing the dishes in the kitchen, talking and smoking. Daisy and I brushed our teeth together and got into our nightgowns, and then she lay down beside me on my bed and went instantly to sleep while I read, looking back first to find the part where it said that ghosts only visit people who sleep alone, going ahead to find out what would become of lovely Eustacia, who wanted so much. I was half asleep myself when I heard a car pull up outside and a car door slam and I thought vaguely that it had something to do with the Morans. And then I heard my father's voice in the kitchen, and then my mother and father both were standing in the doorway.

My mother whispered, "Get dressed," and they both turned away. I pulled on my shorts and a T-shirt and went out into the living room, where my mother was standing, holding my raincoat. "You need to go over to the house," she said, her face calm and severe, maybe annoyed, the look she wore in adversity. "One of the cats got hit by a car and the little girl won't let it go. The Swansons want you to talk to her. Where are your shoes?"

My father was standing in the kitchen, holding a black umbrella and my grass-stained sneakers. Mrs. Clarke had her wrists in her hands and was saying, "Poor Curly," tears in her voice, and my father simply turned to me and said, "Let's go." I slipped into my sneakers. The smell of the exhaust from the car outside had filled the kitchen.

It was Mr. Swanson's car, a big Cadillac, and he was at the wheel. Oddly enough, my father opened the front door for me and then got into the back himself, as if Mr. Swanson and I were peers, or as if I were more of Mr. Swanson's world than his own. The car smelled of its new leather and of Mr. Swanson's cigars. "Sorry to get you out of bed," he said. He wore a windbreaker and corduroy pants, a crew cut going gray at his temples. He had the kind of looks that made you believe he was powerful. "But you were the only person we could think of. She won't listen to us."

Apparently, just as the Swansons were packing their car this evening, getting ready for the drive home, Curly had run out the door, and they had spent the better part of the past two hours searching for him. They had even called Mr. and Mrs. Clarke's apartment on the North Shore to solicit their help, but of course they weren't home. Not half an hour ago they were all in the house, debating whether they should spend the night or go on home, with the hope that Curly would simply come back on his own (they were going to stop by our house on the way out, he said, just so I would know to look for the cat in the morning), when they heard the screech of tires on the road outside the house, and sure enough—their worst fears—there was the poor cat in a heap by the side of the road.

Debbie, their daughter, was the first to reach it, and she scooped it up and cried out that it was still breathing. Mr.

Swanson had put his hand on the bloodied thing and felt a bit of a pulse, but he told her to take it under the porch light so they could see how badly it was hurt. "Badly," Mr. Swanson said, but nothing he could say or do would make his daughter let go of the thing. She just held it and rocked it and insisted it was still breathing and would probably be all right soon. It was clearly dead by the time Mr. Clarke and my father came along, but still she couldn't be convinced to let go. It was Mrs. Swanson who had suggested they come and get me.

Mr. Swanson swung the big car into the drive. The house was all lit up on the inside, looking more than ever like something conjured by fairies, although the group gathered on the porch steps was stooped and mostly in shadow. I could hear Debbie wailing. She had a deep, guttural voice for a child, even when she was laughing, and behind her wailing I could hear her mother and her brother and even Mr. Clarke offering soothing, ineffectual bits of comfort. Her mother looked up when we approached and said, "Thank God," and then turned to place her hands on her son's shoulders and steer him back into the house. Mr. Clarke stepped away, to a far corner of the porch. Mr. Swanson and my father stayed at the bottom of the steps, well behind me.

Debbie was sitting pigeon-toed on the steps, her sneakers and her socks and a bit of her bare knee touched with shadows that may have been blood. She had poor Curly in her lap, her arms clutching him to her chest, his head just under her chin, and she was moving back and forth with him, keening, crying, "He's fine, he's fine."

I climbed two of the steps and then sat down beside her. The floorboards were wet and slick from the rain. In the porch light I could see her shoulder, smeared with blood, and what was left of Curly's face—an ear, an eye, the awful bit of sharp cat teeth, as many as might have been revealed by a snarl. It was not only a lifeless thing, but, sodden with rain and with blood, it was not even close to something that had ever had life in it. And yet Debbie, as I sat beside her, buried her face in its fur.

I touched her arm. The blood was sticky on her skin. "Hey, little swan," I said.

She raised her head to look at me. The blood was smeared on her cheek and her chin, she may even have had some of it in her mouth, and I wondered for a moment if she might have bitten her own tongue with her crying. "It's Curly," she said, in her hoarse voice, her body shaking with her tears. "A car hit him."

I nodded. "Poor little guy," I said. I could smell the blood, something like the metallic smell of the rain, rising from the darkness in her arms.

She lowered her face into his fur again. And then looked up. "I think he's still breathing," she said. "I felt his heart. Before."

I reached out and stroked him, feeling the blood stiffening on his fur. Debbie watched as I did, growing still, or at least stopping her keening for a moment, though her shoulders still shook. "I think he'll be okay," she said, looking at me to confirm this.

I continued to pet him, not sure just what I was running my hand through. I said, "It was nice of you to hold him."

Another car pulled into the driveway, a police car, and I heard Mr. Swanson and my father move toward it. I saw an officer get out, but I didn't look long enough to see if he was the new Mr. Moran. I heard Mr. Swanson say, "Didn't even stop . . . had to be speeding . . . thought we should tell the police."

I moved my hand off the cat and placed it on Debbie's knee. "Little swan," I said, leaning toward her but trying to keep my eyes off the terrible skull, "Curly might like it if you let Mr. Clarke hold him awhile, too. Don't you think?"

I looked over my shoulder toward the house. Mr. Clarke was standing by the bay window, in the multipaned light cast from the living room onto the porch, looking small and wet and bereft himself here on the prow of his magical inheritance. "Mr. Clarke," I said, "do you think you could hold Curly for a while?"

I felt Debbie flex beside me, every little-girl muscle in her body ready to protest, but as I slid my arms into her lap, under the limp and heavy body of the cat, I felt her fall back, too. She let go, and I lifted the heavy thing, handing it to Mr. Clarke, who cradled it in his arms like his own lost child, turning away.

Now Debbie began to cry in earnest, but it was that helpless, pliable brokenhearted crying of a less determined child. I touched her elbow and she got up slowly, her bloodied arms outstretched, her wrists limp, and I led her as she cried up the steps and to the front door, which I tried not to mark with blood, into the light of the hallway and up the ornate Victorian stair. From the living room I heard her brother say, "Eeewww!" and we were only halfway up the stairs when her mother called softly, from behind us, "Try not to touch anything."

I took her into the hall bathroom, a small pink-and-black linoleum bathroom with a thick, shaggy bath rug and the cloying scent of rose-shaped decorative soaps mixed with Mrs. Swanson's decaying wildflowers. First I unbuttoned her shirt as she cried, the material so soaked with blood that I could barely work the slick buttons through the sodden holes, and then I unbuttoned her shorts and pulled them down to her ankles and asked her to step out of them, pulling off her bloodied socks and sneakers as she did. The blood had pooled in her lap, the shorts were no doubt ruined, but I put them in the pink sink anyway and ran cold water over them. "Always use cold water on bloodstains," I told her, washing my own hands in the cold stream. I smiled at her, pushed back her thin hair, which also had blood in it. "Future reference," I said.

I took her hand and helped her into the tub. She began to bend her knees, but I said, Not yet, and instead ran the water, getting it warm enough. I found a washcloth and soaked it and first ran it across her face, over her mouth and her cheeks and her still falling tears, rinsing it again and again, and then I ran it over her arms and her shoulders and between her fingers, until most of the blood, the sad, wet smell of it, had gone down the drain. I told her to sit down. Then I filled up the tub and swished the warm water around her body, which was tanned and beautifully healthy and showed the perfect outline of her bathing suit. I let her hold on to my wet arm, her mouth against my skin, and cry some more. "Poor little swan," I said. Her mother peeked in twice while I bathed her, the second time to deposit a pile of thick pink towels, and then went away. I shampooed her hair, rinsing it with the pink plastic cup on the sink, and then helped her out, wrapping her body in one towel, her hair in another. We walked together down the hall to her bedroom.

Her small valise lay open on the bright pink bedspread, just a few pieces of clothing folded into it, her damp bathing suit still on the floor. Seeing it all, she began to cry again, and I realized that this, of course, was what she had been doing when the benign day shifted on her and someone called up from downstairs that Curly had run out the door. I hugged her and tried to see the room with her eyes—the colorful drawings and the bright-eyed stuffed pets, the new seashells scattered across the dresser in a little pool of sand, the old ones painted yellow and blue and bright green on the shelves. I thought it must seem to her a very long time ago that she was here, simply getting ready to go home, busy and naïve and sun-tired, vaguely contented. A Sunday afternoon in summer a very long time ago.

I found a nightgown in her dresser and slipped it over her head. And then sat her on the bed and combed out her hair. "Moe and Larry are going to be so sad," Debbie said softly, and I said, "Gosh, I know. We'll have to be extra nice to them."

Debbie said, "If only he hadn't run out the door like that."

"That wasn't really like him, was it?" I said. "Sleepy old Curly."

She was pulling at her fingers, one after the other. "I should have locked him in up here," she said.

I laughed. "He wouldn't have liked that."

"I should have, though." She turned to look at me, tears coming back into her eyes. "He was right on my bed when we got back from the beach. I should have locked him in."

"You didn't know," I said. "No one could have known."

I lowered the valise to the floor and pulled back the bedspread. Wearily, she climbed under the covers. I put her stuffed

animals around her, every one I could find, although she usually slept with just a bear and a worn-out calico cat. She didn't
seem to mind. Looking out from among them, she moved her
eyes all over the room. I leaned down to kiss her. "You couldn't
have known," I said again. "You couldn't have known what you
know now."

The Swanson kids didn't say prayers at night. They didn't,
as far as I could tell, have any kind of religion at all. So I said
nothing about Curly among the angels, or Curly as a kitten
again, rolled up against his mother's fur. I simply said that
Curly was probably very grateful to her for the way she had
held him all night. Curly always liked being held. It seemed a
rather insubstantial consolation, and as I offered it I had a
funny recollection of Petey's rabbit trap in the yard—of the
thin twig he'd used to prop up the cardboard box, of something slight and fragile holding back a weighty darkness. But
Debbie nodded, and then threw her arms around my neck.
"Can you babysit for us next weekend?" she whispered into my
hair. "Can you come over and babysit?"

"Sure," I said, and kissed her again.

As I went toward the door, she said, "Do you think my
mother will come up?" and I said I was sure she would.

In the living room, Mr. and Mrs. Swanson seemed to be ar-
guing, but when I got all the way down the stairs I realized
they were actually agreeing with each other, albeit angrily.

"This is why I never wanted them," Mrs. Swanson was
saying. And he was saying, "I never thought she'd get so
attached."

They both turned to look at me when I stood in the doorway, and Mrs. Swanson said, in that same angry tone, "Jesus,

look at your nice coat. You leave it with us and we'll get it cleaned for you." I looked down and saw that my raincoat was smeared with Curly's blood.

As Mrs. Swanson advanced toward me, determined to get my coat, Mr. Swanson said, "George and your dad went on home. I said I'd give you a ride. You were a godsend, really."

"Oh God, yes," Mrs. Swanson said. She had my raincoat by the collar and I let her slip it off. She looked at it with some disgust. "Poor Debbie was just beside herself. I've never seen her like that. She even frightened Donny, and God knows he was crazy about that damn cat, too. Honestly, it was just too much."

She was a thin, attractive woman, a frosted blonde, with one of those high foreheads and straight hairlines that I always associated with smart, wealthy women. Newly tanned, like her daughter. Given to wearing shades of orange and pink and bright green. The Clarkes had told us that she didn't stay out here during the week because she was afraid to sleep alone in this house, without her husband. Looking at her now I found it difficult to believe she was afraid of anything. She folded my coat inside out, as if to avoid looking at the stains. I told her I had left Debbie's clothes soaking in the upstairs sink, and she waved her hand, grimacing. "We'll just throw those away," she said. "My husband's already hosed down the steps." She shuddered, and then glanced at him. "This is exactly why I never wanted pets." And he nodded and held out his hands, to show he wasn't disagreeing with her. She turned back to me and eyed my T-shirt and my cutoffs. "Let me just get you a sweater," she said.

Mr. Swanson and I walked into the hallway. I saw Donny in

his pajamas peering down from the top of the stairs and I blew him a quick kiss. He grinned, and then, as his father followed my eye, he backed away and disappeared. Mrs. Swanson brought me a cardigan, a bright yellow cashmere. "You can return this next weekend," she said. "We'll need you Saturday."

I nodded. I told her Debbie had asked if she would go up, and she said, Of course. But then she folded her arms across her chest and leaned against the banister. She wore a gold charm bracelet on her tanned wrist. She looked at her husband again. "Christ, it was all out of proportion, wasn't it? Her reaction. Just madness."

He nodded. "I'm afraid there's more to it than meets the eye."

She pulled her arms tighter across her chest. "I told you, I'm calling Dr. Temple as soon as we get home." She said this somewhat defiantly, her chin raised. "He did wonders for Sue Bailey's kid, the one who wet the bed. We need to know what we're dealing with here."

Her husband held his arms out once more to indicate he was not objecting.

I draped the sweater over my shoulders, shades of Flora's mother. I threw back my hair. I said, "Curly was her favorite," and the way they both looked at me, you'd think I'd claimed he was her sibling. "It broke her heart," I said.

They both studied me for a moment, as if to decide which side I was on, or what other dimension I came from, and then Mrs. Swanson said, "Well, we don't need this kind of grief."

Mr. Swanson said, "And it had been such a nice weekend up until tonight."

When he dropped me off at home, my mother was still

awake, although my father had gone to bed and the Clarkes back to the North Shore. She was sitting on the couch with Larry on her lap and Moe on the cushion beside her. The Swansons, it seemed, didn't want the cats there in the morning, as a reminder to the children. As if, I said to my mother, the kids are just going to forget. My mother shrugged. It seemed the Swansons were debating this whole idea of letting their children have pets, even if it was just for the summer. Unfortunately, the apartment complex where the Clarkes were renting didn't allow pets, either.

"Well, Daisy will be pleased to see them," I said. "Though I hate to have to tell her about Curly."

My mother lifted Larry off her lap and placed him beside his brother. "Just tell her he ran away," she said. "Just tell her you're sure he'll be back any day now."

I took a quick shower to wash off any other traces of blood, and then got into bed beside Daisy. My mother had told me that she'd slept soundly the whole time I was gone, but when I got in beside her and put my arm across her hip she whispered, "Poor Curly," and put her hand over mine. I could tell she'd been crying. Together, we said a prayer for him in the dark, Curly among the angels.

The Moran kids must have had their radar out, because all five of them had their noses pressed to our screen door the next morning, asking to see the cats. I wondered if the news had reached them somehow through the policeman. I let them in after swearing them to utter silence—Daisy was still asleep—and they knelt in our living room for a while as Moe and Larry strutted among them, rubbing jowls to knees and accepting the long strokes down their backs, the eye-closing luxury of a patient and unending scratch behind the ear. True to their word, the Moran kids, even baby June, mouthed and pantomimed their exchanges. (My turn. You petted him enough. Let me.) And in the odd, and oddly graceful, silence, the cats' luxuriant purring took over the room. It was sort of wonderful, the silence and the cold-cave smell of the fireplace, the towheads and the tanned limbs of the Moran kids as they spread themselves across the living-room carpet. The new light of a summer morning after a night of rain. When Daisy emerged from my bedroom, she was wearing my old seersucker outfit, and her socks and pink shoes were already in place. She stood in the doorway for a minute, the sunlight behind her wiry hair. She watched for a while before quietly joining the Moran kids on the floor, and it seemed to me they took just a minute too long to notice her. Suddenly I'd had enough quiet. I clapped my hands and cried out, "Work to do," which suddenly got them all talking and quarreling again, although Daisy said little. Later, she told me she was surprised, and, I thought, disappointed, to see Moe and Larry in such happy form.

I toasted nearly a whole loaf of bread on cookie sheets in the oven, sprinkled each slice with cinnamon and sugar, and filled their hands as I herded them out the door. Petey's rabbit trap was still in the corner of the yard, the cardboard box sagging now and somewhat lopsided after last night's rain. I could see the limp lettuce leaves still inside. Like so much of the detritus in the Morans' own yard, it had taken on the look of an abandoned enterprise.

Without the Clarkes' house on the morning agenda, we

were able to take longer with Red Rover and the Scotties, and still get to Flora's house while the grass was wet. Daisy was convinced that Flora's mother would be back today—her own experience did not allow for mothers to be so long gone from their children—but Flora was once more placed out on the porch in her stroller. When she saw us, she tossed aside the bottle, which was mostly empty anyway, and strained against the stroller strap. "Out," she cried, leaning, her face nearly to her knees. "Get me out." As I bent to free her, I saw the cloth strap had been reinforced today with a man's leather belt that I had to go to the back of the stroller to unbuckle. She needed to be changed, of course, and when I brought her inside, the house was once again utterly silent, the kitchen empty, the doors to all but Flora's bedroom closed. Only a pair of woman's red espadrilles under the glass coffee table in the living room. The counter in the kitchen was littered with glasses, wineglasses and highball glasses and the short juice glasses he used for his Scotch, as well as a half dozen empty but still smudged ashtrays. I sat the girls at the table with some crayons and paper, filled the sink with soapy water, and washed and dried everything. Then I wiped down all the counters and found some eggs in the refrigerator and scrambled them with lots of butter and cream. I was just spooning the eggs onto saucers for Daisy and Flora when I heard the screen door open and the fat cook appeared in the kitchen door.

"Bless your heart," she said when she saw me. "I would have done that." She was breathless and her lip was beaded with sweat. Her husband, she said, had dropped her off at the head of the drive. She'd been here yesterday, there was a get-together—she took an apron from the shopping bag she carried and tied it on, then sat beside Flora at the table—some people from the city, quite a crowd. There had been an argument of some sort. "I was back in Flora's room, but I heard it going on." One of the men hauled off and socked another, and one of the girls got on the phone to call the police. Quite a commotion. Things seemed to settle down after the police came, and there had been only a few people left by the time her husband fetched her at three this morning. She suddenly lowered her voice. "Have you seen Frenchy yet?" she asked, and I said no, although, I told her, Flora had already been dressed and set out on the porch when I got here.

She nodded. "She served at the party, but then went off to her room without doing a bit of cleaning up. I did what I could, but I was dead on my feet." She gestured, raising her plump arm to indicate the cleaned kitchen. "I thought I'd leave a few things for her. Not for you."

"I didn't mind," I said. I heard footsteps out in the living room, coming forward and then going back. I suspected it was Ana, perhaps just checking to see that I had arrived to take Flora. But then I heard a car pulling into the gravel driveway and Flora and Daisy both looked toward the window with the same bright expression. "Your mommy," Daisy said, and Flora squealed. Both girls went to the window together.

It was indeed a station taxi, but it was empty. It sat for a few minutes, its engine idling, and then we heard the footsteps again and the screen door open, then a woman in a rather loose and flowing dress emerged from the shadow of the house. The dress was a pretty shade of dark red swirled with black, more suited to evening than morning. The woman was not thin, but she moved elegantly in the dress, and though it was impossible to tell how old she was—she wore long bangs and dark glasses and pitch-black hair that was cut to her chin—there was something about the brisk way she got into the cab and leaned forward to speak to the driver that proved she was not terribly young.

Behind me the cook said, "Oh brother," and I turned to see her eyeing me cautiously. "One of the party guests," she said in a soft voice, as if the girls wouldn't hear her. She was looking at me carefully, trying to gauge, it was clear, how well I understood the situation. She knew my mother, she went to our church, she knew I went to the academy. With last night's party fresh in her mind, wineglasses and highball glasses and loaded ashtrays, loaded men socking one another and a young woman summoning the town police, she was considering whether this place was any place for a girl like me to be. She was considering whether my parents should be informed.

"Lucky they have a guest room," I said, and the cook smiled as if to say, You're not fooling me. "It's a wild life they lead," she said, getting up slowly to collect the girls' plates. "These artists. If they don't die young, they go on acting like teenagers till they're seventy."

Daisy took Flora out to the yard while I made her lunch and packed it in the beach bag with our own. Today, I had no inclination to linger, although I had already begun to rehearse what I would say to my parents if the cook did indeed call. I was at the beach with Flora every day, I would tell them. What did I care what else went on? He was a nice man, especially nice to poor Daisy. What did some servant's gossip matter?

As I went to the door, I heard Ana's voice coming from the back bedrooms, loud and fast. I paused for a moment, and then turned and walked into the living room. It was difficult to know, given her French and its natural changes in pitch and speed, but she might have been sobbing, or just telling him off. Either way, the more I listened, the more I realized that whatever she was saying, the frenzied sound she was making was a kind of duplicate of his painting on the wall, the one of the woman in parts. I thought it should serve as a reminder to him to stick with pictures that were of nothing at all.

That morning, my father had gone down to the beach before work to set up the umbrella for us—I loved thinking of him barefoot in his suit and his rolled-up trousers, securing the big umbrella in the sand. He'd told Aunt Peg on the phone Sunday afternoon that with the two of us fair-skinned beauties in the house, he'd have to buy stock in Noxzema. When we got to the beach, we lowered the top of the umbrella down into the sand, and then hung our beach towels from it, anchoring them against the quilt with our shoes and our lunches and my book, making a little towel-shaded cave for our changing room. We changed together, all three of us, in a game I called tops off, bottoms up, the girls laughing as all three of us pulled our shirts up over our heads and pulled our shorts off. Wearing nothing at all, I paused for a moment to help Flora into her suit and then turned to find Daisy sitting beside me with my old shorts set in her lap and her hair fallen over her thin arms and chest, taking me in. I pushed my own hair behind my shoulders. "I haven't got anything you aren't going to have someday, Daisy Mae," I told her. "I just hope you get more." And she smiled, she may have blushed, in the muted light. "I get to see the old me in you," I said. "When you wear my clothes. You get to see in me the you to come. It's only fair."

"I guess," she said, and giggled. Petey's bruise was still on her shoulder, might even have begun to spread.

"Sure," I said. I turned to Flora, who was leaning against me, her hands in my hair, plump and rosy in her skirted suit. "You and Flora both, someday."

I picked up Daisy's suit from the quilt between us, rolled it down a bit. "Let me help you," I said, and leaned toward Daisy's feet and pulled the suit up over them. Even in this light, the bruises looked bad again, maybe worse than they had been. I closed my eyes. I pulled the suit up over her knees and then whispered, Stand up, and pulled it up over her body, one strap and then the other, pushing her hair away. With my eyes still closed, I put my arms around her waist and put my head to her chest, and Flora at my back reached her arms around my head, as if to embrace her, too. "Hug sandwich," I said; then the girls said it, too. I could hear Daisy's heartbeat in my ear, I could feel the quick, lively rhythm of it against the more stately sound of the ocean. For a moment, it occurred to me that it was Dr. Kaufman I had trumped, sitting here behind our beach blankets with nothing on, the voices of other bathers drifting toward us, someone walking right past us on the sand, the sound of the gulls and the feel of the warm terry-cloth-filtered sunlight on my skin. Dr. Kaufman and his dire warnings about baring my breasts on the beach, about my pallid cousin, had been trumped: I had bared every bit of myself, I had shut my eyes, I had shown my cousin what her healthy future held.

I whispered to the girls that it was time to swim, and we broke our embrace and I opened my eyes again. I reached for my suit and dressed quickly, Flora still leaning heavily, comically, against me, as if she were reluctant to lose contact with my skin, Daisy no longer turning demurely away.

At the end of the day, I folded the umbrella down and carried it to the edge of the parking lot as my father had instructed. He would pick it up on his way home from work and replant it for us again in the morning. Saving himself a bundle, he said, on Noxzema, saving us girls from an old age of wrinkles and leathered skin. We pushed Flora in her stroller back to my house so we could show her the two cats, and just as she was climbing out, along came Rags, running at a mad pace, circling us, nearly knocking Flora over, and then darting away, up the Morans' driveway. We heard a shout and a curse from the old man, saw Rags come tearing down the drive again. He skirted us, Daisy and Flora laughing, headed up the street, saw something that interested him on another driveway, and disappeared behind a summer neighbor's hedge.

"That dog really is going to get himself shot," I said. I saw that Petey's limp rabbit trap was knocked over on its side, the lettuce gone. I saw, too, first having the impression that someone had scattered a handful of straw across the grass, that Flora's mother's hat had been torn to pieces over the side lawn. "Poor Janey," I said, and the girls shook their heads solemnly. "I guess I'll have to buy one hat for your mommy, Flora," I said. "And one for Janey, too."

Inside, Moe and Larry greeted us with their tails up and their motors already running, no worse for the wear of a new house and a new routine and a change in their number. Flora and Daisy crouched on the floor, Daisy greeting them, perhaps with not quite the warmth and enthusiasm she had once had, disappointed as she was with their indifference. For the first

time, I felt a little repulsed, too, as I petted them, remembering the snarl on that horrible skull. It was not Curly anymore,
that lifeless thing Debbie had cradled, not in my recollection
of it. It was the worst thing. It was what I was up against.

I washed off three ripe peaches and wrapped them in paper
towels, and we ate them as we walked back to Flora's. Both
lights were on in the studio and the cook was gone and Ana
was not in the house, although the place had been recently
cleaned and still smelled strongly of furniture polish and
bleach. Flora was sticky from the fruit, so I put her in the
bathtub and then slipped her nightgown on while Daisy, still
too sandy for a clean house, waited for me on the porch. There
was no sign of dinner in the kitchen. I carried Flora out onto
the porch. I was prepared to go into his studio again if I had to,
but he was sitting in one of the canvas chairs, Daisy in another. They were sitting quietly, he in that way he had, with
his fingers splayed across his cheek. Both of them were looking
at the sky above the trees, and at the changing light. Flora and
I watched them for a minute, and then Flora said, "Daddy"—
or maybe, "Daisy," it was impossible to tell—and they both
looked at us briefly. He put a finger to his lips. "My redheaded
friend and I," he said, "are waiting for the first star." And even
before he could finish, Daisy had lifted her arm and said,
"There."

I heard the crunch of footsteps on the gravel. Ana was scurrying along the path, wearing the same silky shirt she'd had on
the other night. She climbed the steps and immediately took
Flora from my arms, scratching me a bit as she did with one of
her polished nails. "Merci," she said, singing it. "Bonsoir, zee
you tomorrow, zame time," and carried Flora into the house so

quickly it was a minute or two before the poor, startled child began to cry.

I took the beach quilt from under the stroller, carried it down to the lawn, where the lightning bugs were already beginning to appear. I shook it out, then folded it up again and carried it back up to the porch. "Let's go, Daisy Mae," I said. In the growing shadow of the porch, I could see him watching me. Maybe it was the glasses, or that white flame of hair above his head, or the way he held his fingers to his cheek, but it was this watching that disturbed me most of all. He put out his hand as Daisy stood. "Stay a minute longer," he said to her. And to me, "Sit down for a minute." I hesitated, holding the quilt against my chest, until he said, in a whisper, "It will drive Ana crazy." Inside, I could hear Flora whining, crying a little, maybe saying my name. I placed the quilt over the porch railing and I went to the third canvas chair beside him and sat down. Now he was really smiling, as if we were once more in collusion.

We sat in silence for a minute, stubborn silence on my part, casual, amused silence for him. It was this watching that disturbed me, because in it I saw his belief that he could penetrate with his amused eyes the person I thought I was and find something more to his liking at the core. Erase me and start over again, out of his own design. His own head. It made me feel buffeted, somehow, as if, from moment to moment, I had to catch my breath, plant myself more firmly, as you do between waves. I had years left, I had beauty, I had the capacity to make uncertainty cross his face. And yet I had also entered into some agreement with him. There was some complicity between us, in the way we had left his studio together and headed for the house. In here first, he had said, as we went into the kitchen, as if we both understood what was to follow. Some unspoken complicity in the way I had drawn him into Daisy's care, in what I was doing now, driving Ana crazy. An uneasy alliance, as Sister Irene would have said in World History class.

I raised my eyes and looked back at him. I wondered for a moment why he didn't have a drink, if his toothache had been cured, and then I saw there was an empty glass on the floor beside his chair.

"So what made you choose *Macbeth*?" he said finally. "Out of all the fairy tales you might recite for my daughter?"

I shrugged. "We did it in school freshman year," I said.

His glasses seemed to flash with the setting light. "I thought it might have had something to do with her mother," he said. He leaned forward a bit. "Don't tell me you were one of the witches."

I shook my head. "I was Macduff. It's an all-girl school."

He gave his true laugh. "Of course," he said. He reached down for the empty glass and turned to Daisy. "Would you run inside, Daisy Mae, and ask the lady of the house to fill this for me?"

Daisy took the glass and slipped off her chair. "Okay," she said. I might have resented him for appropriating my nickname, except that it so clearly pleased her. We both watched her go through the door, the pink shoes clicking on the floorboards.

He turned back to me. "Lots of room for histrionics," he said. "Playing Macduff. Great sorrow, bloody revenge. Are you that kind of actress?"

I let the silence come back for a second and then I said, "I didn't play it that way. That was how the nun who directed wanted me to do it. She kept yelling at me to wring my hands. She wanted me to get all pop-eyed when he hears about his family. But I didn't." His head was to one side, against his artist's hand. I was aware of him watching me, his own world whirling inside his head. "Well, I did in rehearsals," I said, planting myself more firmly, "but not when we put it on, when she couldn't do anything about it. I just said it like it was something he always knew was going to happen. I just said"— I gave a kind of nod, as I had done that night on the stage— " 'All my pretty ones.' I said, 'Heaven looked on, and would not take their part'—not a question, like he always knew."

His chin was in his palm, his elbow on the armrest beside me, his long legs spread out before him, crossed at the bare ankles. Something regal in his slouch, his white shirt rolled at the sleeves and open at the collar, the white flame of his hair. "Always knew his children would be slaughtered?" he said softly.

I straightened my spine, aiming for something regal myself. "In a way," I said.

Daisy came out again with the drink in her hand, gave it to him, and slipped back into the canvas chair. He touched her shoulder as he accepted it, said, "Thank you, dear." He placed it in the tall ashtray and turned back to me, as if he were not yet ready to drink. As if first something had to be settled between us.

I was silent again. There was another star and a sliver of moon in the deep blue sky, a few torn shreds of clouds, red and gold. For a moment, I only looked out across the darkening lawn. There was the sound of Flora's voice from inside, Ana's musical if terse replies. The drill of summer locusts in the trees. I felt him studying me, fingers along his cheek, although I still kept my head turned toward the lawn and the weeping cherries.

"I didn't have him scream at Macbeth at the end, either," I said finally. "I didn't make it a triumph. I made it look like he was crying. Like he was sick of all this blood." I had a momentary recollection of that wet and tinny smell. "I had him drop Macbeth's head, at the end. This papier-mâché thing. I had him look like he was sick of the whole thing. Everybody dying."

I turned to him and he lifted his chin out of his palm. I couldn't tell if he was bored. "How'd that go over?" he asked.

"She didn't like it," I said. "She gave me a C."

He chuckled. "Understatement is a hard sell," he said.

I took my arms from the armrest and folded them across my lap. "Some of the other girls said I made Macduff seem like a fairy." I recalled the slow dawning; Mr. Clarke's house suddenly sunk back onto solid, sordid earth. I looked at him to see if he knew what I meant.

He wasn't smiling. "Nice girls," he whispered.

Daisy, just beside him, was gently swinging her feet, utterly patient. "We should go," I said, although I didn't want to, somehow. I stood, and she stood. He raised his glass to us both, still slouched in his chair. "Bonsoir," he said, and nothing more, although I knew he watched us as we walked across the lawn to the drive.

Petey was on the back steps when we got home, the light

in the kitchen behind him already on and my mother inside making dinner, our folded beach umbrella leaning up against the house.

Petey stood as soon as we approached, something behind his back. I looked quickly to see if his rabbit trap was still there. It was gone.

He said to Daisy, "This isn't what I told you about. The thing I really want to get you, but"—and he thrust out his hand. It was a bracelet made of caramel-colored stones, looped in rings of something that even in the dim light I could tell was not real gold. Daisy seemed to have no idea what to do, and so he shoved the bracelet toward her and said, "It's for you."

Hesitantly, she took it from him. I wouldn't ask him, in front of her, where it had come from, but I suspected the worst. And then Petey said, looking up at me, as if he well understood an explanation was needed.

"The cop gave it to my mom, but she didn't like it at all. She said I could have it." He scratched at an already-broken mosquito bite on his arm. "I don't know if you like it," he said to Daisy.

Daisy looked at it and then looked at me. "It's pretty," she said.

I asked, "Are you sure it's okay with your mom?"

"Oh yeah." He was absentmindedly picking at the scab, a string of blood running down his arm. "She was going to throw it away. Honest."

If this was true, it could not bode well for the policeman.

I reached out and gently moved his hand from his arm. "Well, that's nice of you, Petey," I said. And Daisy said, "Thank you," and Petey explained once again that it was not the thing he intended to give her, the thing he was still working on.

I asked him if he wanted to come into the house and put a Band-Aid on that and he looked at the place he had been scratching as if no part of it were his own. "No," he said. "It's all right." And wiped off the blood with his shirt. He motioned toward the bracelet again. "Put it on," he said.

I put the beach bag on the ground and took the bracelet from Daisy. "Hold out your hand," I said, and then turned her wrist over to fasten it. We were in shadow from the porch light and the kitchen light but I knew what I saw along the inside of her arm was another spreading bruise. I fastened the bracelet and turned her arm over, and the thing immediately slipped over her hand and onto the grass. We all bent to pick it up, Petey beating us to it.

He held it, looking pained and disappointed. "It's too big," he said. And I said, no, it could be fixed. I slipped it back over Daisy's tiny hand and then pinched it to show how it could be made tighter. "I can have my dad take out a few links," I said.

Petey seemed skeptical, and his shoulders sank into that disintegrating slouch. But Daisy held her wrist up so that the bracelet slipped nearly to her elbow and shyly said, "Thank you very much," once more, and Petey walked off with his hands deep in his pockets but his step light, somehow, as if not quite convinced of the success of his offering but neither resigned to its failure. He was barefoot and his shorts came nearly to his knees and his white T-shirt might well have been left behind by one of the fathers. "Sometimes," I told Daisy as we walked into the house, "I think Petey's the loneliest kid on earth."

I thought she would object, given his brother and his sisters and all the various temporary residents, animal and human, of his house, but she only nodded and said, "I know what you mean."

Larry and Moe followed us into my room, where I took off the bracelet, and I held her arm under the lamplight. The bruise was there, but it had been exaggerated by the shadows and might only have been something caused by Red Rover's pulling when I let her walk him. Daisy watched me quietly as I examined her, said, "Both," solemnly when I asked her which hand she used to take the leash, and then, when I assured her it was nothing, she grinned her goofy grin. "Out, damned spot," she said. And I put my finger to her lips. "Darn," I said. "Out darn spot."

While she was in the shower I sat with my father at the dining-room table, the cats about our feet, counting the links on the bracelet and trying to figure out the best way to remove them. There was another rattle at the screen door, and then Janey came in through the kitchen, a small paper bag in her hand and her chiseled face dirty and streaked with tears. Her blond hair was still braided, probably the braid I put in it last week, although the ribbon was gone. Moe and Larry came out from under the table to greet her, but she had nothing for them today. "Rags tore up your hat," she said simply, and handed me the paper bag. Inside were the remnants of Flora's mother's hat, only a bit of the crown, and the chewed-up leather hatband, the remains of a bright red ribbon. Janey glanced at my father as if he were somehow inanimate. He had his miniature leather-bound tool set on the table in front of him, his glasses well down on his nose.

"I don't know if you can fix it," she said, her eyes on the air between us, as if she were uncertain of just whom she was appealing to. And then her eyes fell on the bracelet. Her pale brows narrowed. She raised her hand, pointing. "I wanted that bracelet," she said, and as she did I saw—I had glanced at the paler inside of her arm, making a comparison with Daisy's—a cuff of red skin around her wrist. I took the finger she was pointing and turned her arm over. "What happened here?" I said.

"Petey did it," she said, raising her chin and her bottom lip, a look that promised, simultaneously, defiance and tears. "Mommy threw the bracelet on the floor and I got it first," she said. And to my father, "I got it." Back to me, "But Petey took it away." She held out her wrist. "He gave me an Indian sunburn." To my father, "He twisted my skin." To me, "Until I had to let it go. Then he pushed me." Now her voice rose into another, tearful register. "I came over to see if you were home yet but you weren't, and that's when I found the hat on the grass, all chewed up." A tear welled and fell. "Nothing's gone right for me today."

I held out my arms and she immediately came to me, and although she held her body a little stiffly, she put her forehead on my shoulder. My mother, a spatula in her hand, came to the kitchen door to see what the trouble was. A few minutes later Daisy, her hair still draped with a towel, came out of the bedroom. I explained to them both what had happened, and then Daisy stepped forward and lifted the bracelet from the table and handed it to Janey.

"You can have it," she said. "It's okay."

Janey looked at her through her tears and shook her head. "Petey will kill me if I take it."

I assured her he wouldn't. "I'll explain it to Petey," I said. "I'll make it okay."

Sympathetically, Daisy put her fingertips on Janey's sore wrist. She said, "Petey has something else he wants to give me. I'll tell him I'd just rather wait for the other thing."

I glanced at my father to see if he'd made the connection between this other thing and Petey's futile rabbit trap. But he didn't. My mother was saying, "That's very nice of you, Daisy," and Janey was tentatively reaching out to take the bracelet.

"I can shorten that for you," my father said as she tried it on. He leaned toward her, counting with one finger the pale brown stones, and then suggested he remove three of them for a perfect fit. "And I'll tell you what," he said to her over his bifocals. "We'll save the three of them for you so they don't get lost, and as you get bigger, you just come over here and one by one we'll put them back. That way, you can wear the bracelet now and the whole time you're growing up."

Janey sniffled and nodded and further streaked her dirty face with the back of her hand. "Okay," she said softly. My mother returned to the kitchen, and we all watched my father as he bent over the bracelet like a watchmaker. (Later he would declare that the thing was hardly worth five bucks, which no doubt is why Sondra threw it to her children.) I put my arm around Daisy to pull her closer and whisper "Thank you" in her ear. She seemed to be shivering, and I reached up and moved the towel over her head to dry her hair.

I suggested that the bracelet should probably stay here until I had a chance to talk to Petey about it and Janey happily agreed, and happily agreed to stay for dinner as well, tasting creamed spinach for the first time (first by a tentative touch of a forkful to the tip of her pink tongue) and declaring it really good.

That night in bed as I curled around her, Moe and Larry two warm weights at our feet, I told Daisy again how nice she had been to poor Janey. And once again I felt that shiver in her spine. "Janey's lucky," Daisy whispered. "She can come to your house anytime she wants, for years, all the way until she's grown up."

Faintly, I could hear my parents' voices on the other side of the wall, their quiet and unending exchange. "Well, you can, too, Daisy Mae," I told her, whispering into her hair. "Just hop on the train."

I felt her shake her head against the pillow. For a second, when she didn't speak, I thought she might have been crying, homesick again. But then she whispered, "I don't think I'll ever be back here."

I laughed, just a puff of air against her scalp. "Why?" I asked her.

"I don't know," she whispered. "I just have that feeling."

I tightened my arm around her. "Of course you will," I said. "Every summer. You could come at Easter, too, if you want, even Christmas. You can come back anytime, all the way until you're grown up." I said it fondly, assuredly, with all the authority I knew she gave me, all the authority I knew I had, here in my own kingdom, but I also said it against a flash of black anger that suddenly made me want to kick those damn cats off the bed and banish every parable, every song, every story ever told, even by me, about children who never returned. The newborn children named for Irish patriots. The children who said, I want to show it to the angels. Children who kissed their toys at night and said, Wait for me, who dreamt lollipop trees, who bid farewell to their parents from the evening star, children who crawled ghostly into their grieving father's lap, who took to heart an old man's advice that they never grow old, and never did. All my pretty ones? All? I wanted them banished, the stories, the songs, the foolish tales of children's tragic premonitions. I wanted them scribbled over, torn up. Start over again. Draw a world where it simply doesn't happen, a world of only color, no form. Out of my head and more to my liking: a kingdom by the sea, eternal summer, a brush of fairy wings and all dark things banished, age, cruelty, pain, poor dogs, dead cats, harried parents, lonely children, all the coming griefs, all the sentimental, maudlin tales fashioned out of the death of children.

"And when you grow up," I said, "you can move out here, with me. And we'll bring our babies to the beach together and teach them to swim in the ocean and we'll have a hundred puppies in the yard and we'll hire Petey to come over every day and clean up the poop."

She laughed.

"And Mrs. Richardson will have us over for tea, and Mrs. Clarke will give you her house because you were almost her older sister's best friend's boyfriend's niece."

"I didn't get that," Daisy murmured, and I murmured back, "Me neither. But I think it makes you her closest relative. And I'll tell you a secret about that house," I said. "If you promise not to tell anybody. This is absolutely true: Nobody ever saw that house get built. One day there was just grass and trees and that little pond with the dragonflies, and then one night there was a house, lit up like a lightning bug. And although nobody saw anyone go in, in the morning the front door opened and out came a man, kind of short and bald, with a round, happy-looking face and a round stomach and wearing a beautiful gold shirt and brown pants and a black jacket so he kind of looked like a lightning bug himself. And that was Mr. Clarke's uncle, and that's how Mr. Clarke came to own the house. And when it's time to leave it to someone, since they haven't got any children of their own, Mr. and Mrs. Clarke will have to leave it to you, so when you grow up, you'll live in a house built by fairies."

She was quiet again, thinking this over, I could tell. Then she asked, "Why will they have to leave it to someone?"

I said, Only because they miss the city so much—didn't you notice, it's all they talk about? Sooner or later they're going to want to go back to the city and leave the house to someone else. "To you," I said. Everyone who misses a place so much, I said, eventually goes back to it. "Which is why I know you'll always come back here, to me."

Now she nodded, ready to leave behind, it seemed, whatever notion she'd had, just moments ago, about never returning.

"Will you live there, too?" she whispered. "With me?"

I considered this for a minute. "I'll be living here," I said. "But I could visit."

"Will you sleep over?"

"Sure," I said. "Sometimes."

"I wouldn't want to sleep there alone," she said.

"What a coininkydink," I said in my best Three Stooges voice. "Neither does Mrs. Swanson." I moved my head to a cooler part of the pillow. "I don't know what there is to be afraid of. Fairies? I'd love to see some fairies dancing around my room."

But Daisy shook her head again. "Ghosts," she said. "Like the book said, if you sleep alone."

I laughed, and tightened my grip around her. "I don't think seeing ghosts would be such a bad thing, either. You might see someone you used to know."

"Like Curly," she said, sleepy at last, and I said, "There you go."

I held her, listening to her breath until I matched it with my own, and then woke briefly to hear Petey's breath as well, and to see his shadowed form against our window.

When Dr. Kaufman came by our blanket at the beach that afternoon, Flora was still napping in the shade of my father's umbrella and Daisy and I were sitting on the edge of the quilt, drawing finger pictures in the sand. As I saw him approach, I quickly erased my picture, throwing the sand over Daisy's feet, pretending I was unhappy with what I had drawn.

He'd just come out on the train. The city was unbearable, he said, 108° in the shade. (My parents had listened to the weather on the radio that morning, had smiled smugly at each other when they'd heard.) He had his beach chair and his newspaper and he dropped both in the sand to sit at my feet. He wore the same black polo shirt and red trunks. The insides of his thighs were still pale. "I have something to show you," he said, opening the paper and pulling out two long envelopes. "And a favor to ask."

They were letters from the twins, camp letters decorated

with stick figures sitting in canoes and dancing around bright orange fires. On wide-lined paper and in their shaky, oversized hands, Patricia had written that she loved swimming, got stung by a bee, and sang Doe, a Deer at the talent show. Colby, less prolific, went fishing and won a prize—although he didn't say, as Dr. Kaufman pointed out, delighted, leaning over my knees as I read, if one was the result of the other.

I folded my legs under me as I handed the letters back. "Tell them I said hi." And he said, buoyantly, "Oh, I already have."

He looked the letters over again and then folded them up and returned them to their envelopes. "They'll be out here August 10," he said. "And here's the thing. I've met this woman, her name is Jill, she'll be here this weekend. I'll introduce you. Anyway, she's going to be out here that week, too. For the whole week. She really wants to spend some time with the kids, get to know them. Which is great and all, but I don't want to overwhelm her." He smiled. The bright sun shone through his thinning brown hair and lit his scalp. It seemed to light his brown eyes as well, and I realized he had, since last week, been relieved of the burden of his loneliness. "So," he said, "can I book you, the week of the tenth?"

I saw Daisy turn her head over her shoulder, listening. "I've got Flora," I said, but he held up his hand. "I know, I know." He lightly touched his fist to my knee. I saw his eyes slip from my face to my chest to my lap, a happy little tour. "This is just for the nights," he said. "We'll do things with the kids during the day, but I'd really like to give her, give Jill, her nights off." He smiled again. It occurred to me that Ana, too, had her nights off. He suddenly reached out and moved away a strand of hair the wind had blown across my mouth. "It'd be a big help to me," he said. "And the kids would love it. I really want it to be a great week."

I recalled the summer afternoon that I had held his children in my lap while he and his wife—their mother—were inside, the rising tenor of her voice: Oh, what happened; oh, where is it? I wondered if I could anticipate something of the same, the week of the tenth, now with a different woman's voice crying out. The sand had slipped from Daisy's instep, I could see through it to the bruise, but I knew, too, that Dr. Kaufman's attention was elsewhere—on himself, to be exact. I thought there was something Red Roverish, something panting and a little dumb about his new enthusiasm, for this woman, for his kids, for his sudden reprieve from his bachelor summer. I knew Daisy, her bruises and her pale skin, would be lost in it all.

I said I'd do it, and he said, "Great," a little too loudly. Flora stirred beneath the umbrella and he hunched his shoulders and put his fingers to his lips. "Sorry," he said, mouthing the word. He leaned closer; for a minute I thought he was going to kiss me again, but he merely whispered, "We'll look for you on the beach this weekend. You'll get to meet Jill." He stood. He waved to Daisy and she waved back. He pointed to his own cheek. "She's getting some nice color," he said, as if that was that. He picked up his newspaper and his chair and headed down the beach, his calves muscular, slightly bowed, his shoulders thrown back, and his head turning, unabashedly it seemed, toward every young woman he passed. With his every step, a happy spurt of sand was thrown up by his heels.

I packed us up as soon as Flora woke. Even this far out on

the Island, it was a hot, hot day, and by the time we got back to Flora's house, we were all cranky. There was a strange car in the driveway and as we walked past the studio I heard another man's voice, and some laughter. Ana was in the kitchen, in her blue uniform. She was putting tiny sandwiches on a tray that already held crackers topped with caviar and bits of hard-boiled egg. There was a table fan spinning in front of the window. She said something in French that I gathered meant "Don't bother me," so I took both girls back to Flora's bathroom and put them in the shower. I got them dressed and combed out their hair and put some of Flora's baby dolls on the floor for them to play with and then went in to take a shower myself. It was not something I'd ever done before. I had been warned early on by my mother, who had learned it from her own parents, that the last thing I should do in the homes of my employers was to act as if it were my home as well. No matter how warm and friendly and welcoming my employers might be, a bit of distance and decorum, my mother and her mother before her had said, is always appreciated. Helping myself to their shower and to Flora's mother's skin cream (a lovely lily-of-the-valley scent that really put Noxzema to shame) was hardly distant or decorous, but I was hot and salty and tired, and more and more I was coming to realize that Flora's house was the only place I really wanted to be. I put on my shorts and, because of the heat, dispensed with a T-shirt and just slipped into another one of my father's crisp button-downs, one that I had taken from his closet that morning and placed in the bottom of the beach bag. I wrapped my hair in a towel and, barefoot, carried the skin cream back to the bedroom to share it with the girls. I was just smoothing

some on Flora's arms when he came to the doorway. He asked
if I would bring her out to the living room, someone wanted to
meet her. I took the towel from my head and shook my hair
like a dog, wetting us all, getting the girls laughing and running. Then I used the towel to dry Flora's and Daisy's hair and
scooted them out the door.

He was a short, thin young man, with dark hair slicked
back from his high forehead and dark eyes and a long, elegant
nose. He was standing by the plate-glass window, looking out
into the trees, with one hand in the pocket of his slouchy pants
and a cigarette he looked too young for in the other. He turned
when we entered and a kind of astonishment came into his
face. "Look at this," he said, taking in the three of us, and then
turning his full attention to Flora when her father said, "This
one's my daughter."

The man bent, as if to shake her hand, but instead waved at
her, just a diddle of his fingertips, and Flora smiled from behind my leg and did the same. He then straightened up and
looked at me. He had large eyes and pale skin and a slight
shadow of a beard. He was the type of guy the girls at the
academy would have called cute, dreamy. I was introduced as
the babysitter, and he took my hand and shook it and then
raised it to his lips and kissed my knuckles. He looked up at
Flora's father. "Fortunate babies," he said, still holding my
hand, and then his eyes took in the damp shirt I wore and
whatever was under it. Daisy was introduced as "the faithful
companion." He shook her hand, too, saying, "Will you look at
this hair."

He turned to Flora's father. "This is a riot," he said. "You
among all these females." And Flora's father smiled and

shrugged. There was something both fond and tolerant in his manner. As Ana swung in with the tray of caviar, the young man took a small notepad and pencil from his back pocket and Flora's father said, good-naturedly, "Oh, for Christ's sake, Bill," but he waved the pencil and then jotted something down. He closed the book with a grin, returned it to his pants. "Just a note," he said.

Over her shoulder, Ana told me that Flora's dinner was ready in the kitchen.

Once again, he raised his hand and wiggled his fingers at us. "Bon appétit," he said. On a plate on the table there were some crackers, some carrot and celery sticks, and a mashed hard-boiled egg. I had a feeling that Ana had just put it all together, perhaps when she'd heard us out in the living room. She didn't return to the kitchen the whole time we were there, coaxing Flora to eat (I finally made her a cream-cheese-and-jelly sandwich, the fail-safe), and it was only after we had gone outside to look for fireflies that I heard the water running in the sink and the clink of ice and glass.

A little while later, I heard the screen door slam, and the young man came down the steps and into the yard. I had a firefly in my palm, but I let it go as I saw him approach, suddenly feeling a little foolish to be playing such games. It was still warm, but a breeze had begun to stir. "Oh, it escaped," he said. He stood beside me and watched it rise into the air. Then he kept his chin raised and said, "How old are you?"

I told him and he nodded, his eyes still on the sky. "Are you too young," he said, "to know what's going on here? I mean, what the arrangement is." I paused for a moment. He had a long neck and a jaw and cheekbones that might have been carved. I still couldn't guess how old he was. Twenties, perhaps. "I just take care of Flora," I said.

He looked down at me, his chin still raised. "I guess that means you are," he said. Then he lowered his chin. "When does Mommy get back?" he asked.

I shrugged. "I don't know."

He put his hands in his pockets, raised his shoulders, and gave a great sigh. For a minute we both watched Daisy and Flora crossing the lawn. "Someone told me she's in Europe," he said, and I felt my heart sink, for Flora.

"I don't know," I said. "I thought she was in the city."

"She is," he said. "Some city. Somewhere or other." He looked at me again. "This may turn into a permanent position for you," he said. We were nearly the same height and he was standing very close to me, our arms nearly touching. I'd had very little experience with boys my own age, but somehow I understood that he was not flirting. The admiration that occasionally showed in his eyes—that familiar prelude to being told I was pretty—seemed entirely incidental. "I mean," he said, as if we were old friends, "the French lady is fine and all. He has a taste for such things. But I've never known him to want a steady diet of middle-aged and plump. There's always got to be something young and lively"—he motioned toward Flora—"child-bearing, for dessert." He swept his gaze over me again. "I don't know," he said. "It's a blood-of-a-virgin kind of thing, I guess." I looked at his dark eyes and his handsome face. He had straight white teeth, thin lips. I blinked twice, and then he suddenly touched my arm and laughed as if there were a pit caught in his throat.

"Oh no," he said, still holding my arm. "Now you're going

to quit. Oh God, he'll murder me. I've lost him his beautiful teenage babysitter. Oh God." He leaned closer, moving his hand to my back. "Don't quit," he said, and I felt his fingertips along my spine. "Tell me you're not going to quit," he said. "Forget what I said. He's a perfectly harmless guy. He'll probably have to marry that maid in there if you quit."

I saw that Daisy and Flora had turned their attention to him, drawn by his spluttering laughter. "I wouldn't quit," I said softly, trying to smile. "Why should I quit?"

He suddenly waved a hand in front of his lips, as if he'd just taken a mouthful of something hot. "I talk too much," he said. "It's what he likes about me." He put his hands into his pockets once again. "Of course, there's no reason for you to quit and no reason he shouldn't stay out here in this perfectly lovely place with all of you perfectly lovely little females." He waited a beat. I heard the screen door open behind us, and then felt his hand on my back again, his nails scratching my spine. "And if you've got nothing on at all under that big white shirt," he said softly, into my ear, "well, that's perfectly lovely, too."

Flora went to her father with her hands cupped around a lightning bug and we both turned to watch them. He bent over her, placed his hand on her head, and then looked at the two of us.

The young man suddenly slipped his arm under mine, laughing. "I just asked your babysitter out on a date. Completely innocent. A movie and an ice cream soda. Do you mind?"

He drew closer to us. "I don't mind," he said. "She should be going out for movies and ice cream sodas," he said. He plucked at the young man's shirtsleeve, moving him away. "But not with you." He looked at me. "He is, you know, what some of your schoolmates might refer to as a Macduff."

The young man laughed, a deep laugh in the back of his throat, and said, "That's a new one." And then Flora was at my knees, reaching up. I stepped away from them both and bent down and lifted her. She immediately put her head on my shoulder.

I looked at her father from over her head, and as if in response he took the young man's arm again and said, "Let's go eat." The man stumbled a bit over the grass, calling, "Good night, girls," as they made their way to the car. He got into the driver's seat, and then Flora's father shut the car door and turned back to us. Passing her, he touched Daisy's head gently, in a kind of benediction, and then he put his arm across my shoulder and leaned to kiss his daughter's hair. "Good night, sweetheart," he said, as if this were a nightly routine. I could smell the drinks on his breath. Flora snuggled shyly against my shoulder. Straightening, he turned to kiss me lightly on the forehead, my own lips just inches from the fragile skin of his throat. The faint odor of aftershave, of bay rum. He touched the back of my hair, still damp from my shower, and lifted a handful of it off my neck. Suddenly it was all I could do not to lean my head into his palm. It was all I wanted to do. But I was aware of Macduff watching, perhaps scribbling something in his little notebook. I was aware of Daisy, too, and Flora in my arms. "I apologize," he whispered. He lifted a handful of my hair and then let it fall through his fingers, catching just the last bit of it and raising it to his lips. Then he turned back toward the car.

Flora, her head tucked into my shoulder, suddenly reached out and put her hand over my heart, as if she had felt the change in its rhythm. Daisy turned to watch the car pull out, returning Macduff's little fingertip wave as he passed. Then she turned back to me. I put my hand out for her. "Let's get Flora to bed." And was grateful for the steadying effect of her grip.

We met Ana just inside the door. She had her black skirt and the sleeveless top on again, now with one of Flora's mother's scarves tied jauntily around her neck. She had her purse over her arm and said, "Bonsoir," and I had to put my hand out and touch her in order to make her pause. Her flesh was cool.

"You're leaving?" I asked. She was wearing more lipstick, more makeup, than I was used to seeing, and I could smell Flora's mother's Chanel.

"I have a dinner appointment," she said, without a pause in her forward momentum. "I will be back later on." She had the car keys in her hand and she raised them a bit, let them jingle. "You are the babysitter," she said as she pushed through the screen door.

"Goodbye, Ana," Flora said to the scented air. And then to me, "Ana's gone."

"Vanished," I said.

I called my parents to tell them I'd be here a while longer, and they suggested they come over and pick up Daisy if we were out much later than ten. Daisy grimaced when I told her this, but I put my arm around her and said not to worry about it. How late could they be?

We read to Flora for a while and then played with her a

while longer on the rug. When she was finally asleep, Daisy and I went into the kitchen and snacked on crackers and celery and hard-boiled eggs, little sweet pickles and Spanish olives and bright red maraschino cherries. We washed what dishes there were and put everything away, and then I made us both grilled cheese sandwiches. The television was in the guest room and we carried our dinner in there. But Macduff had a thick leather overnight bag opened on the bed—a pair of trousers hung over the back of the chair—and although I spread a towel out on the floor in front of the TV and we put our plates on it and ate our sandwiches there, neither one of us felt comfortable enough to linger. Instead, I took a blanket from Flora's closet and spread it over the white leather couch in the living room and told Daisy to lie down awhile. I sat on the floor beside her and let her braid and unbraid my hair until her responses grew shorter and her hands grew still. I crossed my arms over my raised knees and bent my head into them, waiting.

I imagined a thousand different scenes. Ana would come home first and I would simply call my father to come and get us. Macduff's car would pull into the drive and he and Flora's father would come in and I would tell them, "I'll just call home," and wake Daisy and wait out on the front porch. Macduff would disappear and Ana would disappear, and with Daisy and Flora asleep, we would sit together, he and I, and he would put his hand under my hair and I would lean my head back into his palm. His artist's fingers on the buttons of my shirt. How many more years will this earn me, he would ask, and Daisy would say, I don't know. How many more do you want, and he and Daisy, in collusion, would simply say, More, breaking aspirin between their teeth. More, more years, years thick as paint laid on with a putty knife. More.

I heard the car first, the wheels against the gravel, and then saw the headlights change the shadows in the darkened kitchen. I got off the floor and sat on the couch at Daisy's feet. I covered her pink shoes with my hand. Then I heard the two men's voices. I was grateful it wasn't Ana. But then they were silent, and only Macduff came in through the screen door. He had one hand in his pocket and he made a casual expression of surprise when he saw me, and Daisy asleep beside me, as if he hadn't expected to see us but probably should have. He walked into the room and sat in one of the white chairs opposite us as if he had just left it. "He's gone off to his studio," he whispered. "I'm supposed to tell Ana he's there."

I told him Ana had gone out for dinner. I didn't know when she would be back.

"Oh dear." He frowned and pursed his lips. Then he leaned toward me. "You could go out there instead," he whispered, his dark eyebrows raised. "That might give him a thrill." He was both coy and devilish, smiling at me as if he saw on my face some remnant of my own recent dreams. His own face as dark and handsome as one would expect of some comic-book Satan. I lowered my head. The point was, I knew, that I could. I could go out there, nearly wanted to, cross the dark path, and the threshold and the paint-spattered floor, Daisy and Flora asleep, Macduff in here with his little notebook, find him on that bed or that bier in the corner of the studio. Rearrange the world to my own liking, out of my own dreams, my own head—better at it even than he was.

I stood up—Macduff's eyes following me, expectantly, I

thought—and said I would just call home to get a ride. He nodded. When I came back from the phone in the hallway, he had lit a cigarette and he was watching Daisy sleep on the couch. As I began to bend over her, he said, "Oh, do you have to wake her up?"

"My father will be here," I said, and he waved his hand. "Just wait a few minutes. I can't remember the last time I saw a kid asleep like this." He leaned forward, his chin in his hand, the cigarette burning. The shadow of his beard had grown darker and it had made his hair and eyes seem that much darker still. "It's so pure," he said. I sat down beside her again, uncertain if it was the right thing to do, to let him watch her like this, but a few seconds later he drew on his cigarette and then said, moving it around, "Does he sleep out there, in the studio?"

I shrugged. "I think he takes naps," I said. "During the day."

He laughed through his nose. "How much is he out there?" he asked. "I mean, on any given day?"

I shrugged. "I don't know," I said. "A lot."

He nodded, touched a finger to the tip of his elegant nose. "And how much does he drink?" he asked.

I shrugged again. "I don't know," I said. "I'm at the beach all day. With Flora."

He nodded. "Flora," he said, and tapped his chin, considering this. "Does he spend much time with Flora, you think? I mean, when you're not here being the babysitter."

I shook my head. "I don't know," I said once more.

He crossed his legs, tucked one hand under his elbow.

"What do you think possessed him," he went on, "to finally have a child, at his age?" I shrugged again, and he said, for me, running the words together, his eyes opened wide in imitation, "You don't know." He leaned toward the wide coffee table between us, flicked his cigarette, shaking his head. "I don't know either."

He looked around the room. "Four wives and God knows how many girlfriends, and finally, at seventy, he has a child." His eyes fell on the painting of the woman. He looked at it fondly, as if it were a recognizable portrait of someone he knew. "The wives and the girlfriends I can understand. He loves women. Truly. All shapes and sizes." He glanced at me. "Insatiably. I don't think he could paint without them, you know, without his daily allowance." His eyes went back to the painting. "But a kid, at seventy? And after all the abortionists he's helped put through medical school." He laughed deeply in his throat and then looked at me and put his fingers to his lips. "Sorry," he said. He fanned his fingers in front of his mouth again. "Just stop me when I get offensive." He nodded toward the wall. "What do you think of his paintings?" He pointed the two fingers that held his cigarette toward me like a gun. "And don't say you don't know. This is an opinion question."

His slicked-back hair had begun to fall a little, over his high forehead and his large and sleepy-looking eyes. I strained to hear my father's car.

"I don't think I understand them," I said.

"You don't like them." He stepped over my words. "That's always what people say when they don't like them. That's okay." He took another drag of his cigarette and looked at me through the smoke. "What I really want to know is what he thinks of them, these days."

I shrugged, keeping my hand on Daisy's shoe. I wasn't going to say, I don't know, again.

He leaned forward, his cheek against his wrist, as if we were exchanging secrets in school. "I think he's feeling kind of desperate, to tell you the truth," he said, whispering. "I think that's why he had the kid. I think it's beginning to occur to him that the work's not going to last, not the way he thought it would." He looked at me, a little smug, a little too proud of his own insight. He reminded me of the gossiping girls at school, the tiny, plain-faced ones, or the overweight and acned ones, even the conventionally pretty but dumb ones—all of them who talked behind their hands, behind my back. "I think his confidence failed him," he went on. "I think maybe he looked at his career, at fifty years of work, and realized it was all laid down, it was pretty much done—and it wasn't good enough. It wasn't going to last." He raised his eyebrows, nearly delighted. "So he had a kid, in desperation." He flicked his cigarette toward the ashtray again. "I mean, at least that's something. A kid. Even if the art ends up being worthless, you can always say, well, there was a kid."

I had a brief recollection of Aunt Peg and Uncle Jack's neat bedroom, the high, tightly made bed, the sympathetic eyes of the Sacred Heart. "He's still painting," I said softly.

Macduff squinted at me through the smoke. "Yeah," he said. "And drinking like a fish. And balling the maid while his beautiful young wife is God knows where. Don't you think that's desperation?"

I resisted saying, I don't know. I said instead, "He gave me one of his drawings once. Just a small one. My parents had it framed. The framer offered them a hundred dollars for it."

He chuckled. "They probably should have taken it," he said, and then he waved his fingers in front of his face again. "No, I'm being mean. Who knows what will happen. Lots of great artists die in obscurity, right? He might just be in a slump now. His prices will probably soar after he dies."

It was quiet for a minute and I could hear Daisy's soft breathing. I imagined I could hear Flora, too, in her crib, softly breathing. "Are you writing something about him?" I asked.

And now his dark eyes flashed. "I am," he said, sitting up rather primly, brushing something from his pant leg. "It started out as an article, but now I don't know what I'm going to do with it. If he dies in the next two or three years, it will be a biography. If he hangs on till ninety, I'll have to make it a novel." He laughed that deep, back-of-his-throat laugh again. "Either way, I figure I'm his last best chance at greatness."

I heard a car on the driveway and I went to the kitchen to make sure it was my father and not Ana. It was, and I waved through the glass and then returned to the living room to get Daisy. She was limp and perspiring, heavier than she would have been awake, and much to my surprise Macduff rushed forward to help me with her, gently moving her arm onto my shoulder, whispering, "Have you got her now?" as I hoisted her a bit to get a better grip. He put his fingertips to the back of her calf as it dangled over my hip, stroked her flesh, and said, "Ooh, bad bruise." I looked over her shoulder to the bruise that rose up out of her white anklet, spreading across her skin. I knew it had not been there this afternoon.

He opened the screen door for me and lifted the beach bag from the porch and carried it down the steps to my father's car. He opened the passenger door, said, "Good evening, sir," to my father, like a seminarian taking me to the prom, and then kept his hand just under my elbow as I got in with Daisy and settled her on my lap. He opened the back door to put the beach bag in, then closed the front door for me.

He leaned into the window, his face right next to mine. "Lovely to meet you," he said, and to my father, "You have a lovely daughter."

My father, tired even in the dim light of the dashboard, a pale windbreaker thrown over his pajamas, leaned toward the steering wheel and said, "Thank you," pleased, and puzzled, and uncertain, it was clear, which expression was the proper one to show.

As we backed out, I said, over Daisy's head, "A man writing an article about Flora's father."

"A reporter," my father said, impressed—the circles I traveled in—and then after a moment's thought, "I hope you weren't in there alone with him." I gave him my "Oh honestly" look and said, no, they'd all just come back from dinner.

"There's the great man himself," my father said. I turned to see Flora's father standing in the door of his studio, a dark silhouette with one arm raised against the doorframe, the other in his pocket. Macduff was sauntering toward him. I thought to say to my poor father, There's more in heaven and hell than in your philosophy, Horatio, but instead I put my lips to Daisy's wiry hair. In a day or two, at least—at most—I knew I would have to tell someone, my mother, my father, perhaps Dr. Kaufman himself, and already I felt the loss of her, taken from my arms.

I woke next morning to the sound of hammering, coming from the Morans' side yard. And when we passed their house on the way to Red Rover's, Petey came running down the drive to ask what time we'd be home. I said, The usual, around dinnertime. He was shirtless and breathing hard, his eyes wider and even paler, it seemed, with his own brand of excitement. "But don't go crazy if we're late," I warned him.

He suddenly grabbed my fingers with one hand and my wrist with another. "Come here for a minute," he said, and then to Daisy, "Wait here just a minute," and began to haul me up the driveway. Over my shoulder I told Daisy I'd be right back. She shrugged and sat down cross-legged on the grass. Today, out of that lingering homesickness, perhaps, she had agreed to wear the plaid shorts set her mother had bought her, and as she sat, it seemed to bloom up around her shoulders. There was a long Chevy parked in the Morans' driveway, and as we came around it I saw that the young policeman, once again shirtless, was standing over a sawhorse table, fitting together a couple of pieces of wood. Tony was sitting at his feet with a hammer and another piece of square wood in his lap. There was sawdust around them and the smell of new pine.

"Can I show her?" Petey said, and the policeman smiled. "Is she the one?" he asked. "The rabbit lover?"

Petey pulled back his head and said, "No," as if such things should be obvious. "She lives right next door," which should be more obvious still. "It's Daisy," he said.

"Oh yeah, Daisy," the policeman said, nodding. It occurred to me that I'd seen him in the village, in his uniform, a new recruit as of this summer. He was broad-shouldered and muscular, with a crew cut and small eyes. An altogether optimistic face. I introduced myself and he said, "Oh yeah, I met your dad," and then Petey was holding up a small wooden box, pushing it into my hands.

"Look at this," he said. "We just made it. We're making three of them."

It was, I quickly gathered, an expert rabbit trap with a hinged door and two wire mesh windows in front and back, and a little latch swinging from the top. "I'm going to man one," Petey was saying breathlessly. "And Tony's going to man one, and the girls are going to man one. We're going to spread them out to different locations so we increase our chances."

The policeman reached over and rubbed Petey's head. He suddenly seemed bashful, as if a little chagrined to hear himself so enthusiastically quoted. "The way I understand it," he said, "no one's keeping any rabbits. Just showing."

Petey nodded. "Yeah, I just want to show her."

"For her birthday," the policeman said, and I saw Petey glance at me, to see if I would expose his lie. Daisy's birthday, like mine, was in April. He nodded, "Yeah," and ducked under the policeman's arm to pick up a scrap of wire mesh. "See?" he said to me, and held the mesh up to his eyes. "We can see through it now. See if it's really in there."

I touched the wire. "Good idea," I said, and the cop

laughed and clapped Petey on the shoulder. Also shirtless, the two boys might have been his sons. "Quite a Casanova here," he said, smiling at me. "Whatever his lady love wants, his lady love gets." Petey ducked his head again and Tony snickered, fitting a piece of mesh to the board in his lap. "Hey, don't laugh," the cop said. "Knowing how to keep your girlfriend happy is an art." And then he leaned down and showed Tony where to place the tack, gently moving his hand to the right spot. I thought of the discarded bracelet.

Beside us, the house was quiet, most of the shades still drawn. I gathered that the cop must have arrived early this morning, bringing these supplies. I had heard the hammering well before I got up. Or maybe he had been here all night and the rabbit traps were only his excuse to linger—this battered place, these ragged kids, transformed for him by the presence of his lady love, asleep behind one of the crooked shades.

"I better go," I told Petey, and he grabbed my arm again and said, "Don't tell."

I smiled at him, and at the cop behind him. "Your secret's safe with me," I said.

I found Daisy on the grass at the foot of the driveway where I'd left her. Garbage, the tabby stray, was circling her, rubbing himself against her back and her knee, purring as Daisy ran her hand down the length of his back and to the tip of his tail. He paused at her shoe, as Curly had, and rubbed his jowls against it. I crouched down beside her to scratch him behind the ear. "What would you do if you got to heaven," Daisy asked, "and you found out there were no pets there, no dogs or cats or anything?"

I stood up, put out my hand to pull her up too. "I'd raise a fuss," I said. "I'd go to the head guy and tell him if he didn't let dogs in, I'd march down to the other place and see what they had to offer." She laughed, pulling the big shorts up at the waist, adjusting her blouse, uncomfortable in her new clothes. "But they do have pets," I said. "St. Francis made sure of that a long time ago."

It was a glorious morning, windy and bright, with clouds moving along so swiftly you might have been viewing them from a train. We skipped Red Rover that morning because Dr. Kaufman was back from the city, and took the Scotties for a longer walk than usual, all the way to the Main Beach, where the black flag was already flying, and then back down to the Coast Guard beach, where they could run, although by the time we got there, they were so tired they simply sat at our feet, panting, their pink tongues nearly luminous in their black faces. We leaned against the steel rail at the top of the parking lot. The waves were huge, and clearly dangerous, coming one after the other, booming emphatically, slamming down their spray. Daisy edged closer to me and took my hand as we watched. We talked about the edge of the world, as we could see it this morning, what it would be like to be in a ship and to watch the receding horizon, to watch it for as long as it took for another shore to come into view, another shore where the waves were also crashing, the foaming water running up onto the beach, a shoreline equal and opposite to the one on which we stood, invisible but not imaginary, where someone might well be on the lookout for us (or at least for the Scotties, I said, since that was where they were born), waving a scarf from a widow's watch or a distant tower, Hello, hello.

I waved, and Daisy raised her hand and waved, too. Leaning against the parking lot railing, I looked down at Daisy's shoes and, pointing, told her, "Now they're totally blue." She looked at them, too. "Like they fell out of the sky," I said.

She laughed. "Not really."

I could see the passing clouds reflected in their jewels. "Really," I said. "It's true. They're perfectly blue. Maybe it means you're about to fly."

At the Richardsons', where the gardens were full of dew and lush with summer flowers, we handed the Scotties over to the maid at the back door and then heard Mrs. Richardson's voice calling, "Tell them to come in." The maid held the door wider, motioning for us to obey, the two leashes still in her hands, and Rupert and Angus both jumped up as we entered, as if to celebrate (although somewhat wearily) our return. We were in a small room just off a kitchen, and we saw Mrs. Richardson in a long white robe, a teacup in her hand, at the far end of it, just sweeping out. We followed. The kitchen was long and narrow, the biggest I—and certainly Daisy—had ever seen. To our right as we left it was a small conservatory, all glass and potted plants, and Mr. and Mrs. Richardson were having breakfast there at a glass-topped table with a lovely bowl of roses in the center. He wore a satin-collared jacket and she was in the white robe—decorated, I saw now, with embroidered sprigs of spring flowers, and tied up right under her substantial bosom with what appeared to be a double knot that she had, no doubt, secured with a hardy tug.

"You girls look absolutely windblown," she said, pulling out one of the wrought-iron chairs and returning to her place. "You must have some tea."

She leaned down to give the dogs a few pieces of buttered

toast, telling us all the while that they hadn't played golf this morning because of the wind but had instead had a good lie-in, which was why we found them still lounging about so late in the day. The dogs sat attentively beside her, looking up, waiting for more bread, and when it didn't come, they both turned and waddled back to me, stationing themselves, with a thump of their stubby tails, right at my feet.

"Ah," Mrs. Richardson exclaimed just as the maid brought me and Daisy our tea. "Will you look at that?" And the poor maid straightened up quickly, prepared, it seemed, to take offense. But Mrs. Richardson was talking about the dogs. "You'll break my heart, you boys," she said, leaning to see them under the table. She looked up at me from beneath her short graying bangs. "You've got something magical about you," she said. "You must have."

"They've just got good taste," her husband said, and then immediately seemed to suck his lips into his mustache, as if he wished he hadn't spoken at all. Still leaning, she turned her gaze on him, her big face thrust forward. She seemed to assess him in a second, fondly but thoroughly, and then she said, "Oh, you old fogey," and turned back to me. "Now you've got the poor girl blushing."

I hadn't blushed, until that moment, because it was only at that moment that it occurred to me that Mr. Richardson was probably somewhat younger than Flora's father. And only a little while ago this plump and comical couple had been "lying in" until 7 a.m.

Now Mrs. Richardson moved her hand across the table and said, more businesslike, "I want to talk to your father about his dahlias. They're exquisite. We've taken to going by your house nearly every afternoon—they do take my breath away." To her husband, "Don't they?" And he said, "Oh yes," and offered Daisy a blueberry scone, which she accepted shyly. "I've even knocked on your door once or twice, but there's been no one home. When would I find him in?"

I told her he and my mother both worked in Riverhead and weren't usually back until after seven. Of course, I said, he was there on weekends. She sat back, as if the information displeased her. "We're so busy with guests on weekends," she said. "We usually pass your house around four-thirty or five, when we walk the dogs, could he manage to be home then?"

I wondered, briefly, if I hadn't made myself clear ("The girl should really be taught to speak up"). I said again that he worked in Riverhead. He and my mother both. They usually didn't get home till after seven.

She straightened up, the information still didn't please her, and sipped her tea. Thinking it over, she said, "Well, I don't want to disrupt the dogs too much, perhaps we'll just drive over some evening. Would that be all right?"

I said I would mention it to my parents, I was sure it would be fine.

Her eyes narrowed a bit and I saw her glance again at the dogs, who were still at my feet. Some thought crossed her face, something that made her mouth tight. "Perhaps I should call first," she said. "To make sure I'm not disturbing anyone."

I sipped my own tea. "Please do," I said. And I heard her husband laugh, a low chuckle. He offered me the plate. "Have a scone," he said.

When we had finished our tea, Mrs. Richardson stood and asked if we would like to see the house. I was about to decline when Daisy said, "Oh yes," and then added, when we all looked at her, somewhat startled (it was, I believe, the loudest reply she had ever made), "please."

It was a large and lovely house, very masculine, very British, with lots of leather and plaid, heavy mahogany furniture with formidable curves much like Mrs. Richardson's, darkly framed pictures of fox hunts and Cotswold villages on the walls. There was, too, under the smell of the roses—and there was a bowl of pretty roses in every room—the unmistakable odor of old people. A fustiness that had nothing to do with how immaculately clean the house was (a woman was dusting, another was washing the kitchen floor), a close, sad, human smell, the odor of breath, and flesh and hair, of worn clothes, of objects held too long in your hands. Daisy walked through the rooms—and Mrs. Richardson showed us only the library and the den, the dining room and living room—with her mouth open and her chin raised, gazing skyward, as if we were at the planetarium. Her unmitigated awe had its effect on Mrs. Richardson, however, and she began to watch Daisy with some amusement as we passed through each room, and then to linger with her. In the library she paused to show Daisy a faded copy of *The Wizard of Oz*, and another of *The Wind in the Willows*. In the den, it was her husband's ship in a bottle that they lingered over, and a pair of cast-iron Scottie doorstops that, of course, bore a remarkable resemblance to Angus and Rupert. In the living room she lifted a small round silver frame from the mantel and said, "And this is my little boy." Politely, Daisy peered into the frame that Mrs. Richardson lowered for her: the old-fashioned face of a boy in what appeared to be a sailor collar, looking pleasantly, if solemnly, into the camera with Mrs. Richardson's own steel-gray eyes. In-stinctively (surprisingly, to me, at least) Daisy put her hand on Mrs. Richardson's wrist. "What's his name?" she whispered.

"Andrew," Mrs. Richardson said in her sure voice. "Andrew Thomas."

"He's very nice," Daisy said, as she had said of the door-stops and the model ship.

Mrs. Richardson chuckled. "Yes, he was," she said. "Thank you."

And then Daisy added, looking straight up at her, "I think I met him before I was born."

Mrs. Richardson moved the photo aside, as if it blocked her view, and gave Daisy another one of her steady, assessing gazes. And then she said, more kindly than I would have guessed from the frown on her face, "What a peculiar thing to say."

Daisy took her hand from Mrs. Richardson's wrist and shrugged, unfazed. "I remember him," she said. For a second the only sound in the room was of Rupert, or Angus, scratch-ing at himself, shaking his collar.

I put my hand on Daisy's head. "We should go," I said, while Mrs. Richardson said, turning to place the photo back on the mantel, "Oh my dear. He would have been much older than you."

I thanked her for the tea and, sorry for my earlier rudeness, assured her that my father would welcome her visit. He was a wealth of information, I added, about his dahlias.

She smiled, leading us to the front door. Something of her mettle, her iron, had softened somehow. She said, "I'm happy just walking by and admiring them."

She scooped up Rupert, or Angus, as we walked out the

door (his white belly, his scrambling feet) and held the other back with her foot, to keep him from following. "Lovely to see you," she said, dismissing us, but then, as we went down the steps, she called to Daisy, "And I do love your shoes." She pointed to the sky. "Such a pretty blue."

Since I was responsible, fully, for Daisy's proclamation, I said nothing about it as we walked to Flora's. I was not about to begin to dismantle whatever it was I had taught her in these past few days. Once she got back to Queens Village, Bernadette and her brothers would be doing enough of that. But I took her hand as we walked, to keep her, I said, from blowing away. She skipped beside me, her hair sailing out over her shoulders. Her shoes blue, perhaps reflecting the bright sky. "You're feeling better today," I said cautiously, and she said, Yes. She said she had loved Mrs. Richardson's house, and the scones (which had tasted rather bland, a little stale, to me), and the room with all the windows where we'd had our tea. She couldn't make up her mind, she said, if she wanted to raise Scotties or Irish setters when she grew up, and I said, Not to mention English setters and Welsh corgis—which she didn't get until I explained it. No matter, I said. The point was, they were all from just on the other side of the ocean, from that equal and opposite invisible shore.

We took the caretaker's gate, and once we were in the woods, the wind seemed to hush a bit, seemed only to skim the treetops, to occasionally part the leaves in order to allow in new shafts of sunlight. Among the trees, it was possible to distinguish once again the sound of the wind from the sound of the ocean. We plotted out the day as we walked: we would go into the village and buy Flora a kite, and maybe—I had to check my wallet——enough candy to decorate one of the cherry trees. We'd give Flora her lunch and her nap, and then take the kite down to the beach to see if we could fly it. We'd ask Ana, I said, or maybe Flora's father (making plans of my own), for some rags to tie together to make a tail.

Daisy said, straight-faced, "Rags wouldn't like us using his tail."

I looked down at her, and watched her wonderful grin blossom. Her little teeth and her wild hair and her narrow shoulders in the oversized plaid shirt and shorts her mother had bought for her. I squeezed her hand. "What am I going to do without you, Daisy Mae?" I asked. "What am I going to do when you go home?"

"I don't know," she said, but I picked her up and put her over my shoulder so her words fell off into a delighted squeal. She was so much lighter than she'd been last night, although a good bit squirmier. I jogged with her over my shoulder, along the path through the trees, and she exaggerated the way the bouncing disrupted her words. "You'll just have to remember me," she said.

When we came out, I was relieved to see that Macduff's car was gone. The lights were on in his studio and the side door open. Although I could smell the paint, I didn't glance inside, just put Daisy down and let her walk along the gravel, her shoes crunching, letting him know we were here. Flora was not on the porch, I was relieved to see, but inside, in the kitchen with Ana, eating a bowl of cereal. Ana was sitting beside her, leaning close, both elbows up on the table, and speaking French to Flora in what seemed to me an overly sweet and childish way. She pretended not to notice us at first, and only sat up after she laughed delightedly, as if over something Flora had said—although Flora had said nothing, only turned to Daisy with her spoon held out—and kissed the child on the forehead. Then she looked straight at me, smiling, as if to say she was prepared to beat me at my own game, to out-babysit the babysitter. "Good morning," she said. She pushed herself out of the chair—she was in her blue uniform, but she had opened it at the collar, enough to show cleavage—and then went to the counter, where she'd already filled a baby bottle with Hawaiian Punch. She waved it in the air. "Are you thirsty, Flora?" she said, in English, and Flora held out both hands. "Red juice," she said. "Give me." Ana walked across the floor and handed it to her. Flora grabbed it, stuck it in her mouth. Smiling, Ana put her hands on her broad hips and turned to me as if to say, Want to make something of it?

I shrugged, refusing to meet her eye. But Daisy spoke up and said, "Her mother doesn't want her to drink bottles."

Ana frowned. She was good-looking, I suppose, that olive skin and those brown eyes, but there were two lines like dark gashes on either side of her mouth. Not laugh lines, it seemed clear, but lines of anger or trouble or grief. They were drawn clearly on her face now. "Her mother is not here," she said to Daisy, her voice going up the scale. She turned to me, her hands on her hips, that coquettish tilt to her head. "When she gets here, you can tell her I give Flora bottles." The lines grew deeper as she pretended to smile. "And I will tell her you have stolen her hat."

We looked at each other for a moment, and then I threw back my head and laughed. I can't say it was a conscious imitation of the way he laughed, his true laugh, but I heard an echo of it in my own voice, and I think maybe Ana did, too. An echo of our complicity, a complicity even I didn't understand, but one that I saw now left Ana, left any number of things, well behind. I was nobody's rival. Daisy, her eyes full of concern, smiled, watching me, and Flora pulled the bottle out of her mouth to laugh, too.

I moved to the table to lift Flora out of her chair. "We're going to take a walk into the village," I said, and then carried Flora, still attached to her bottle, out to the porch. Daisy followed. "Why's she so mad at you?" she asked as I put Flora into the stroller. I shrugged. "That's what I get," I said, "for driving Ana crazy."

Daisy thought for a moment, looking toward the canvas chairs. Then she said, as if recalling his words, "Oh yeah."

I pushed the stroller down the steps on its back wheels, and then over the gravel drive the same way, Flora's little feet straight up in the air and her voice, from deep within the stroller, from behind the scarlet juice, humming and bouncing. It was a good walk to the village, and whether it was from the wind or the walk, halfway there, I heard the breathlessness come into Daisy's voice. I took Flora out of the stroller and told Daisy to get in, and then put Flora on her lap and pushed them both. Looking down at the two pairs of little-girl legs, I saw that Daisy's, in contrast to Flora's plump and browned knees and calves, were not only thin but colorless, despite the time we had spent in the sun, as if the Noxzema had bleached not only her sunburn but any trace of natural color as well. I stopped to ask Flora if she wanted to walk, and so for a while she scurried ahead of us while I continued to push Daisy in the stroller. At one point, I reached down to feel her forehead, but she pushed my hand away. She said she was just tired.

At the five-and-dime we bought a kite and some string and enough lollipops and licorice shoelaces to decorate one of the weeping cherries. As we left, I saw Dr. Kaufman just coming out of the A&P across the street. He had a brown grocery sack in his arms and a woman beside him. She was holding on to his free arm with both hands and she was laughing, they both were. She had dark red hair, something like Red Rover's, teased into a high crown at the top of her head. She was short and a little heavy, dressed in gold pedal pushers and a gold top, a black sweater thrown over her shoulders—about as different as he could get, I guessed, from his wife and their mother. Erase it and start over again. I suddenly recalled seeing the web of white stretch marks on Mrs. Kaufman's chest that summer I had been their babysitter, like the lines left on a piece of paper that had been crumpled up and then unfolded. It was skin, of course, that resisted, refused to relent: Daisy's bruise, Flora's growing, her father's arms turning to dust. You could reimagine, rename, things all you wanted, but it was flesh, somehow, that would not relent.

I paused to put our purchases in the basket beneath the stroller, waiting for them to round the corner into the parking lot, hoping they wouldn't see us, but we were barely out of the village, had just paused to let Daisy sit in the stroller a while longer, when he pulled up in his car. She was in the passenger seat, smiling at us, and he leaned across her lap to call my name. He began to say something, but the wind was still gusting and he held up his hand to say, Wait a minute, and turned off the engine and got out. He ran around the back of the car and then opened the door for her. She got out slowly, as if she were at the end of a long ride. She wore black high-heeled sandals and her toes were painted bright red, and she was smiling at us all the while, the black sweater over her shoulders and her gold clothes nearly iridescent in the sun.

"This is Jill," Dr. Kaufman said, his chest puffy in his pride over her. "She just got in on the train. This," he said, introducing her to me, "is the girl I was telling you about, Theresa. She'll be taking care of the twins that week."

Jill held out a well-manicured hand, her wrist full of bangles. She asked me a sudden series of questions—pointless, most of them: what grade are you in and what's your favorite subject and what singers do you like—as if she felt obliged to interview me there on the spot. She was perfumed and overly made up, but pretty, already tanned, a general impression of red and gold and auburn. As she grilled me, Dr. Kaufman crouched down on the sidewalk to talk to Flora, who was showing him the candy bracelet I had bought her, and then, still squatting, he turned his attention to Daisy, and I saw her hold out her candy bracelet, too. He took her hand to look at it, and then he reached up and put his fingers to her throat, just briefly, as if he were taking her pulse. He straightened up and interrupted Jill's conversation to introduce her to the two girls. "What grade are you in?" Jill asked Daisy. "What's your favorite subject?"

Dr. Kaufman turned to me. I found myself not wanting to meet his eye.

"Do you girls want a ride?" he asked softly, as if this were something just between the two of us.

I shook my head. "No," I said. "Thanks, though." I told him this was our morning excursion, meant to get Flora ready for a nap.

He nodded, his hands on his hips, as if he understood. "She okay?" he asked. I knew he meant Daisy.

"Yeah, fine," I said. The wind was blowing my hair across my face. "She may be getting a little head cold."

He frowned. "You mention what I said? To her parents?"

I let the wind obscure a yes or a no. "As soon as she gets home," I said.

This seemed to satisfy him, because he looked at Jill, who had run out of things to say to the two girls, questions to ask. "Shall we go?" she said. And then to me, "I'm glad we got a chance to meet."

We waved to them as they pulled away, and then Flora and I pushed Daisy for a while, and then Daisy helped me push Flora. When we reached the driveway, I felt the wind fall away, much as it had this morning, when we took the caretaker's gate and the path through the woods, and the feeling was so much like coming into harbor that I said to Daisy and Flora, as my father always said when he docked his boat, "All ashore that's going ashore."

He had the sawhorses set up in the driveway, the old door stretched over them, but there was no other sign of him.

Flora climbed out of the stroller eagerly, and Daisy said, smiling at me, "Finally returned." The girls wanted to decorate the tree first, so we pushed the stroller right over the grass, right up to the middle of the three trees, the one they had chosen. I took the beach quilt from the porch and spread it out, and then the girls spread the licorice and lollipops across it. I went into the house for a pair of scissors—Ana walking past me as I took them from the desk drawer, looking over my shoulder to see what I was up to—and then sat with them on the quilt, unwrapping lollipops and tying each with a little piece of kite string. One by one, they carried the lollipops to the tree and tied them to its lower branches, Flora holding the thin branches still while Daisy tied the bow, then coming to me to help them, all of us with lollipops in our mouths as we moved back and forth from the quilt to the tree, "working."

Once or twice I became aware of him behind us, as he stood in the doorway of his studio or carried small cans of paint out to the driveway. I let Flora stand on the seat of her stroller to reach some higher branches, and then lifted her up when she wanted to go higher still, Daisy on the quilt, tying more strings to the remaining lollipops. He carried the canvas through the door of the studio and placed it against the wall, the sun catching it as he did, making it seem to me as I hoisted Flora into the leaves that someone was waving to get my attention. I turned and saw what it was. He had a cigarette in his mouth, his shoulders were stooped, and there was something of Petey's boneless, disappointed slouch to his stance as he looked at his handiwork, the canvas filled with black and gray and white paint, slashed and smeared. He threw his cigarette on the driveway and went into his studio again.

Daisy brought us the licorice strings, and we began to add these to the thin branches as well, draping them just above each lollipop. Although the wind here was only a breeze, Daisy's cheeks were bright red, but then, I noticed, Flora's cheeks, and eyes, and lips were bright, too. Positively windblown. We tied the red licorice to the branches, which seemed heavy now with the weight of the candy, even threw some in the air to get them caught at the top of the tree. He came out of the studio again, carrying a few more small cans of paint, and in an instant, it seemed—I had only turned to take some more licorice strings from the quilt—there was a red stroke across the canvas. The girls were laughing now, doing a little dance around the tree as they tossed the remaining strings of licorice as high as they could. I touched their shoulders and told them to stand back, to get the full effect of their work, and to check for any bare spots, as you do with Christmas trees. We made a circuit of the tree, its branches hanging a bit lower now but full of odd colors, purple and green and bright orange, that caught the sun as the breeze passed. I pulled the quilt out from under the tree a bit and we stretched across it, our backs to the house, and viewed our masterpiece. Then we all three fell back and studied the sky. The clouds were high and still moving swiftly, and we spotted a face and a fish and a crocodile's shape, a lady floating sideways in a long dress that became a tall ship with its sail being bent by the wind. Flora was between us, and Daisy and I raised our arms, pointing, while she followed suit. A castle, Flora said, her little arm in the air, a birthday cake, a pig—although Daisy and I couldn't see them. "Are you making this up?" Daisy finally asked her, and Flora said, "Yes, I am." Delighted, Daisy curled herself sideways, holding her stomach while she laughed, knocking together the hard sides of her magical shoes.

Flora sat up and said, "Daddy, do you see?"

He was standing just behind us, and as he moved closer in his soft shoes, Flora leaned over me. "Do you see the clouds?" she said.

I'm not sure he understood her, because he simply stood there beside us, his hands in his pockets, and said, "Pretty fancy tree."

Flora leaned closer to me, her hands on my stomach. "Look at the clouds, Daddy," she called.

He looked down at her and then up, and for a moment he lost his footing. But then he steadied himself and slowly crouched down, and then sat, a little awkwardly, and then stretched himself out on the grass beside me, on his back. He raised one leg, in that familiar pose of his, and cupped his hands over his eyes.

As if she understood the effort this had cost him, Flora said, "Good, Daddy," and then lay flat herself.

"I see a boat," he said, and Daisy said, "Yeah, us too," delightedly, as if the sighting had been confirmed.

"I see the outlines of a great city."

"A castle," Flora said, but he didn't understand her and I had to interpret the word for him. I turned my head and raised my chin to see him. "A castle," I repeated. His white hair was against the grass. His arm was right beside mine, the other still covered his eyes as he looked at the changing sky. He said, "Yes, you may be right."

And then, as if he had only located me by the sound of my voice, he moved his hand to rest his fingers against my hip. We were all silent for a moment and there came the hollow sound of the ocean, the waves too rough for swimming today. "A shoe," he said, and raised his hand from his brow to point at the sky. Flora's arm went up, too. "A shoe," she said.

"Daisy's shoes," I said.

"With jewels," Flora said.

The wind rose again and shook the bright lollipops on the tree; one fell to the grass as if it were ripened fruit. He had just the edge of his palm on my hipbone, his fingertips lightly touching my leg. "A castle," he said again, still pointing. "A turret, a spire, a lookout tower."

"A widow's watch," Daisy said.

And I heard him laugh, softly, lying in the grass. "Yes," he said. "A widow's walk." He moved his hand down my hip and over my bare thigh and held it there, only the slightest pressure in his fingertips. I felt the wind run over the grass. I placed my hand on my belly, not sure if I meant to hold down the hem of my shirt or to raise it. I lifted my knee to match his.

"A widow's walk," he said again, chuckling. Lying beside me in the grass, he stretched out his artist's fingers and brushed the inside of my thigh. "Watching and waiting," he said, or seemed to. "Longing," he said. And then took his hand away and raised himself up on his elbow to say, leaning over me, "You're something else, Daisy Mae."

And to his daughter, "You as well, little girl." He reached his arm across me to smooth her hair and then drew his hand back and placed it over mine. He leaned forward, pressing both our hands into my flesh, and bent his white head gently, in what at first seemed a kind of obeisance. "And you," he whispered, the branches of the weeping cherry moving in the wind, the earth beneath Flora's mother's blue quilt seeming to press itself against the small of my back.

He moved away. I kept my hand over my eyes, but I could tell by his shadow across me and on the grass that it was difficult for him to stand. From under my palm I saw him press his knuckles against the grass, leaning first on his arms—strained and sinewy, scrubbed clean, marked with the red paint he had added to the canvas just this morning—then drawing his knees under him. Then he raised one knee, sat back on his heel. Touched his hand once more to the grass. I sat up and the two girls sat up, and without a word we all stood and went to him, Daisy and Flora laughing, to take his elbows, I to stand above him as he knelt and to hold out my hand. As he took it, I was surprised to see blades of grass falling from his fingers, as if he had been torn away from the lawn where we'd been lying, had tried to hold on, as if he had struggled not to raise himself but to stay. Letting the blades of grass fall from his fingers, he leaned heavily against my hand, and then placed his fingertips on my shoulders as he straightened himself, stepping backward once to regain his footing, and then stepping forward again, his hands on my shoulders, his chin brushing my scalp. With the wind at my back, obscured by my blowing hair, I put my lips to the papery skin of his throat and felt his pulse against my mouth. I felt his laughter. I turned to see that Daisy and his daughter were offering him the lollipops that had fallen to the ground, Flora saying, "Here, Daddy, here."

"First fruits of the harvest," he said. He had his arm around me, his shoulder against the back of my head, his hand on my hip. He took a lollipop from each of them, and then they offered the rest to me.

Leaning, he said into my hair, "Come out to the studio when you get a chance."

I turned to look over my shoulder as he walked back to his painting. An old man, shuffling a bit in his soft shoes, his white hair rising off his head, his white shirt moving in and out as if with his breath, with the beating of his heart; moving, in truth, with the buffeting wind.

We went into the house for lunch. Both girls looked wind-blown and weary, and Daisy's cheeks were still brighter than Flora's. We ate our sandwiches at the kitchen table, and Ana came in twice to ignore us and once to fix her brown eyes on mine as she roughly wiped some chocolate milk from Flora's mouth with a dish towel. "No beach today?" she asked, and I said there was a black flag, no swimming.

She clicked her tongue and rubbed Flora's mouth again as if she were washing a window. "I think you can still sit on the beach," she said, as Flora began to cry. Stepping away from the child, Ana held out both hands, as if to say, Voilà! "You see, you wait too long to give her a nap."

I picked up Flora, still crying, and, with Daisy trailing, carried her into her room. I changed her, still crying, and rocked her a bit in my arms, Daisy sitting at our feet and rubbing her legs. Still, Flora cried and squirmed and arched her back, slapping away the book Daisy brought her, and the stuffed animals, angrily putting her little hand over my mouth when I tried to sing. She said she wanted her mother. She wanted her mother, and once the chant had started, there was no stopping it. I held her in the rocking chair, said, Hush, hush, but the crisis was full-blown. She wanted her mother. Daisy looked at me and shook her head, tears coming into her own eyes. "Your mommy will be back soon," she told Flora, stroking her arm. "Mommy's coming," although her words were lost against the sound of Flora's wailing. When Ana stood in the doorway, waving a bottle of punch, Flora held out her hands, and Ana entered the room and smugly handed it to her. Flora took it greedily and then let her head fall back against my arm. In a minute her eyes began to close.

Ana left the room with her hands on her hips, her backside wagging. A minute later I heard her shoes against the gravel, and then a faint conversation between the two of them, in French. I heard the front door open and close again, Ana's footsteps in the kitchen. I pulled the bottle from Flora's mouth, her lips moving with the memory of it for a few seconds before she settled further into sleep. I lifted her, placed her in the crib. Daisy was curled up on the floor, her hands under her cheeks but her eyes wide open. I leaned down to touch her face and knew for certain that the color in her cheeks was not from the wind alone. I went to Flora's closet, but the aspirin had not been returned to the shoebox. I told her to wait just a minute and went down the hallway and through the bright living room and out the front door. I was aware of Ana's face at the kitchen window.

The painting was now streaked with yellow as well. There was another paint-stained diaper tucked into his back pocket, and for the first time I saw him holding a palette as well as the putty knife. Smoothly, intently, he was applying a careful line of yellow to the canvas, following some precise design, some dictate, whose source, of course, and intention, I couldn't begin to tell. He had one of the lollipops in his mouth, his glasses on top of his head, and he was squinting at his work as if the little white stick were a cigarette giving off smoke. There was something sure in his movements as he applied the paint, something in his manner that reminded me of the change in Dr. Kaufman when he stopped thinking about me and asked about Daisy. The certainty of his profession, the habits of his profession, making all his gestures definite, as if there were no other course, as if it were not all arbitrary, conjured up out of his head. I wondered how often he had done this, how many pictures he had made like this, over his long lifetime. And if Macduff had been right to say that they might come to nothing at all. Not work at all, but play, pretending.

Backing away from the canvas, he placed the palette on the sawhorse table, threw the putty knife on top of it, then took the diaper from his back pocket, wiped his hands, and threw that down as well. He took the lollipop out of his mouth and threw it on the ground, then walked toward the door of his studio. He only turned when he was about to step inside, turned and gestured that I should precede him. It was the first I knew that he realized I was there. As I walked past him, he put his hand to the small of my back, following me into the studio, which was full of the filtered sunshine of the skylight. He didn't close the door behind him, but then, I had never seen that door closed. He went to the cluttered shelves and took another clean cloth and wiped his hands again; he took the glasses off his head and wiped them as well. "The babes are asleep, then?" he said. And I said, "No."

He looked up at me, and there was that uncertainty once more.

"No?" he said.

"Daisy's awake," I said. "She's not feeling well, I think. I was wondering if you had the aspirin."

He bowed his head, wagged it, laughed softly to himself. He walked across the room to the stool beside the bed and lifted the aspirin bottle from it. He tossed it to me and I caught it. "Good old St. Joseph," he said. "Poor schmuck."

He sat down on the high, jumbled bed. "Is she really sick," he said, smiling faintly, "or are you just being an indulgent mother?"

I was standing right under the skylight, but the room still felt cool, as if it were in shadow, a cool, bright shadow. I was aware of the smell of the paint and, for the first time, of the number of other canvases, some empty, some barely painted on, stacked up along the walls. False starts, I supposed, futile efforts, unfinished masterpieces. I wondered what distinguished them from the ones he pursued.

"I think she's really sick," I told him. I was aware of the windburn on my own cheeks and lips, and the weight of my hair on the back of my neck. "She's been feverish since she got here, I think." I paused. He had crossed his legs and put his chin in his hand, his fingers covering his mouth. His eyes were the darkest thing about him, steady and deep behind his glasses. All else was pale, fading. "She has bruises that don't heal," I said. "On her feet, and her back. One on her shoulder that she got from a little boy last week, which actually seems to be getting worse." He didn't take his eyes from me or turn his head. "I haven't told anybody," I said. "All they'll do is take her back home. Her summer will be over."

I said, "I want to keep her here a little longer."

He took his hand from his chin and laid his arm across his leg, as if he were about to respond. But he said nothing. We were a good ten feet apart, but in the odd, cool, opaque light of his studio we might as well have been as close as we'd been earlier, on the lawn, when I put my lips to the pulse at his throat, felt the vibration of his laughter in my mouth. The door was open and there was no need to pull it closed. I could hear the wind outside and perhaps, faintly, the sound of the ocean, the waves too dangerous for swimming. But in here, in this pale light, our complicity closed out everything else.

Finally, he said softly, his voice hoarse, as if he had indeed just spoken, and at some length, "Go bring her the aspirin. Make her drink something, too, juice or something. Or water."

I nodded.

"And come back," he said. "If you can." He paused. "If you're so inclined." And then he laughed, hesitant, and I saw by his hesitation that I was, still, better at this than he was. "Or not," he said.

Daisy was asleep on the floor when I returned, but I woke her up and gave her the aspirin and had her drink a glass of water. Then she rested her head on my thigh, and I stroked her cheek and her hair while we planned in whispers the rest of the afternoon, and the evening, and the days to come.

When she drifted off again, I moved her head to the stuffed animal she used as a pillow and covered her with one of Flora's light blankets. I walked back through the hallway and the living room, where his paintings were. Ana was at the kitchen table with a sandwich and a magazine and she looked up as I went out the door but did not go to the window. I walked down the path. The painting was still outside, against the wall, the red paint looking wet in the sunlight.

I stepped inside, into what was our own light. He was standing over another small table, sketching in long strokes, as he had done the first night I was here. As he had done the first night I was here, he continued for a while, as if he were alone in the room, and then, idly, put the charcoal down and pulled off his glasses and turned to me. What those drawings might be worth, I knew, remained to be seen. His art would come to nothing because it had been done out of desperation, or it would change everything, because it could.

"She's asleep?" he asked, and I nodded. "Poor kid," he said, as if he fully understood what was coming for Daisy. And then he added, "Both of them. My poor kid, too." As if he saw Flora's troubled life as well.

He moved toward me. He pushed the hair off my shoulder, gently, and as he did, I put my fingertips to his wrists in what was Daisy's gesture of affection and sympathy. I thought I could feel how thin his skin was, textured only by some drops of paint.

"And what about you?" he said, looking down at me.

"I'm fine," I told him.

I kept my fingertips against his wrists as he undid each button of my blouse, then I reached back to sweep the shirt over my arms and onto the floor. Only a little hesitant, and with the softest intake of breath, he bent to kiss my throat, his hand in my hair. He kissed my shoulders, and as I leaned my head back into his palm, he kissed my mouth again, the taste of alcohol not nearly as strong as it had been the last time, mixed as it was now with the sweet flavor of the lollipop. He moved me toward the bed with his hand at the small of my back. He moved his hands down my hips and then slowly knelt in front of me while I put my hands on his wild white hair. I leaned back on the bed, onto the jumbled bolts and blankets of damask and silk, and shaded my eyes as he slipped out of his clothes and then stretched himself beside me, his flesh surprisingly cool, his long, pale limbs light, nearly weightless against mine. But all his movements were sure, and I trusted whatever design he followed, out of his own head, relieved, for just a few minutes, of the need to follow any design of my own. At one point there was some disruption of the sunlight that came through the open doorway, but it was momentary, a shadow passing as it will in a dream, unable to get in.

When it was gone, I got up and slipped back into my clothes, standing for just one moment under the opaque light with my shirt in my hands. He was still stretched out on the bed, the damask draped over his shoulder and his thigh. He turned to me, the back of his hand on his forehead, and watched, and I watched back. Finally, he said, "Although I can hardly see you, from here, without my glasses, I suspect you're beautiful, standing there."

I pulled on my shirt, lifted my hair up over my collar, and slowly closed each button. "Back to my work," I said.

Daisy and Flora were still sleeping. Only twenty minutes had elapsed since I'd left the room. I put the back of my hand to Daisy's cheek, she seemed cooler, and drew the blanket up over Flora's shoulder. I glanced at the three sketches in their gold frames and considered what their worth might be, when they had been claimed by the future and all that was pretty and charming about them was transformed by all that had intervened——the infant grown into a troubled woman, the mother never returned, the father and all his efforts turned to dust. But then, I supposed, with more time, all that would be forgotten as well, and they would once again be charming and pretty portraits of a mother and a child—not a biography, as Macduff might have said, but a novel.

I found I preferred modern art, pictures of nothing, after all.

I went out to the porch with my book. I moved one of the canvas chairs under Flora's window. I realized that every bit of my body, every inch of my skin, felt windblown, weather-worn, pleasantly weary, except for some pain at my center, a dark, sharp jewel of it. I turned the book over, thought I heard Ana's voice coming from the studio, perhaps crying again, or crying out. Then it was silent, only the distant breeze, the distant ocean, the birds on the lawn and in the high hedge. And then, softly, I heard Flora and Daisy. They were talking to each other, something about the tree, and the licorice, and Mommy in New York City, something sweet and calm in the rhythm of their voices, in the gentle exchange of their words, that reminded me of my parents' muted conversations, the perpetual sound of their voices coming through our bedroom wall as I woke or drifted to sleep. I felt a sweet, deep, sorrowful nostalgia for them, and for the days I had been in their care.

Then I heard Flora say my name, and Daisy repeat it. I called over my shoulder, toward the window, "I'm out here, girls," and got up and went to them.

We had a snack in the kitchen, glasses of Hawaiian Punch (telling Flora, "Doesn't it taste better in a glass?") and some crackers, and then I went to the broom closet and found some of the old pillowcases Ana used to clean with. We carried them out to the quilt under the trees, and after we had each picked a lollipop and a licorice string, I used the scissors to cut them into long strips that the girls knotted together to make a tail for our kite. We put the kite together on the porch, to be out of the wind, and then Flora got into the stroller and we headed for the beach, Daisy carrying the gaudy kite on her back to keep the wind from bending it. A modern-art version, it seemed to me, of angel wings.

We had used a good deal more kite string on the lollipops than I had figured, and so while the kite took off immediately, it seemed to end its ascent rather abruptly, and while with plenty of tugging and running I was able to keep it aloft pretty well, it never lost the impression, as kites sometimes will, of being tethered to the earth. This bothered me more than it bothered the girls, who chased after the kite and tried to grab its tail each time it dove toward the sand. The waves were high, coming close upon one another's backs and crashing with that hollow, angry sound that I usually associate with bad weather. But the sky remained bright. The clouds had grown higher but they were still pure white and lit by the sun. As we stood at the edge of the water, letting the foam spill around Daisy's feet, we spotted a ship out on the horizon, just the grayish silhouette of what seemed like a tanker heading east. We watched it moving, imperceptibly, it seemed, and then Daisy said, "I think it will be safe out there. I think the water's pretty calm. It's just dangerous here, where we swim."

I looked down at her, Flora on my hip. "You think?" I asked.

She nodded. "Yeah, I'm pretty sure," she said. And then did a gentle little two-step, just as I had instructed her, moving her feet out of the wet sand that covered them to a new spot where they could be covered again. She looked up once more. "Yeah," she said, as if to reassure us, "those sailors will be fine."

Up in the parking lot, as was our routine, I had them both lean against the railing while I bent to wipe the sand off their feet. I slipped Flora's white sandals on, then brushed off Daisy's feet. With her clean, bruised foot resting on my thigh, I held up one of the shoes, and it caught the sun, iridescent and, I insisted, still pale blue, the very color of the sky. I held it out to Flora. "Haven't these turned blue?" I asked, and Flora shook her head solemnly and then told us, "The babies were crying."

Daisy and I looked at each other and frowned. Then Daisy smiled her "Let's indulge Flora" smile and said, "What babies, Flora Dora?"

"The babies," Flora said, and reached out and put her fingernail to one of the little fake jewels. In an instant it was off and fallen into the sand. I leaned over to pick it up and then held it out to Daisy in the palm of my hand. It was turquoise and diamond-shaped, and the glue that had held it had left its shape on the shoe. "We can just glue this back on, Daisy Mae," I said. "I'm sure we can."

She seemed stricken, and if she had been another child— Bernadette, for instance, or one of the Morans—she might have slapped Flora's hand. But she only shrugged, used to this kind of disappointment. "I know," she said.

I slipped the jewel into the pocket of my shirt, slipped the sock and the shoe over Daisy's foot. Gently ran my hand over the bruise on the back of her calf. We walked home quietly, the sky becoming a pale orange in the west, although above us it was still bright blue. On one of the great lawns, just our side of a long split-rail fence entwined with roses, we came upon a tiny rabbit, close enough to the road that we could see its mouth moving, the reflected light in its round black eye. With a finger to my lips, I told the girls to be quiet as we crouched down to watch him, getting as close as any wild rabbit will let you get, a very young rabbit, it seemed to me, not wise enough yet to be startled.

When he'd finally hopped away, we began walking again, and I said to Daisy, "You must have told Petey you liked rabbits."

She said, "Yeah. Remember my first day. That morning when we saw all the rabbits, when Red Rover ate my muffin?"

I said I did remember. It wasn't so very long ago.

"We were sitting with the Scotties," Daisy said. "Petey told me he wasn't allowed to have a dog and I said we weren't either. But I was thinking of asking my father if I could have a rabbit. Because you could keep them in your room and they wouldn't run away. And they're so cute. I said I'd just like to pet one."

I laughed. "You may have started something," I said.

At Flora's house the car was gone and the painting was still propped up against the studio wall. There was green in it now, the color of grass, flecked here and there into the black and the gray. The cook was in the kitchen, shaking a torrent of tenderizer onto a thick steak, picking it up with her bare fingers and slapping it down again, her forearms jiggling. The overhead light was on although it was only six o'clock and the light outside was still bright. There was a pot of water boiling on the stove and some dough rolled out on a cutting board on the table. Something lovely and ordinary about the scene, and about her solid presence in her hairnet and calico apron, the beads of perspiration above her lip. What had happened this afternoon, in that pale, enchanted light of the studio where he painted, suddenly struck me as imaginary, a place and time and series of events that were only conjured, recited, wished for, dreamt about, a fanciful antidote to what was real and solid and inevitable—this kitchen, this food, this woman, the preparation of yet another meal at the closing of yet another day. For a moment I found myself trying to recall that little bit of pain, somewhere at my center, fearful, for a moment, that I had lost it.

"Hello, my dears," the cook said over her shoulder. Daisy and Flora went to the table, looking at the rolled-out dough as if it would form itself into biscuits or cookies or pie right before their eyes. "Frenchy's gone," she said to me. "He took her to the station." She rolled her eyes, breathing heavily with her efforts in the kitchen. "All of a sudden she remembers she hasn't seen her husband in three weeks." She chuckled, flipped the steak over. "Thank God I'm a Christian," she said.

Daisy and I got Flora into her pajamas and then delivered her to the cook, who had already set out a dinner of applesauce and warm biscuits and carrots and peas. She told us we might as well go on home. She'd get Flora to sleep. She'd brought her overnight bag, she said. Not that she didn't think it would do him good to take care of his daughter by himself, but at his age, and with the way he liked his drink, it probably wasn't the safest thing to leave the two of them alone.

She chuckled again to herself, and whispered to me, "I don't suppose I'll have to bar the door."

Flora cried when we said goodbye, and as Daisy leaned over to kiss her good night, I noticed the brightness had returned to her cheek. "One minute," I said to Daisy at the door, and then went back to Flora's room to retrieve the aspirin I'd left there this afternoon. I shook a dozen of them into my palm and then slipped them into my shirt pocket. Flora's mother's scarves had been taken out of the kitchen and placed neatly on Flora's dresser. I lifted one, and saw beneath it a folded piece of heavy beige cloth, the painter's backdrop damask that covered the studio bed. It was no more than a twelve-inch square, rough-edged, cut rather quickly and unevenly by a dull scissors. In the center there was a stain, a smear of dark color.

I folded the cloth carefully, and returned it to the pile of scarves.

We walked home together in the fading summer light, holding hands, mostly quiet. At one point Daisy said suddenly, "I know what Flora meant—about the babies." I looked down at her. The windburn, the fever had painted her cheeks, and her eyes were bright against them. "That was the story you told, about the babies at Lourdes who drink the water in their bottles and then their tears turn to jewels. Remember? You told Flora. And their mothers put them on their shoes. That's what she was thinking about when she picked the jewel off my shoe. The babies crying."

I stood still for a moment, then dropped my head back and closed my eyes. "You're right," I said. "You're absolutely right."

Daisy nodded, proud of herself.

"Gosh," I said. "I can't tell you kids anything. You remember everything."

We began walking again, and softly Daisy said, "I remember Andrew Thomas."

I put my hand to the back of her neck, lifted her thick red hair. Another gust of wind picked up the rest of it and Daisy squinted, walking into it. "Margaret Mary Daisy, Daisy, tell me your answer true," I said. "I have no doubt that you do."

We had just turned the corner onto our road when we heard the commotion: Rags barking and Petey and Tony shouting, and maybe Janey's voice and the old man's mixed in there, too, mixed and carried by the wind. We had not reached the Moran place yet when out of their driveway came Tony, and then Petey, with one of the wooden rabbit traps held aloft, high above his head, and Rags leaping and jumping and barking beneath it, and Janey and Judy following, trying to bat the dog away. Tony was the first to see us and he pointed, and then Petey saw us and came running, knees high, triumphantly holding up the rabbit trap, Rags snapping at his heels, the girls following, screaming and yelling, all joyous, all oblivious to the old man's voice, which was still coming from behind their hedge, shouting and swearing. Baby June following up behind.

They descended on us, Petey yelling, "We got one, we got one," his face flushed and perspiring, his eyes crazy and bright. He thrust the rabbit trap into Daisy's hands as Rags followed along under it, barking and spinning, the wind blowing his fur. "For you," Petey shouted. And Tony, like an echo, leaning over her, repeated, "For you, for you." And then the girls were upon her, Janey crying, "Let me see, let me see," Judy trying to swat the dog away.

They engulfed Daisy, with their brown limbs and their

blond heads, their voices and their quick breaths, their hands on the cage, on her arms, all of them pressing together, Rags barking and leaping. I saw Daisy's foot go up behind her, either to regain her balance or to move the dog away, and then I saw Rags with his teeth sunk into her ankle. She cried out and Rags was jumping toward Janey and Petey, who were suddenly holding the cage, suddenly stepping away from Daisy as she bent, screaming, both hands to her leg. I saw the blood blossom into her thin white anklet.

I scooped her up and ran to the house. She was crying, holding her leg, screaming in breathless bursts. "You're all right," I told her. "You're all right, Daisy Mae. You're all right." I was aware only of the sound of the Morans running behind me. Then of Petey shouting in his adult voice, "I'll get the cop." I pulled open the back door and ran through the silent kitchen, through the living room, where the cats bounded from the couch to welcome our arrival.

"You're all right, you're all right," I kept repeating, through her panting tears. "You're all right, Daisy Mae."

I carried her into the bathroom and sat her on the edge of the tub. I pulled off her shoe and the white socks. The bite was precise, two deep toothmarks already beginning to swell and then a smaller set of punctures between them. I turned on the water in the tub. She had her arm around me, she was gripping my hair, burying her face in it. I told her to move her leg under the water, to rinse off the blood, while I pulled a towel down from the rack and wrapped it around her calf. Moe and Larry padded gently around my knees.

"It hurts it hurts it hurts," she said. I said, "I know, I know. It'll be all right."

I leaned back and found the bottle of hydrogen peroxide my mother kept under the sink and poured it over her ankle as well, making the blood foam. She screamed and tightened her grip on my hair. "I know," I said, holding her. "I know."

I was hardly aware of the Moran kids, piled like a logjam in the bathroom door, until I heard Mrs. Richardson's voice saying, "Move away, you children, move away." And then, "Scat, scat," to Moe and Larry.

And then—with a dream's inappropriate and nonchalant merging of people and place—Mrs. Richardson, in her tweed skirt and sensible shoes and her wide, capable body, was behind me in our narrow bathroom, her hand on my shoulder as she leaned to see Daisy's leg. "Oh, that's bad," she said, drawing in her breath. "Terribly discolored." She patted Daisy's shoulder as well. "We're going to get you to a doctor, my dear," she said, shouting a bit to be heard over the running water. And to me, "She should go straight to the emergency room."

I felt Daisy's arm tighten around my neck, her fingers gripping my hair. I leaned to scoop the water over her foot, over the blood, handful after handful. "It'll be all right, Daisy Mae," I told her, trying to keep my voice sure. "It'll be okay."

"The man next door has gotten hold of the dog," Mrs. Richardson was saying. She seemed to be bustling about, as much as she could in such a narrow space, opening and closing the vanity doors. "That's the important thing, in case of rabies. I gather it's a stray."

Daisy was crying so hard by then, I doubt if she heard. I hardly heard myself, with the water running and Daisy leaning over my back, her mouth against my shoulder. One of the Moran kids said, "It was Rags," and I think there was a sound that I associated with the wind—I had the image of a tree limb breaking, the clap of a black wave—and a few minutes later Tony was shouting, "Here he comes."

Then I recognized the cop's voice saying, patiently, "Get out of the way, guys." Now the cop, Mrs. Moran's boyfriend, was in the bathroom as well, leaning past Mrs. Richardson's solid front. "I'll drive you to the hospital," he said. I continued scooping the water over Daisy's leg.

He moved closer. Mrs. Richardson pressed up against the sink. "Let me carry her," he said.

But I blocked him with my elbow and my shoulder.

"The sooner the better," Mrs. Richardson said.

I looked at Daisy, her little chin raised and her eyes shut tightly against the pain. "I'll carry her," I said.

Slowly, I turned off the water and asked someone to hand me another towel. Mrs. Richardson already had one in her hands. I turned Daisy around and had her place the bitten leg on the towel, and then I wrapped it carefully, bending over her, my hair against her bare legs.

"Apply pressure, dear," Mrs. Richardson said.

And the cop said, "Let me get my car."

He squeezed out through the door, herding the Moran kids in front of him, saying, "Come on, guys, give her space. She'll be okay."

I carried her through the living room, where the light had begun to take on its peachy, golden hue, through the kitchen, and out into the yard, where the Moran kids were all standing, Janey and Tony dumbfounded, their mouths open, Judy crying into her hands, Petey with his fists balled up tight, his face both furious and full of tears. Mr. Richardson was out there, too, with Angus and Rupert held short-leashed, close to his side. Even old Mr. Moran. He was unshaven, wearing a gray-looking undershirt and baggy pants, leaning wearily on our back fence, above my father's dahlias. He was holding baby June in his arms. The cop pulled his car out of the Morans' driveway and then swung up to our gate.

Mrs. Richardson placed her broad hand on my shoulder. "When will your parents be home?" she asked me, and I said, "Soon." She called across the lawn to her husband. "They'll be home any minute. Tell them we've gone to the emergency room in Southampton. We'll meet them there." And then, to her dogs, "You be good boys, now."

The cop got out and opened the back door for us. Holding Daisy in my arms, I slid into the back seat, and then Mrs. Richardson slid in right beside me. The cop took a red light out of his glove compartment, wires trailing from it, and put it on the dashboard.

"Well, isn't this fortunate?" Mrs. Richardson said pleasantly. "To have a policeman right next door."

There was a small black radio under the dashboard as well, and as he drove, he pulled a microphone from it and, in an efficient and nasal voice that did not seem his own, reported that he was taking a child to the Southampton emergency room, dog bite, ankle, and then turned over his shoulder to ask us if she'd been bitten anywhere else. Daisy and I both said, "No."

Then, with his voice lowered, he said, "A stray" and "taken care of." He gave the Morans' address. "Under a tarp and some pine boards," he said. "West side of the house, toward the back."

Mrs. Richardson was unwrapping the bloodied towel from

Daisy's foot. "We want to keep some pressure on this," she said, as she wrapped it again, more tightly, her solid gray bangs moving over her steely eyes. And then she said, in the same determined voice, "Such a pretty shoe, Daisy, you'll have to tell me where you found them."

Crying, her head under my chin, Daisy whispered, "It hurts, it hurts." I stroked her arm. "I know," I said. "I know." Then I remembered the aspirins I had taken from Flora's room. I slipped my fingers under her head, into the pocket of my shirt, and slid out as many as I could, finding the turquoise jewel as I did. I held the aspirins out to her in the palm of my hand, and she took them one by one.

We were in the hospital only twenty minutes or so when my parents arrived. Daisy's parents were there by ten. By then the conversations had begun, whispered conversations between the doctors and the parents, mine and Daisy's, conversations to which I was not privy.

She spent the night there, Aunt Peg and Uncle Jack sleeping on chairs beside her. My parents and I went home and gathered her things, all the new and unused outfits, the hairbrush and toothbrush, the new sneakers still bound together with their plastic string. I added a few of my old clothes to her suitcase—the red-and-blue-checked sundress, the white Sunday dress with the green sash, the red Gypsy skirt, on a whim, certain somehow that it would not meet with Uncle Jack's approval. There was only a bit of blood on the inside of her pink shoe and I scrubbed at it with cold water until it was gone. Then I glued the jewel back into place and brought the shoe to her in her hospital room the next morning. Uncle Jack shouted, "Hey, Cinderella," but then turned to Aunt Peg, frowning, to say, "Maybe she shouldn't have been wearing these," a last attempt to find something he might add to his lengthy list of prohibitions, to find an ordinary and avoidable cause that would yield an attainable antidote for whatever it was that troubled poor Daisy.

They left for Queens Village that afternoon, and for another hospital, in the city, by the following morning. Driving back to our own house, my parents told me, hesitantly, vaguely, but speaking together and for each other, as was their way, that the doctors were afraid there was some trouble with Daisy's blood. Had I noticed her bruises, they asked, and I said I had. Perhaps, they said, I should have mentioned them to someone. I said I figured it was just the result of being raised with so many siblings. "Like the Moran kids," my parents said together, and I was absolved.

I took care of the Scotties and Red Rover for the rest of the week. And on Saturday night I babysat for the Swanson kids. Mr. Clarke had returned Moe and Larry to them that morning. They were, apparently, ready to take on the experience of owning pets again. The two cats curled around my legs when I came to the house, oblivious to all, and when I asked Debbie how she'd managed to change her mother's mind, she gave me a sly look and said she had just asked nicely if the cats could come back. But Donny laughed. He was straddling the back of the wicker couch where we sat. "Yeah, right," he said. "She told the doctor she goes to that she'd kill herself if the cats didn't come back."

Debbie turned on him with all the vehemence of a woman betrayed. "Did not," she said.

"You know you did."

I held up my hands. It was another lovely summer twilight and we were on the wide front porch, just below the widow's watch, waiting for the fireflies to begin to appear once more. "I don't even want to know," I said. "Don't even tell me."

I didn't go back to Flora's. When we ran into the cook outside church on Sunday, my mother was the one to explain what had happened to Daisy and why I had been missing. The good lady clucked her tongue and shook her head and said the poor little thing never did look right to her, so pale. She said it was perfectly fine that I hadn't been by—absolution all around— she was quite enjoying the little girl, Frenchy had returned just yesterday morning, and her own mother was due back next weekend. "No doubt," she said to me, "she'll be giving you a call, to get back into the routine."

But she never did. That evening I had a call from Mrs. Carew, my first employer. Her sister was visiting from Princeton with two young children and she wondered if I'd be free for the week. Then the Swansons moved in for the rest of the summer, and I was busy with them. Then the Kaufman twins and Jill arrived. She had now become "my fiancée" and wore a huge ruby ring about the size and shape of the English muffin I had folded over Daisy's finger, back on that morning in June. She slept in the guest bedroom, I was happy to see, and was modest around the pool. She winked at me once, after she had rebuffed Dr. Kaufman for placing his hand on her thigh. "Three words to live by," she told me, shaking her bangles, counting them off on her manicured fingers, "after—the— wedding."

I spoke to Daisy every Sunday, just a word or two when she was sick, longer conversations when she was feeling better. She always asked about the dogs and the cats, and I told her stories about all of them, Rags included. I told her the Moran kids were always asking for her. And that poor Petey sent his love—which was always met by a purposeful silence that brought more vividly to my mind her freckled blush and her goofy grin than any words she might have spoken. In March she left us—as all the family took to saying, harking back to some ancient, ancestral turn of phrase none of us, separately, could have claimed as our own, although Bernadette and I, alone in our beds, might over the years have thought to say, She left me. Uncle Tommy was visiting us when the long-expected phone call finally came, and he was the first to point out (determined to be happy) that she had left us in the season of the Resurrection, the beginning of spring.

Late in August of the summer Daisy came, just after my parents had left for work, I carried a plum and my book to the front porch, and when I had finished them both, I went down the steps and around to the back of the house, my feet bare in the wet grass, the sun warm enough on my shoulders and my hair to portend the hot, humid day that was to come, despite the pleasant ease of the morning air. I peeked behind the hedge that ran beneath our bedroom windows but could find no evidence that Petey had been there, although I'd thought I'd heard him during the night. I went up the back steps and, just as I pulled open the screen door, saw the blurred gray bundle that I knew immediately, even before I bent down to examine it, was a living thing. Three baby rabbits, newborn, blind, wrapped in what appeared to be their own sticky cocoon.

I went into the house, through the kitchen and the living room and into my bedroom, where I dumped the ribbons out of my ribbon box—just a shoebox covered with fabric—and carried it outside. I went around the perimeter of our lawn, pulling at the long grass, filling the box. I knew without asking that this was Petey's gift, indistinguishable as it was from a burden. Petey, who always used to ask, challenging and pleading at the same time, "Do you like me? Do you like my family?" Who had wept with his fists tight. Who would be plagued all his life by anger and affection, by gifts gone awry, by the irreconcilable difference between what he got and what he longed for— by the inevitable, insufferable loss buried like a dark jewel at the heart of every act of love.

I tore at the grass around our yard, handful after quick handful, and as if the sound of it had drawn them, when I looked up, the Moran kids were slowly moving through our gate. Judy with baby June in her arms, Janey with a box of sweet cereal clutched to her chest, Tony and Petey bumping arms and hips as if battling to share the same space.

Without a word, I carried the box to the steps and bent down, and with the Moran kids gathered around me, I gently lifted the hopeless little things, still breathing, into the nest of torn grass.